GUPPIES FOR TEA

Marika Cobbold

Chivers Press • Thorndike Press
Bath, Avon, England   Thorndike, Maine USA

This Large Print edition is published by Chivers Press, England, and by Thorndike Press, USA.

Published in 1995 in the U.K. by arrangement with Transworld Publishers Ltd.

Published in 1995 in the U.S. by arrangement with St. Martin's Press, Inc.

U.K. Hardcover ISBN 0-7451-2961-7 (Chivers Large Print)
U.K. Softcover ISBN 0-7451-2963-3
U.S. Softcover ISBN 0-7862-0385-4 (General Series Edition)

The text of this Large Print edition is unabridged.
Other aspects of the book may vary from the original edition.

Set in 16 pt. New Times Roman.

Printed in Great Britain on acid-free paper.

British Library Cataloguing in Publication Data available

Library of Congress Catalog Card Number: 94–61863

Do not go gentle into that good night,
Old age should burn and rave at close of day;
Rage, rage against the dying of the light.

Dylan Thomas, 1914–53

ACKNOWLEDGEMENTS

I would like to thank Elizabeth Buchan and Hilary Johnson for their invaluable help. Warmest thanks too, to Diane Pearson, my editor, for her belief in this book and to Sarah Molloy, my agent, for her support.

Special thanks to Richard Cobbold, Lars Hjorne, Anne Hjorne, Liz Bebb and Ann Drake for their help and support and to Jeremy and Harriet Cobbold for their constant encouragement.

For Richard
with love

CHAPTER ONE

'And there's the Admiral.' Sister Morris gave a cheery wave into the gloom of the Residents' Lounge. 'We like to sit him by the aquarium; reminds him of his seafaring days, I always think.'

Standing behind Sister Morris, a firm grip on the handles of his mother's wheelchair, Robert Merryman looked around him approvingly. Had it not been for the smell of disinfectant one could almost believe one was in a private house.

Sister Morris led the way upstairs. The walls of the first-floor landing were painted soft grey-green and on each white glossed door hung a ceramic tile, a number painted on it, garlanded with pastel flowers. She stopped at the third door on the right where a five tangled with a blue clematis.

'And here it is!' Sister Morris sounded as if she was about to announce the winning ticket in a raffle, 'Number Five.'

She lowered her voice and added, 'If you knew how many enquiries we've had about this room since it became vacant . . .' She flung open the door.

Robert leant over the wheelchair and peered inside.

'It's a very well-appointed little room,

Mother, you'll see,' Robert said heartily, feeling like a Ford car salesman who knew that at the end of a day he'd be driving home in a Jaguar.

Selma Merryman, hunched in her wheelchair, tried to turn her head to look at her son. 'Robert, I don't wish to see. I have a perfectly comfortable room at home.' Her voice trembled, 'There really is no need for me to be here, my toe is healing very well.' But the protests by now had become mechanical, hammered too feebly into the wall of family decisions surrounding her. She was wheeled inside.

Number Five was a small room, the shape of a shoe box, and the smell of disinfectant was stronger in spite of the open window at the far end. The walls were off-white and there was a narrow bed with an orange nylon bedspread. High above the dressing-table, with its easy-to-clean melamine top, hung a bright watercolour landscape adorned by an ice-cream-pink sunset. Under the window with its moss-green curtains stood a chair, its seat striped beige and brown. It was the kind of chair, Robert could not help thinking, that you would never find in anyone's home.

'We've had new curtains put up, and there's a new floor. Well we had to, with the floor.' Sister Morris pursed her thin, cyclamen-pink lips. 'Even with the toilet just round the corner.'

'It's not a bad room,' Peggy Merryman whispered to her husband as Sister Morris busied herself around the place closing the window and fluffing up a cushion. 'Very clean.' Peggy, looking unhappy, pulled the collar of her green husky closer around her thin neck.

'You'll be much more comfortable here, Ma, you'll see,' Robert said, his voice like that of Sister Morris, a little raised.

'I'm in a wheelchair Robert, it does not automatically follow that I'm deaf.'

'Of course not, Mother, of course not.' Robert smiled nervously at Sister Morris, whose sandy eyebrows had jerked upwards at Selma's words. He walked around and squatted down, level with his mother. 'We'd better be off, I'm afraid. Time and tide wait for no man and we've got a long drive home.' He took Selma's hands.

At the word home, Selma looked up, fixing him with eyes like pebbles, dulled by sand. She snatched his right hand back against her chest and held it there. Robert tried to ease himself free. 'Dagmar will visit while we're away, and Amelia of course; it's a good thing she's back in the country.' Still, Selma would not let go of his hand, her grip was surprisingly strong.

'Well, off we must go.' And with a yank Robert finally managed to pull his hand away. He kissed Selma on both cheeks, then gave her an awkward little pat on the head before leaving the room, his shoulders a little hunched

3

as if he was avoiding a low beam. Peggy embraced her mother-in-law, tears in her eyes, and then they were gone, followed out by Sister Morris.

'Don't go yet, dear,' Selma called out, sitting where they had parked her, unable to turn around even to see them leave. 'Don't go.' But as she sat listening to the silence, she knew it was no good. Just as it had been no good when she had stood on the large stone steps at school calling after her parents; just as when, later, she had pleaded with Daniel at the quayside not to sail for Germany. If they wanted to go, there was nothing, nothing at all, she could do to stop them.

Sometime later, she was not sure how much—she got confused over time—there was a yank at the back of the wheelchair and she felt herself being moved.

'I'm Nurse Williams, Mrs Merryman. You come along with me and I'll introduce you to our other residents. You'll soon make friends, you'll see.'

'I'd rather not.' Selma raised her voice. 'If you don't mind, I'd rather stay in my room.'

'Nonsense,' answered Nurse Williams cheerfully. 'You don't want to sit here all by yourself.'

'I hated boarding school as a child,' Selma said as she was wheeled out of the room.

'Did you dear?' All the staff were told to use the residents' names, not 'dear' or 'love', but

4

Nurse Williams tended to forget.

'Hated it!'

'Well, this isn't a boarding school, it's Cherryfield.' Nurse Williams sounded as if a problem had been solved.

They passed the kitchen, its swinging door allowing the smell of boiled fish to mix with that of the ever present disinfectant. 'That will be your cod for tea,' Nurse Williams said.

Selma straightened in her chair. 'Cod for tea?'

'Fish is food for the brain,' Nurse Williams chanted briskly.

'I don't have cod for tea. A sliver of smoked salmon on thin brown bread, yes; a small sardine sandwich maybe; but not cod, not for tea.' Selma's voice, with its breath of a Swedish accent, was firm.

'Call it supper then if you prefer.' A note of irritation crept in amongst Nurse Williams' determinedly cheerful tones. 'Here we are anyway, this is the lounge.' She pushed Selma's wheelchair into the centre of the room.

Wine-red Dralon curtains were half drawn against the spring afternoon and, from a huge television set, *Blue Peter* blared into every corner. Two upholstered armchairs flanked the French windows at the far end of the room, and opposite the television, lined up against the wall, stood a row of beige, imitation leather chairs, each occupied by an elderly resident.

Selma looked with mounting panic at the

5

row of old people, some returning her gaze with little nods and smiles, the others continuing to stare ahead at the television.

'... and then you fold it like so.' The *Blue Peter* presenter, a purple tinge to her long hair, flipped back the corners of an empty box of cornflakes. 'And here you have it.' Her young face beamed out across the room. 'Your own stables!'

'If you don't mind, I'd like to go to my room now. I can't read with all this noise.'

'Funny how the old dears will get on their high horses all of a sudden,' Nurse Williams would say later to Sister Morris, over a cup of tea.

'Who are all these people?' Selma fretted. 'What is this place?'

*   *   *

In the still, auntly drawing room of the Old Rectory, Abbotslea, Gerald Forbes looked up from the file on his knee. 'A café! No, I don't think that's a very good idea, Amelia. You very sweetly gave up a perfectly good career to come and look after me, and to be free, you said, to write on your own terms. Not to become a café owner.' He looked down again at his file.

He's going bald, Amelia thought. His hair is all black and silky, and just at the top of his head there's a little pink patch. She said, 'Don't say café in that way.'

6

'In what way? How should one say it?' Gerald looked irritated.

'You say café meaning, "Nasty little place where you stop reluctantly for a greasy sausage because the pubs are shut." What I'm going to have is a haven. A place where writers write, artists sketch, shoppers rest and aspidistras grow.' Amelia was smiling again as she perched on the arm of Gerald's chair.

'If you expended a tenth of that imagination and energy on your articles, you'd be appearing in every magazine in the country,' Gerald said.

Amelia appeared not to have heard. 'And I must have a trio. You know, an old boy at the piano and two large, grey-haired ladies playing the cello and the violin. They have to be large so that one can see them above the aspidistras.'

She kissed Gerald absent-mindedly on the bald patch on his head. 'In the old days in Gothenburg, Selma would meet her friends in a place just like that, twice a week on a Monday and Friday, and sometimes in between.' Amelia leant back against Gerald's shoulder and looked dreamily ahead.

'Of course they wore hats. I'm not sure I could enforce a hat rule. What do you think, Gerald?'

Gerald sprang up from the chair, giving her a little shove on the way. 'I think you're waffling. I thought you said supper would be ready at a decent time tonight.'

Amelia sat down in the vacant chair and looked at him, hurt. 'Two years ago you were a struggling artist looking for a muse, your head full of pre-Raphaelites and artists' communes. Now you're back to being a country solicitor, the rules are changing.' She added, 'If at least we had children,' managing to seem longing and encouraging both at once.

'I can't see the rush. Lots of women have their first baby in their thirties. One of the girls at the office was reading this article the other day which actually said that older women make better mothers.' Gerald had walked over to the drinks tray and was pouring himself another gin and tonic, 'Top up?' He held the whisky bottle up to Amelia who shook her head.

'Poor Aunt Edith only left you the house in the hope that we'd fill it with the children she could never have,' she said.

'Aunt Edith was a dyke.'

'That's what I said, she couldn't have children. Anyway, you can't be a country solicitor without having a big family. Watch any television series and you'll see.'

'You watch too much television. Clarissa Edwards, our new clerk, gave her set to Oxfam the other day.'

'That's kind of her,' Amelia said. 'But she'll regret it in a day or two, people who get rid of their sets nearly always do. They have a honeymoon with themselves, reading all the

8

books they always meant to read but never found as engrossing as *Dallas*. They play patience and discover silence, and after two weeks you'll find them next door, watching their neighbour's set.'

'When did you say supper was?'

Amelia sighed and got up from the chair. 'In two minutes.'

*　　　*　　　*

'Is this wise, my darling?' Selma had said when Amelia had told her she was moving in with Gerald. Sitting in the bay of her Devon drawing room pouring strong coffee into two tiny, gold-encrusted cups, Selma looked at her granddaughter over the spiralling steam.

As she moved, Amelia sniffed the air, drawing in the comforting scent of tea-rose, as much part of Selma as if she had been the rose itself. 'I'm doing it for love,' she had answered simply.

She reminded herself of that now, as she stood in the kitchen of the Old Rectory taking a casserole out of the combination micro-oven that had been Aunt Edith's last purchase. Amelia hated it and wished it was an Aga.

'Anyway, is it wise do you think ...' She turned as she heard Gerald's voice uttering Selma's lines. '... For you to have children, with your family history, I mean?' Gerald stood leaning against the kitchen door, drink

9

in hand, his eyes carefully avoiding hers.

Amelia looked at him appalled. 'What do you mean, "my family history"?'

'You know. Your mother, she's bonkers after all.'

Amelia continued to stare at him. She felt like someone who had shared her innermost secret with a friend only to find the same friend busy pinning it up on the school notice-board.

Then the telephone rang and Amelia hurried from the room. There were tears in her eyes, Gerald could see. With a mournful look at his near-empty glass, he drained what was left of the gin and tonic and thought of Stewart.

Stewart, his boyhood friend, had owned a pretty red setter and one day he beat it. It had been a careless beating, delivered with scant vigour, the cause of it soon forgotten. But before long Stewart was giving the dog regular whippings harder and harder, his face red with guilt and pleasure.

Until the first beating Stewart had been fond of the dog, but soon he hated it.

Gerald got up and put the casserole dish back in the oven. I could never hate Amelia, he thought, any more than I could hit her, but she irritates the shit out of me.

When he first met Amelia, at an art exhibition preview a little over two years earlier, she had just come back to England after three years away. 'Why Sweden?' he had asked, thinking that a long absence abroad

10

would explain the air she had of looking at, rather than participating in, the scenes around her: an air of being permanently surprised.

'My mother's Swedish. Also, I fell in love with the son of her oldest friend,' she had said almost in passing, as they admired a large, gouache nude. 'He was married,' she had added. 'And one day I bumped into his wife and three children. Three children, all small and golden haired.' She had turned and looked at him directly now, her almond-shaped eyes opened wide at the unfairness of it all. 'They were feeding the seals at Slottskogen and that was it; I left him and came back here.' Then she had wandered across the room to study a seascape.

As he got to know Amelia better, Gerald found that her air of being a little at odds with her surroundings was constant and a source of regret to her. It seemed she had spent most of her childhood curled up in a chair reading and dreaming, feeling more at home in the world of her books (where children came in fives, mothers smiled serenely and fathers, stern but loving, steered their children through a life of mild adventures and cosy morality) than in her progressive boarding school or the immaculate flat where she lived alone with her mother.

'My father buggered off and left us when I was two,' she told Gerald on their second meeting, her soft voice enunciating the swear-word in clear, precise syllables. 'Then he died.'

When they made love for the first time it was her turn to surprise him, first by her passion, then afterwards by her obvious distress, as she dressed hurriedly and refused to speak of their lovemaking.

Weeks later he had said to her accusingly, 'Each time after we've been in bed together you behave like a deflowered virgin.'

She had thought a while before saying wistfully, 'I always hoped to be a virgin when I married, but it didn't work. Actually,' she went on, answering his question thoroughly, as usual, 'I was only sixteen when I first slept with my boyfriend. It was very odd,' she sighed. 'At school all my friends were desperate to lose their virginity but few of them actually did. I, who had a drawer full of white lace cotton nighties, fell practically into the first pair of outstretched arms. I didn't seem to be able to help myself.' She looked intently into his eyes, as if she hoped he might be able to explain her life to her.

'I just wasn't prepared for it. I mean look at them; Pollyanna, Anne of Green Gables, the lot of them, cruising from girlhood to mother of multitudes with a purity that would have impressed the Virgin Mary.

'I ran off to my grandparents and locked myself away with Winnie the Pooh for a week. I lay on my bed there, crying for hours on end, banished by every upstanding, God-fearing character in every decent novel I had ever read.

Banished to the world of *Kitty, a Teenager in Love,* and *Sister Barton Gets a New Doctor*.' Amelia had smiled weakly and shrugged her narrow shoulders.

Gerald could hear the soft, slow voice speaking, could remember everything it had told him, but now the words only annoyed him. He got up from the table and slammed the glass down on the sink. 'Why does everything always have to be so bloody complicated?' he shouted. 'Why the hell can't you just be normal?'

Out in the hall where the last shafts of evening sun were still coming through the leaded window, Amelia stood with the phone in her hand. 'Miss Lindsay? Miss Amelia Lindsay?' The voice on at the other end did not wait for confirmation of this before continuing in an aggrieved voice, 'Miss Lindsay this is Sister Morris from Cherryfield Residential Home for the Elderly. I know we are expecting you at the weekend but I'm afraid that won't do.'

As the voice paused for breath, Amelia asked, 'You don't want me to visit my grandmother?'

'Oh, but we do. We most certainly do. But at once. It has to be at once I'm afraid,' Sister Morris said with the grim satisfaction of the bringer of bad news.

'She's not ill?'

'She might well have a sick mind after what

13

she said to that young nurse, but physically your grandmother is as well as can be hoped. I can expect you tomorrow then.' And Sister Morris hung up.

CHAPTER TWO

All that evening Amelia fretted. What could be wrong with her grandmother? What made Uncle Robert think he had the right to scuttle off to Brazil, leaving Amelia and a useless Dagmar to cope? On and on she worried until Gerald snapped, 'Why don't you just call up and find out exactly what is wrong, not that you know anything is, instead of sitting round whinging at me?' Then he strode up to bed.

'I can't call now, it's too late, I'll wake them all up,' Amelia called feebly after him, remembering the days when he would have put his arms round her and told her gently not to be such a worrier.

*   *   *

The next morning she drove to the station in Basingstoke, having first fed the hens and watered the tomato and aubergine seedlings in the greenhouse.

Rich, black soil clung to the heels of her red court shoes and she had forgotten to put on the belt that, Gerald said, really made the skirt and jumper she was wearing. Amelia well knew the value of the right accessories but she often had her mind on other things. Not always more important ones, just different.

She arrived at the station in good time, she always did at railway stations and airports, and found a seat in a no-smoking carriage.

As the Plymouth train pulled away from the platform, Amelia picked up a novel from her large black velvet bag. Finding the right page, she gazed over the top of it, out at nothing in particular.

She thought of Willoughby, Selma's husband, dying in the Kingsmouth Cottage Hospital, the curtains drawn round his bed, separating his dying from the supper-time chatter on the ward. It was the night before Willoughby died that Uncle Robert first brought up the idea of a Nice Home. Amelia had been trying to sleep, lying in the high, mahogany bed where great-grandfather Jocelyn had died forty years earlier: peacefully, Amelia had been told. But she had always hated the bed; she knew that Jocelyn had lain tied to that bed by his own withered limbs, silently screaming, unable to fight off death's unsolicited advances. Now, she had thought, it was Willoughby's turn to lie fighting the Grim Rapist.

She had switched on the light and looked at her watch, it was three-fifteen. She had been about to switch it off again, when she saw her grandmother in the doorway, the two cats, Tigger and Tim, circling her feet.

'There you are darling,' Selma said. 'I don't seem to be able to get this damned thing open. Here, you try.' She held out a tin of Whiskas. 'There's the opener, it's terribly stiff.'

'Mother, what are you doing up.' Robert, his hair ruffled but his tartan dressing-gown tightly belted, had appeared on the landing. He looked into the room and saw Amelia sitting on the bed, a tin of cat food in her hand. 'What's going on, Amelia?'

'The cats dear,' Selma said in a patient voice. 'They haven't had their dinner.' Robert had stared after her as she took the open tin and disappeared out on to the landing, the mewling cats in her wake. It was then that he had mentioned the idea of a Nice Home.

The next day, Willoughby died. The family, Robert and Peggy, Amelia's mother Dagmar and Amelia herself, had stayed on for the funeral and Selma was grateful to them all.

She shouldn't have been, Amelia thought as she turned back from the train window and flicked over yet another unread page of the novel, because that week she had been on trial. The fridge filled with out-of-date yoghurt and small, carefully wrapped remnants of long-ago meals, the endlessly repeated questions, the fruitless shopping expeditions that turned into hours of aimless wandering, everything was

16

taken down and used in evidence against her. Taken down by the loving, spying eyes of her family.

Peggy had stood speechless, peering into a greaseproof-paper parcel.

'Lamb chops,' Selma, who had just appeared in the kitchen, said helpfully. 'I wondered where they had got to.' She picked up a fork and stabbed one of the chops. Lifting it out of the paper she had looked thoughtfully at the mould that clung to it with spindly tentacles. 'I think they might be a little off. I really wouldn't eat them if I were you, dear.'

Then there had been Dagmar, wandering backwards and forwards to the bathroom to wash her hands and carefully spreading Kleenex tissues over the seats of the comfortable, shabby armchairs, before sitting down.

Robert, who didn't see much of his half-sister, had taken it all as further proof that their mother's days as a housekeeper were over. Amelia wondered at how her mother's obsession could once again spread like an ugly stain across other people's lives.

'I miss him, I miss him so terribly.' Selma's tears, her eruption into grief after days of stoical control, had interrupted *The Nine O'Clock News* and embarrassed them all.

Robert turned the sound of the television down, before turning to his mother with an air of infinite patience. 'You know, we all feel you

17

would be so much happier at a Nice Residential Home, rather than wandering around this great barn of a place all on your own and with constant reminders of Pa.'

'I'm not likely to forget your father,' Selma had looked at her son with a small smile. 'Whether I'm here or somewhere else; I was married to him for nearly fifty years.'

Then Peggy found out that Selma had not had a bath since the day of Willoughby's stroke, since the day he had not been there to lift her into the tub. 'You must see that you need looking after,' Robert had said more sternly this time.

Amelia had turned to Selma. 'What do *you* think?' she had asked.

Slowly Selma had lowered the coffee cup towards the saucer, concentrating on her shaking hand, willing it to still. Her movement accelerated and the cup clattered on to the saucer. She looked up at Amelia with eyes that seemed to have faded, as if all the tears had finally washed the colour away. 'I want to stay here. This is my home.'

A month later, five days ago, Selma's house had been sold and Selma herself moved to Cherryfield. Amelia's objections had been strongly felt but weakly supported by word or action.

So, sitting on the Plymouth train, Amelia worried as much about herself, about her lack of loyalty and strength of purpose.

18

*   *   *

The taxi ride through the small town of Kingsmouth took Amelia past Ashcombe, once Selma's and Willoughby's house, now soon to be the residence of Mr and Mrs Desmond Hamilton, a local builder and his wife. Amelia looked up at the whitewashed house on the hill above the creek, its green lawns sloping down towards the water, yellow with the hundreds of daffodils that Willoughby had planted. The car turned a corner and Ashcombe disappeared from view.

Cherryfield stood square in its own grounds at the other end of the small town. It too was on a hill, it too was white painted with green windows, and Robert had debated whether the proximity and likeness to her old home would pain or please his mother. Would it comfort her to see across the river her home of fifty years? Would the view over the water from the green windows of Cherryfield make her feel secure? Or would it be to her, gentle, well-meaning torture?

'I think a move right away from here would be worse,' Robert had declared finally. And Selma, with the ill-fitting deference of an old woman to her son, had said to him, 'I know I'm a nuisance dear, but can't I just stay here, at Ashcombe? I promise I won't be any trouble.' She had given a little laugh that meant, 'As if I ever would be,' but her eyes were fixed intently

19

on Robert's.

Robert had exchanged glances with his wife who, when Selma rose laboriously from her chair, nodded towards the spreading dark patch on the seat.

At Cherryfield a pretty, blonde nurse opened the door. As she stepped out to greet Amelia, a white petal from the cherry tree at the side of the porch drifted across on a gust of wind and settled in her curls. The nurse looked charming and very young. 'If you'd like to wait here,' she indicated a chair in the hall, 'Sister Morris will be with you in a second.'

Amelia sat down, feeling all at once quite calm. Nothing seemed to be seriously wrong and Cherryfield was at first glance as nice as Robert had described it.

She looked approvingly at the large vase filled with blossoming cherry branches that were reflected in the highly polished mahogany table, and at the Redoute prints on the whitewashed walls. The sun shone through the coloured glass at the top of the door creating a drifting pattern across the brown carpet. There was a certain tranquillity about the place, Amelia felt, as she leafed through last month's copy of *The Field*.

'Leave me alone you bloody woman! I'm not sitting on that thing.' Amelia scrambled to her feet as she recognized Selma's voice, accented and furious.

'I'm telling you for the last time, I'll sit where

I want and I'll pee where I want and that's all there is to it. I pay you enough.'

The inner door of the hall opened and a round woman in her fifties entered. 'Miss Lindsay, I'm Sister Morris.' She held her hand out, then withdrew it the moment it touched Amelia's. 'I assume you heard our little outburst. We have them all the time.' Sister Morris's sandy eyebrows jerked upwards and she clamped her lips together, as if to say that although far harsher words were queuing up to leave her mouth, she was manfully stopping them.

When Amelia said nothing, Sister Morris drew her breath in between her teeth and said 'I'm afraid it's all having a very disruptive effect on our other residents, not to mention the staff. Only yesterday one of our girls actually went home in tears.'

'I'm sorry,' Amelia said at last. She could think of nothing better. Then, as Sister Morris looked expectantly at her, pale green eyes protruding, she added, 'What can I do?' clinging a little longer to a world where grandparents disciplined their grandchildren, not the other way around.

'It's quite simple,' Sister Morris assured Amelia. 'Your grandmother must, I emphasize must, be made to understand that as a guest with us here at Cherryfield she has a duty to behave according to our rules and regulations...'

Amelia had a vision of Selma manacled to the wall of an immaculate torture chamber with Amelia herself standing beneath, shouting out the rules of Cherryfield Residential Home for the Elderly.

'. . . and that includes sitting on an inco pad on the chair especially allotted to her.' Sister Morris's voice quietened and her cheeks ceased to vibrate. Almost confidentially now she added, 'It's very strange how upset she got at my suggestion that she discuss her little problem with her family. I fear you can't be very close.'

Amelia was about to object that feeling close to someone didn't automatically mean you cared to have little chats about your urinary tracts with them, when Sister Morris spoke again. 'You know, I'm sure this refusal to look her incontinence in the eye and face up to it is half the problem. Now if it was me,' her face took on an expression of awe-inspiring jollity, 'I would say, "I'm afraid I'm incontinent so where would you like me to sit?"'

Sister Morris tore herself back to a less amiable reality. 'It's all about facing up to things, you know. You'll find your grandmother in the conservatory, she seems to like it out there. Have a heart to heart.'

'About peeing?' Amelia asked, but Sister Morris had already disappeared through the double doors.

In the conservatory, where scarlet begonias

22

trailed from white plastic pots along the sills, Sister Morris stopped to point an accusing finger at the far end of the room. 'There she is, still in her wheelchair I see. Her toe was in a frightful state, I don't know what her doctor can have been thinking of.' And she bustled back into the lounge.

Amelia looked past the row of Cherryfield residents, most of them connected like electrical appliances to bottles and stands, towards the far corner where Selma sat like a baby elephant, her bent, chubby back half turned to the room.

She did not look up as Amelia walked towards her along the row of chairs. A couple of the old people, 'Old Folk' she felt sure Sister Morris would call them when in a better mood, responded to her 'Good afternoon', the others continued to stare wordlessly out at the garden or inwards, to their own vaguely remembered, subsiding pasts.

Gently, Amelia put her hand on Selma's shoulder. Like an old-fashioned computer, slow to load the new information, Selma took her time reacting. Her head turned and as her matt-brown eyes focused, the expression of angry confusion gave way to a wide smile. She straightened a little in her wheelchair and put a small hand to her hair. It had lost its blue-toned smoothness and was set in the little scalp tightening curls she had always despised.

'Amelia darling, how lovely to see you.' She

turned her face up to be kissed and Amelia flinched at the sight of the hair on Selma's upper lip and chin normally smooth and petal-pink powdered. Embarrassed for them both, and attempting to disguise the gesture, Amelia swatted at a non-existent insect that disturbed her with its imaginary buzzing.

'When was it we saw you, last week was it not?' Selma added with studied nonchalance as she looked intently at Amelia. 'You'll think I've gone dotty but I can't seem to remember.'

Amelia paused before answering. It was tempting to say in the same casual tone, 'That's right, last week,' instead of the truth, that she had not seen her grandmother since the funeral four weeks earlier. That same evening, Selma had sat at the head of the table, still pretty in a black velvet dress, dignified in her laced-up sorrow. She had adored her husband but there she had sat, making conversation, facing her balding middle-aged son across the table in his father's chair.

But she was still the mistress of her own house then, and senility could be called forgetfulness as she moved around her own, comfortably arranged, household.

'It's been a little longer than that I'm afraid,' Amelia said finally, 'I seem to have been terribly busy.'

'Haven't we all?' Selma on autocue agreed as she was flung back to the days where she had indeed been busy.

'Jane Austen again.' Amelia picked up the thick paperback omnibus edition that perched on top of Selma's handbag.

'Have a sweet?' Selma bent down over the bag with a movement as if filmed in slow motion. Her hand shaking, she fished for the handles. Amelia was wondering if it would be tactless to help, when Selma caught the bag, only to lose it halfway in the air. As it fell, a bunch of keys dropped out followed by three boiled sweets, unwrapped and covered in fluff, a selection of copper coins, a flurry of credit card receipts and a Chanel lipstick. Last, a white lace handkerchief floated down, settling on the coins like a shroud.

'Silly me,' Selma said with a little laugh, then, 'You take the keys to the house darling, make sure the heating is put back on.'

Amelia was about to reply when she heard the sound of crying, snuffling, abandoned weeping. She turned to see a big-boned woman wedged into a dainty chintz-lined basket chair, like a large child in a doll's seat, tears rolling down her smooth cheeks.

A nurse appeared with a watering-can and began watering the begonias. After a couple of minutes Amelia went up to her, tapping her softly on the shoulder to catch her attention. 'She seems distressed,' she said pointing to the weeping woman.

The nurse turned round and smiled soothingly at her. 'Oh that's all right, that's

Mrs Wells.' And that apparently explained all. She continued to water the plants, and after waiting a moment, Amelia went back to Selma, looking surreptitiously as she passed at the still weeping Mrs Wells.

'I'll take you outside.' Amelia picked up Selma's things and began pushing the chair, careful to avoid the rubber tubes and thin legs stretched out under crocheted blankets.

Selma looked around her with distaste. 'Who are these people?' she asked in a carrying whisper. 'I can't remember asking them here.'

Amelia brought Selma into the dappled shadow of a large cherry tree. She secured the brakes and sat down herself on the wooden bench splattered with bird-droppings.

'Ghastly lot of old people in there,' Selma said conversationally. Then, 'How's the poetry?'

'Oh that,' Amelia said, surprised that her grandmother should remember. 'They say it's difficult being a genius. I would say not half as hard as not being one.'

'Don't I know, don't I know.' Selma rocked in her wheelchair, laughing quietly. 'When I was a girl, how I longed to hear people say, not, "Doesn't Selma play well," but, "Listen to Selma, she plays like an angel."'

And Amelia felt happier; her grandmother was not so much changed after all.

A cherry blossom fell from the branch above, landing at Selma's feet, then another.

Like a snowflake, Selma thought. How long since she had seen snow.

As she closed her eyes she could almost feel the crunch under her soles of the crisp, early morning snow as she ran through the streets back home, late for school as always, her breath ahead of her like a smoky standard. That piercing scream from above, a sound, she had thought, like that of the peacocks at home being chased across the lawn. When she looked up, she had seen Mrs Hollander, all dressed in white, standing on the roof of the great apartment house. Another piercing scream and Mrs Hollander lifted her shrouded arms and leapt. In front of Selma's eyes she fell through the air like a giant snowflake, down, down, spinning, before hitting the pavement, turning the fresh snow red. 'Poor flying Dutchman,' Selma said out loud.

'What was that, Grandma?' Amelia leant forward on the bench. But before Selma had time to answer, they heard a voice calling.

'There you are.' Sister Morris stepped determinedly towards them through the daisies in the damp grass. 'Had our little chat?'

'Mrs ... ? Oh you must think I'm dotty but I can't remember your name,' Selma laughed merrily.

'Sister Morris, Mrs Merryman, I'm Sister Morris.'

'Of course you are. I don't believe you know my granddaughter.'

27

'Oh yes, we have met. In fact we've only just had a little talk. About our problem.' Sister Morris bent down to come face to face with Selma, her expression one of jollity. She's going to pinch her cheeks, I know it, Amelia thought, but Sister Morris straightened up, contenting herself with a conspiratorial little nod in Amelia's direction. Selma looked uncomprehendingly at her.

'Our toilet difficulties,' Sister Morris explained helpfully.

Selma couldn't turn away, but for a moment she closed her eyes. Then she said slowly, 'I'm afraid I don't know what you're talking about. Now if you'd excuse us, I'd like to give Amelia some tea. Amelia darling, could you help me into the drawing room?'

Inside, Selma hailed an auxiliary. 'Would you be so kind as to bring us some tea.'

'Tea's not until half six Mrs Merryman, you know that.'

'I was not referring to supper.' Selma, crumpled in her wheelchair, hand shaking, attempted haughtiness. 'If it's not too much trouble we'd like a cup of tea please and a slice of cake and a biscuit or two.'

'You'll have your biscuit with your cocoa, Mrs Merryman.' The young nurse spoke firmly now, but she turned to Amelia with a friendly grin. 'They get ever so greedy you know,' she said in a stage whisper.

'I'm so sorry,' Selma said to Amelia, 'I don't

28

seem to be able to offer you tea.'

'It doesn't matter,' Amelia said quickly. 'I had an enormous lunch on the train.'

By the fish-tank something stirred. 'Nonsense, damned cheek. If you want a cup of tea, you should have one.' And the Admiral sank back in his chair.

'Good afternoon everyone.' A small figure being wheeled into the lounge, raised an emaciated arm and gave a cheery wave.

Selma looked up with distaste. 'There's that tiresome woman. She never stops talking.' Ignoring her furious shaking of the head, the nurse transferred, first the inco pad, then the woman herself, to the chair next to Selma. 'Here's Miss White for you.' She sounded congratulatory.

Miss White was aptly named, Amelia thought, as the tiny woman continued to beam at her. Her large eyes were of such a watered-down blue that they seemed almost colourless, and the face, its complexion the texture of crumpled tissue paper, was framed by white curls tumbling over her tiny shoulders. She sat upright in the chair, the edges of the inco pad showing at the sides of her baby-blue polyester dress.

'I'm Phyllis White.' The little woman reached out a surprisingly large hand for Amelia to grasp. 'I'm a new girl like your nan. It's lovely here, don't you think? Always someone to chat with. Of course some of the old things are a bit quiet, but even a quiet one is better than no-one, that's what I say.' She laughed uproariously and Amelia looked across at Selma who sat scowling and jealous at Miss White's hijacking of her visitor.

An hour later, Nurse Williams came in with a young auxiliary in tow. 'Tea-time,' she announced cheerfully, as they began helping the residents back in their wheelchairs. The Admiral and some others needed help only to get out from their chairs, then with the aid of walking frames they proceeded with surprising speed towards the dining room.

The evening meal, any meal, Amelia thought, must be a break from the monotony of the Cherryfield day, a Geriatric Happening, even when it consisted of three pilchards and half an egg on a lettuce leaf.

'Darling, don't go yet.' Selma's voice was light but her podgy hand gripped Amelia's wrist like a trap.

'I'll walk you to the dining room,' Amelia said. 'And I'll be here again tomorrow morning before I go back.'

Once at the table though, seated between the Admiral and Miss White, Selma seemed not to mind Amelia going. She obediently turned her face up to be kissed then, as Amelia walked off, she lifted a piece of hard-boiled egg carefully to her mouth. Pale yellow crumbs settled on her lips and chin as she chewed and picked at her food.

'Now then Mr Hurst!' Amelia turned in the doorway to see a nurse hurrying over to the table next to Selma's, where Mr Hurst, a fit looking elderly man with a mild, faraway expression stuck his fork purposefully into his neighbour's pilchard. The nurse directed his hand back over his own plate before hurrying over to another table, where some milk had been upset. As Amelia left she saw Mr Hurst calmly attacking his neighbour's plate once more.

CHAPTER THREE

Amelia lay on the bed in her room at The Anchor Inn, a picture of sloth.

It was ten o'clock at night. She had had dinner in the small dining room: roast shoulder of lamb with potatoes and two vegetables. She had called home. Gerald had sounded in a hurry but said he was staying in watching television. He had used that voice too, his Star Wars voice, able to destroy any attempted intimacies before they hit him. These days everything she did seemed to irritate him. Take the other evening. She had run herself a hot bath, scenting it with half a bottle of gardenia oil. Then she had waited for his car to turn up the road before running to the bathroom and jumping into the tub, only to leap out again as she heard the front door slam. All so she could greet him in the hall, wrapped only in a towel, her body warm and scented from the water. Of course it had been a bloody silly idea, she thought now, wiping a tear from her eye, but still, there had been no need for him to be so unpleasant. She winced at the memory: 'Have you got nothing better to do with your day than lounging around in the bath. I would have thought the least I could expect after a hard day is to find you dressed.' So embarrassing. And so unfair: on that particular day she had started and all but finished a major article on the Hampshire watercress beds she was doing for a Swedish magazine.

She sighed, Gerald was right though, generally she was disorganized, completely lacking in any sense of urgency. She lay on the hotel bed, weighed down by the heap of things she ought to be doing: about Selma, about the collection of poems Gerald had rightly predicted would never be completed, and about the unanswered correspondence that piled up with the unread books on her bedside table back at the Old Rectory.

This lack of self-discipline was what Amelia most disliked about herself, the way she had of floating away from tasks, of knowing exactly what needed to be done, and then doing nothing.

Sighing, she sat up on one elbow, staring out of the window and at Ashcombe across the harbour. The house was in darkness. Had Selma still been living there, lights would have come on in room after room like bright beads threaded on a dull string, as she pottered through the house in her emerald green, velvet dressing-gown.

She would feed the cats, dust a little if the urge took her, chatter to her husband, her voice sometimes within hearing distance, sometimes not. Neither of them minded, it was the comfortable knowledge of the other being there that mattered.

Soon she would pour hot milk into two mugs, hers, twice mended and decorated with a marmalade cat, and Willoughby's owl with the hairline crack running through. Both mugs had been Christmas presents from Amelia over twenty years earlier.

Willoughby had been good at mending china. The restoring of an object to usefulness always gave him great satisfaction.

Amelia had always loved the oldness of the things in her grandparents' house, the familiarity of them. In the bright flat she shared with her mother things never grew familiar, they were thrown out before there was time. As Dagmar's obsession with cleanliness grew stronger, the life expectancy of possessions, clothes, shoes, ornaments, kitchen utensils, became shorter. Once when Amelia was nine she had asked her mother, half jokingly, half apprehensively, if she, Amelia, got really dirty,

33

would her mother throw her out too?

Dagmar had looked at her and laughed for such a long time that Amelia had got bored waiting for an answer. Then, suddenly, the laughter had turned to crying and Dagmar had fled the room.

'You must be patient with your mother,' Selma had said later when the child told her what had happened. She took Amelia's hand. 'She's frightened you see.'

Amelia liked the feel of her grandmother's hand, soft like the chamois leather she used to polish the windows in the flat. Her mother's hand felt more like a nutmeg grater. 'Frightened of what?' she had asked.

Selma had shrugged her shoulders and looked sad. 'Life, I think. And that is too big a fear for anyone to cope with. So what does your mother do?'

Amelia, her slanted eyes fixed intently on Selma's face, shook her head.

'She carves the fear up, like you've just cut that big piece of chocolate cake I gave you, into manageable pieces. She creates little fears, bite-sized ones and concentrates on them. So many times I've talked to her, tried to winkle the problem from her like meat from a crab claw.' She shook her head.

'I wish she was more like you,' Amelia had said, looking adoringly at her grandmother.

Selma had been a child's, or a man's, idea of beauty. There were no edges to her, everything

34

was rounded, arms, chin, even the tip of her nose. She wore soft, flowing dresses and Amelia had never seen her in trousers. Her hair, black, then slowly turning bluey-grey, was brushed smoothly from her forehead and behind the ears, cut in softly at the nape of the neck.

Amelia always saw her visits to Ashcombe as a boat ride in the sunshine down a smooth lazy river. With her mother the boat was out at sea and you never knew when the next storm would gather. Maybe it was because Ashcombe had for so long been a refuge from the newness and brightness of the flat that Amelia had not noticed when it slid from cosy disorder into squalor. Dagmar, of course, had stopped visiting after Tigger the Tom had been sick in her suitcase as it lay open on the spare room bed, waiting to be unpacked. But as silent dust settled layer upon layer on every surface, dulling the colour of the china ornaments as passing centuries muted Old Masters, Peggy had said something would have to be done.

Then Willoughby died and the thin mask of competence had been torn from Selma, revealing a frightened and confused old woman who did not always remember to grieve for the husband she had adored.

Reluctantly, yawning, Amelia heaved herself off the bed and walked into the bathroom to remove her make-up. She slapped

35

a large clot of expensive night cream on her clean skin and wondered why people said 'as natural as brushing your teeth'. Brushing teeth was a bore, particularly when there was no-one next to you in bed to repel with your bad breath.

Alone or not, Selma would never have gone to bed without brushing her teeth, Amelia thought. Dagmar, strangely enough, would. Amelia's mother was selective in her quest for cleanliness, she had to be. When you have disinfected all the hangers in your wardrobe twice in a day, there is so little time and energy left for normality.

Amelia pottered back to bed feeling angry. Gerald was right; her mother was bonkers. Selma, therefore, had no right to abscond into old age; Amelia needed her. Drifting down a stream of self-pity, she fell asleep.

*   *   *

'I've brought you some clotted cream fudge from the Dairy.' The next morning back at Cherryfield Amelia kissed Selma and handed her the small, wrapped box.

'What a sweet girl.' Selma smiled, then began to untie the string. It seemed impossible that, with her shaking right hand, she would ever succeed, but Amelia knew better than to offer her scissors; her grandparents had never been mean, but string was untied and carefully rolled and stored.

'I haven't got my glasses on,' Selma said. 'You try.'

The box was opened and placed on the teak-veneered coffee table. Selma was silent as she bent over the fudge, carefully choosing the largest piece. While she chewed it, slowly at the front of her mouth, her fingers were already searching for another one.

Amelia looked away, out over the garden where the wind strewed the cherry blossom across the grass. She could not bear to watch Selma, frowning, rapt with concentration as if a box of fudge was an event.

'You have one, darling,' Selma said finally, putting yet another sweet in her mouth before giving the box a little push in Amelia's direction. Then she looked at her hard and added with studied nonchalance, 'Of course Robert promised I would be back home by my birthday.'

Amelia, about to have a piece, stopped, her hand halfway to her mouth. 'Robert said that?'

'I don't see why you should be so surprised. You weren't surely expecting me to stay in this place for ever.' Selma laughed a little at the absurdity of the idea. 'My toe is healing very well as a matter of fact.' She stretched her bandaged left foot in its Scholl sandal out for inspection, wincing as it touched the leg of the chair.

'They are trying their best here, I can see

that,' she conceded. 'The staff on the whole are very nice, but I couldn't live here. Those dreadful old people.' Selma paused meaningfully, rolling her eyes in the direction of a couple of her fellow residents propped up in chairs along the conservatory wall. 'The only one worth talking to is Admiral ... Oh dear, I can't seem to think of his name.'

Amelia sat quietly, feeling as if she was talking to a robot who'd had a small but essential part from its control panel removed, making its behaviour just one step to the side of normal. 'So Robert said you would be home for your birthday?' she repeated.

'I just told you so, darling. Are you not paying attention? Oh look, there's the Admiral now.' Selma raised herself up a little in her chair and gave a small wave.

Admiral Mallett was steered through the conservatory doorway by a large young man in his mid-twenties, with untidy brown hair and a strong-featured, but amiable face.

'I don't believe you know my son, Henry.' The Admiral looked on proudly as Henry shook hands first with Selma and then Amelia. As if he was doing something outstandingly clever, Amelia thought, amused.

'Sailor, like his old man,' the Admiral said, as Henry helped him into the chair next to Selma. 'I married late you know. Henry here came along when I was practically in my dotage.'

'I was just telling my granddaughter that I'm not expecting to stay here for very long,' Selma said rather grandly.

'Good for you,' said the Admiral. 'Jolly good for you.' He cleared his throat noisily. 'Of course I've sold my house. Voluntary confinement this. The old place became much too large once my sister kicked the bucket, bless her soul. And of course Henry isn't around very much.' He shrugged his shoulders and grinned. 'Well that's the Service for you.'

'The Navy could stand on its head and blow raspberries at my father and he would smile indulgently and say, "Well that's the Service for you,"' Henry said, smiling indulgently himself. He had a surprisingly boyish, light voice coming from such a large frame, Amelia noticed.

'Well this isn't a bad place, food's all right, what there is of it. The nurses are nice enough gals.' Admiral Mallett spoke with all the determination of a man persuading himself. 'Of course the place advertises itself as "For the Active Elderly". Can't say that I've seen much of the active so far, present company excepted of course.' He indicated Selma with a little bow.

'It's my wretched toe,' Selma said.

'And then there's Death Row,' the Admiral continued.

'Death Row?' Amelia shot Selma an anxious glance.

'That's the other part of Cherryfield, the Annexe,' Henry explained with a little smile, choosing his words carefully. 'For the less active residents, the ones needing a little more care.'

'For the chronically dying, shall we say,' the Admiral intercepted with a hoarse laugh that ended in a loud cough.

Selma stirred uneasily in her chair. 'Of course I haven't played tennis for months,' she said. The Admiral and Henry looked a little surprised.

'Look, coffee.' Amelia pointed to the door where Nurse Williams came in, carrying a huge tray of blue, plastic cups and saucers. Behind her followed a procession of wheelchair-bound residents in various stages of awareness, a kind of geriatric pageant, Amelia thought.

'I said to Sister Morris, why don't we have our coffee in the conservatory, it's such a lovely morning!' Nurse Williams exclaimed to anyone who cared to listen.

'Over here, Orderly,' Miss White commanded with some authority, 'with my new friends.' She was placed between Selma and the Admiral. 'And who is this?' She twinkled at Henry who had stood up as she arrived. 'Navy like your father, I say. Have you been to Crete? You must have been to Crete. I had such a wonderful trip there. We went by bus, the whole way.'

Henry smiled encouragingly at her and

Amelia wished he hadn't. 'Of course there was the ferry ... But we were still on the bus, if you see what I mean. Lovely people they were on that trip. Then I've always been lucky that way. Some were not as nice as they could have been though, I must say, a bit offhand. That courier girl. She wasn't what I would call nice. No ... I told her I liked a seat at the front, but after the first day she changed me right to the very back of the bus. I felt the motion of the vehicle very badly. But people are ever so nice.' Miss White paused at last, to help herself to a biscuit from the plate Henry held out to her.

Selma's cup clattered as she placed it back on the saucer, Miss White dunked her biscuit and sucked noisily on it before munching it between thin lips. 'I wrote travel features for the *Hereford and Worcester Gazette*,' she said, having finished her biscuit and established there were no more to come. '"A Spinster's Journey: Europe Through My Bus Window". Very popular they were. Until the fashion changed.'

'Amelia dear,' Selma said, 'take me out in the garden, there's a sweet girl.'

Amelia stood up with an apologetic smile.

Outside, Selma lifted her face to the sun, closing her eyes and sighing contentedly. The warmth of the sun on your skin, Amelia thought, was one of life's few enduring pleasures.

Until Willoughby died Amelia had never

worried about what happened to a corpse once inside the grave; she only knew she didn't like the thought of being cremated. But, since the funeral, she had been unable to ward off images of Willoughby's kind face and short-sighted blue eyes at various stages of decomposition that haunted her with no warning.

Not so many weeks ago, on a day like this one, he would have been gardening, she thought. His square hands, like a mole's paws, digging away at weeds, planting out seedlings for a summer he would not see.

'Amelia,' Selma's hand gripped her shoulder, the long nails digging in hard. 'How did grandpa die? I know you must think I've gone completely mad, but it's all so confused.' Selma's eyes pleaded with her to understand.

Amelia thought of Willoughby lying in the narrow hospital bed, as breath by laboured breath he approached death. She thought of Selma visiting and of her calm as she sat stroking his hand, talking all the while. At times something close to irritation had crept into her voice; for so long he had been the strong one, the trellis round which she had entwined the branches of her contented existence. 'So what are you doing,' she seemed to ask, 'lying here broken?'

'He had a stroke, he died in hospital a week later.' Amelia's voice was gentle but, as she looked at her grandmother's pinched face and anxious eyes, she felt as if she was shooting her in the heart with arrows dipped in cotton wool. 'He went into a coma and he just never came round. It was pneumonia that actually killed him.' 'The old man's friend,' the young doctor had called it.

'He was never uncomfortable, one of us was always there.' Amelia took Selma's hand, forcing the constant shaking to cease for the moment.

'Thank you darling,' Selma sighed. 'I miss him so much, you know. It's worst at night. I dream about him all the time, and when I wake up I believe he's still there. Then I remember.' She stared out over the garden, in silence. Amelia sat feeling useless, aware that the one thing her grandmother wanted, her husband, she could not give her.

Selma's eyelids fluttered and closed, her chin falling against her chest, then she snorted loudly and, with a little shiver, opened her eyes again. She stared at Amelia for a second—she's wondering who the hell I am, Amelia thought—before saying, 'I know it's very kind of these people to have me to stay, but I'd much rather be home. I'm sure once I'm back with my own things I'll be as right as rain.'

Amelia smiled weakly, thinking that it might be worth the air fare to Brazil just to go and throw something hard at Robert. Selma fell asleep again, her grey-toned cheek resting against the back of the wheelchair.

'My father's asleep too, in there.' Amelia turned round to find Henry looking down at them, smiling.

'It strikes me,' Amelia said fiercely, 'that there will have to be an awful lot of good things in one's life before it compensates for this.' And she gesticulated at Selma who gave a loud snore before closing her mouth and making little chewing movements with her lips. 'I wonder if being born is at all a good idea if, at the end, there's got to be Cherryfield.'

'Luckily one's not asked,' Henry said briskly.

'The worst time of all,' said Amelia, not listening, rubbing her eyes with the back of her hand and getting it streaked with mascara, 'is when there's no-one left who loves you best. Selma has been lucky; at the peak of her existence, she was loved by her parents, husband, children, she was the centre of their world. But look at her now, what is left of all that love, where is the security? At the end of the day, you're just an old teddy that everyone's grown out of.'

'There's always God, He never stops loving you,' Henry said, somewhat startlingly.

'Ah, you're born again.' Amelia nodded.

'Certainly not,' Henry said. 'I'm a Naval Chaplain.' And he sat down on the grass by the bench.

'Goodness,' Amelia said looking at him properly now, 'how comforting for you.'

44

'Actually, it's meant to be sort of comforting for others.' He smiled mildly at her.

Well, comfort Selma then, Amelia thought, irritated by the smile. But she said, 'Is your father happy here?'

Henry lay back resting on his elbows, staring up at the sky. 'Not happy exactly, but he's used to community life, institutions if you like; Dartmouth, ships, Naval bases. It's not really Cherryfield he minds, it's being old.'

'My grandmother is very unhappy.' Amelia looked at Selma whose mouth had fallen open again as she snored gently. 'She thinks she's going back home. Would you believe,' she turned to Henry, willing her outrage on him, 'my uncle didn't tell her the house had been sold. And now he's buggered off to Brazil, leaving me to tell her.' Then she blushed, remembering the invisible dog collar that should shield Henry Mallett from that sort of language. 'Sorry,' she said.

'That's all right, I have been down the odd sailors' mess deck you know.'

'I think this is a dreadful place,' Amelia sighed. 'Everything about it upsets me. It's unfair I know, they seem to try their best. Couldn't you just see the headlines? I'm a journalist by the way; I even think in bold, **"Ill-treatment at Retirement Home:** Nurse wipes old woman's bottom." Not much of a story in that!'

A snore turned into a hiccup and Selma

45

awoke. Her eyes flickered between Amelia and Henry, uncertain and unfocused, then her gaze fixed on Amelia. 'Darling, how lovely to see you. When did you arrive? And who's your young man? You must introduce us.' Selma stretched out a chubby arm and smiled coquettishly.

Henry stood up and took her hand. 'I'm Henry Mallett. I think you know my father already—Admiral Mallett.'

Amelia smiled at him gratefully. She did not go to church much herself, but had inherited from Selma a respect for men of religion, were they Chaplains or Rabbis: an expectation of goodness. She approved of Henry.

'Grandma,' she said, 'Henry's a Naval chaplain.'

'Now isn't that interesting.' Selma beamed at them both. 'And tell me, how did you come to meet my granddaughter?'

CHAPTER FOUR

'That's what's so disconcerting.' Amelia stirred the earthenware pan filled with vegetable soup. 'One moment she's the old Selma; with it, sensible, the sort of person you feel you can go to with your problems. Next thing you know, whoosh, she's gone, replaced by this large, malfunctioning child.' She

46

looked across the kitchen at Gerald. 'It's really very upsetting.'

'Well there you are, it was obviously right to put her in a home,' Gerald said, picking up the *Independent* and turning to the sports pages.

Amelia slammed the spoon down by the side of the cooker making Gerald wince. 'It wasn't all that long ago that she enthralled people with her piano recitals. You know, back in Sweden a young man actually shot himself underneath her balcony because her parents wouldn't let her marry him. And now, now she's someone who's "put" places. What the hell help is it knowing that "it was obviously right"?'

'A lot I should think,' Gerald said sourly.

How her vagueness irritated him, he thought, her habit of making illogical remarks in that rather slow, deliberate voice of hers, a voice that, just like her grandmother's playing, had once enthralled. Even her prettiness annoyed him these days. Her grey, slanted eyes, the soft wavy hair that framed the oval face, all reminded him of how much in love he had been with her once.

Oh Amelia, he thought, looking at her moving about the kitchen, wiping down the cooker, using three matches to light the candle on the kitchen table, you're altogether too languid, too useless. Suddenly angry he snapped, 'Why don't you do something about the situation if you think it's so terrible.' And he slammed down the paper and strode from the room.

Amelia cried as she kept the soup warm on the stove, stirring it slowly. She cried bitterly, because now she really feared that Gerald had stopped loving her, but she also cried carefully, so as not to smudge her make-up, because he was not lost to her yet, and he could come back in to the kitchen any moment.

'There's a sweetness about you,' Gerald had said soon after their first meeting, and he had shaken his head with a bemused air as if to say, I might seem strong, but against you I'm helpless. He was so good natured too, like over that silly business with the modelling. He had been as hard-working and serious a painter as he was a solicitor now. Yet he had shown no irritation when, after having promised to sit for an important canvas, she had turned up in his studio only to end up wasting his day. She hadn't intended to, of course. She had watched him set up his easel, she had undressed and sat down where he wanted her to, and then she had panicked like a fool when he asked her to part her legs for the pose. But Gerald had been only kind and understanding. She had sat crying in his huge blue armchair, her knees pressed together as if they had been welded that way, and he, kneeling by her side, had just smiled and said, 'You're a sweet, fragile, dreamy girl, and I should never have asked you to do this.'

'Sweet, dreamy, fragile,' Amelia hissed,

splashing the wooden spoon round the soup. 'Try wet, gullible and inconsistent.'

The soup had simmered so long she knew there would be no flavour left. She took it off the stove and went to look for Gerald. She found him in the bedroom, speaking on the phone. As he looked up to see her in the doorway, he said a loud and hurried goodbye and hung up.

Amelia took a deep breath and walked over to the bed. She sat down next to him and, giving him a little smile, she put her hand out, running her fingers through his hair. Ignoring his irritated flinching, she kissed him lightly on the cheek. 'Gerald, I love you.'

Gerald looked at a point somewhere over her left shoulder. 'And I love you too,' he mumbled.

Grateful, she hugged him and, after a few moments, she felt his arms round her back.

* * *

In a small but beautifully furnished flat not far from the Cathedral in Exeter, Dagmar Lindsay shone a torch into the back of her wardrobe, making sure it really was clean, that it was just a shadow she'd seen earlier, not dirt. Again she rubbed her finger against the back wall of the cupboard, checking. Her long-fingered hands—pianist hands Selma always said delightedly—were raw, the skin chapped and rough, not fitting the creamy complexion of her face and the soft skin on her slim arms.

'I just haven't got the time to go off to Kingsmouth,' she muttered to herself, as she removed hanger after hanger from the rail, wiping them with a J-cloth drenched in Dettol. 'I can't see why Robert should get away scot-free, I really can't.' She went over to the basin and rinsed the cloth carefully, turning it under the hot tap, then she washed her hands. She pushed a strand of pale, blond hair from her forehead and, taking a deep breath, smoothed down her cornflower-blue, silk skirt before returning smiling to the sitting room where her guests were having coffee.

'So sorry,' Dagmar said, 'I had to call to see how mother was.'

*　　*　　*

'Miss Lindsay, Miss Amelia Lindsay? I hope we didn't wake you up.' The voice on the phone was nasal and apologetic. 'I told your grandmother it was much too late to call anyone up, but she would not listen I'm afraid. Miss Lindsay, are you there?'

'Yes. No you didn't wake me up, it's quite all right. Are you calling from Cherryfield?'

'I'm sorry, didn't I say. It's Nurse Kelly, I'm duty tonight. Your grandmother has quite a temper when she wants.' The voice laughed uncertainly. 'Here's your gran now.'

50

'Amelia darling.' Selma's voice sounded faint, there was a crashing noise, nothing, then, 'Oh bugger!'

'Miss Lindsay, Mrs Merryman dropped the phone but here she is again now.'

'Amelia,' Selma's voice was small and frightened. 'I wanted to make sure I had your number.' There was a pause and Amelia could hear Selma breathing heavily into the phone. 'It's 0962 3628 ... Bother, I can't read the last number. Is it nine ... Or one?'

'But grandma, you've just called the right number, you're talking to me now.'

'Yes of course, silly of me. What did you say the number was? 0962 ...'

*   *   *

Gerald, however irritated he got with Amelia, found it impossible not to continue giving her advice, attempting to sort her life out for her. The next evening he looked up from his brief and explained that it was a form of arrogance believing that no-one but she could look after Selma. 'You just can't go running off to Devon every other week. You have your own life to lead, responsibilities here, a home to run. Then there's the question of the cost of all these trips, hotel rooms ...' He turned a page in the brief. 'You're not your grandmother's keeper you know.'

Still Amelia couldn't stop thinking of Selma

51

alone and confused at Cherryfield. Friends with new babies had said that suddenly the world seemed populated almost exclusively by infants in prams. A member of the family, not recently arrived in the world, but on the way out, tottering into certified old age, had the same effect, Amelia felt. Old people, harassed by a blinking green man turning all too fast into angry red, crossed in front of her car at pedestrian crossings. They were found in their own cars at every roundabout, sitting paralysed by the stream of traffic pouring from every direction. There they were again, fumbling for the right change in the check-out queue at the supermarket, apologizing for their outmoded habit of carrying real money.

Two weeks after her first visit to Cherryfield, Amelia was again boarding the train to Plymouth. She wondered, as she looked for a seat, what had made Gerald suddenly quite happy with her decision to go. Could it just be that she had sold another couple of articles and was able to pay for the weekend herself?

An old man settled like a large shabby bird on the seat opposite, his dark brown mac flapping round his scrawny limbs. 'All right, all right, I don't need any more reminders, I'm going down, aren't I?' Amelia muttered in an inaudible voice.

When the train passed a large and heavily populated graveyard the old man and Amelia both stared out at it.

The stones, mostly marble, rose from the ground, new and shining like giant teeth, or old crumbling white, streaked by years of rain like powdered cheeks by tears. Amelia looked over her book at the old man and wondered if he felt the pull of the graves, or if death, even at his age, was something that only happened to others?

'Nice day,' smiled the old man, showing a perfect set of white dentures.

'Lovely day,' said the nurse who opened the door for Amelia at Cherryfield.

Selma sat in a chair in front of the television, her face half turned from the programme on learning difficulties in adult life. On her lap lay her copy of the Omnibus Jane Austen. Amelia had to go right up and put her hand on Selma's arm before she looked up, a frown on her face. Resting the back of her head against the chair she gazed at Amelia, then, with a sudden delighted smile, she put out her hand. 'Darling, what a lovely surprise.'

'I phoned and told them I was coming, they should have told you.'

'The maid's been in and out of my room all morning, but she never said a word.' Selma frowned, 'I do wish I'd known, I haven't been to the shops at all this week.'

'We'll go out for lunch,' Amelia said quickly. 'Is your toe better? Are you able to walk a little?'

'It is a bit sore, but of course I can walk on it.

53

Just give me a hand up darling.'

Amelia braced herself and began to pull. For a moment Selma stood tottering on both feet, her dress riding up at the back showing the edge of her flesh-coloured knickers, then with a shriek of pain, she toppled back into the chair.

'Why don't I get the wheelchair, just for today, give the foot a bit of a rest?'

'This is quite ridiculous,' Selma muttered. 'There's absolutely nothing wrong with my foot, a small cut that's all.'

As Amelia came through the door a few minutes later, pushing the wheelchair, she heard Selma's laugh, soft and flirtatious like a girl's. At her side, chatting, stood the Admiral and his son. Henry, looking relaxed, was leaning lightly against the half-empty bookcase behind him, his father, on the other hand, attempting the same easy pose, looked strained; his elbow resting on top of the bookcase the only thing preventing him from collapsing.

'I'm going to sit down, won't you join me?' Amelia hurried forward. The Admiral shot her a grateful glance and said he'd love to.

'I get very tired standing,' she added, wondering if she might be overdoing it.

'Amelia darling, you didn't tell me your young man was here.' Selma smiled graciously at Henry.

'Grandma, that's Henry Mallett, Admiral Mallett's son.'

'What a coincidence!' Selma looked gratified. 'I believe the Admiral is staying here too.'

'Well, seeing we're all here,' Henry said, 'why don't we have lunch together?'

Amelia didn't notice the make of Henry's car, but it was burgundy coloured and they all fitted inside quite comfortably. Selma, fresh lipstick and scent applied, was hauled from the wheelchair into the front seat of the car and Amelia sat in the back with the Admiral.

Henry suggested they went to a hotel he knew on the edge of Dartmoor. They drove for half an hour, through nearby Totnes and out again on to narrow winding lanes flanked by tall hedgerows. Selma wound the window down and sighed happily as the air blew through her washed-out curls. The Admiral looked out at the passing landscape.

'You almost forget there are such creatures as children.' He smiled at three small girls on bikes.

As they parked in front of the hotel, there was a slight fracas when Selma could not release the seat belt. 'The stupid thing,' she fumed pink faced. 'It's completely stuck. No,' she said to Henry as he leant across to try, 'it doesn't matter what you ... Oh, thank you.' And she was helped out and back into the collapsible wheelchair. 'I can't wait to be back on my feet again,' she said over her shoulder to the Admiral, as Henry wheeled her towards the

55

hotel entrance.

At the table in the restaurant, the Admiral was in expansive mood. 'I'll do the wine shall I, dear boy?' he said as he peered short-sightedly at the wine list.

They had stilton soup to start with, and a glass of dry sherry. This was followed by lamb chops and new potatoes and what the Admiral called 'a robust claret'. Selma and he then ordered trifle. 'None of this nouvelle stuff,' the Admiral sniffed, 'a fellow could starve to death.' He hailed the waiter, 'Be liberal with the cream.' And he winked at Selma who giggled happily.

'You are a dreadful man.' Her chubby shoulders heaved with laughter.

It was, Amelia thought, as if the atmosphere at Cherryfield was too thin to sustain real life and that now, back in the world, Selma and the Admiral filled out and coloured in, ceasing to be old people, and becoming just people.

She looked up to see Henry smiling at her. 'How long are you home for?' she asked him.

'Most of the summer, then we deploy to the Gulf for six months. At least my father will have had a chance to settle in at Cherryfield first.'

'I wish I wasn't so far away,' Amelia sighed. 'My mother lives in Exeter but without a car it's no good staying with her.' Amelia didn't say that the thought of spending time alone with her mother in the flat made her feel like an escaped convict hauled back to prison.

'... and of course they couldn't believe their eyes at the High Commission when I dived into the pool in tropical mess dress.' The Admiral laughed loudly at the memory as he raised a spoonful of cherry-topped trifle to his lips. Suddenly there was silence and the Admiral's long face turned pink, then purple. Amelia stared as he gave a strangled cough, his pale blue eyes bulging, tears rising. Henry leapt from his chair.

At the table opposite, a young girl stared and nudged her mother, and the lunching family at another, carried on their conversation in carefully loud voices, as if to show that they at least were minding their own business.

The Admiral sat rigid in his chair as Henry prised his lips apart. He had stopped coughing and was making rasping, staccato noises, his face turning a bluish hue.

Selma didn't move but sat silent, gripping the table edge with both hands.

'An ambulance, quick!' Amelia called to the waiter.

Beads of sweat appeared on Henry's face as he pushed his fingers inside his father's mouth. Suddenly the Admiral yanked free and, with a loud belch, disgorged his dentures on the plate of trifle.

Henry dabbed his father's face with a napkin dipped in mineral water. 'It's all right Pa,' he whispered, 'I'm here.'

57

The guests at the next table left, gingerly carrying their cups of coffee, and, opposite, the teenage girl dissolved in giggles.

'It's not funny,' Amelia whispered near to tears, 'it's not funny.'

'He'll be fine now,' Henry said, looking up at her. 'I don't think we need the ambulance. Don't worry he'll be fine.'

CHAPTER FIVE

The Admiral had rested a while on a chaise-longue in the Ladies powder room, a pink towel, with 'For Our Guests' embroidered in gold thread, dampened and placed across his forehead. Now he sat in the front seat of the car, next to Henry. His head was resting against the seatback and the sun, shining though the car window, showed up little patches of colourless stubble on his chin, where he had not seen to shave.

To make room for Selma's bad foot, Henry had pushed the driver's seat forward, almost as far as it would go, and, as he was driving, his knees were pressed right up against the wheel.

Amelia was chatting, thinking it the best thing to do. 'Oh look,' she exclaimed, 'just look at those lambs. Aren't they adorable? Spring really is wonderful, so full of promise, a new beginning ...' She stopped. I'm being tactless

58

she thought.

'I mean whatever one's age,' she tried again, 'spring is . . . well sort of promising.' She caught Henry's face in the rearview mirror. A smile flickered in his eyes.

Back at Cherryfield, the Admiral was put to bed. Downstairs, Selma said, 'Don't go,' and she took Amelia's hand. As Amelia said nothing, she added as if she had just thought of it, 'Why don't I come and stay with you for a few days?'

If Selma had been ten years old, Amelia thought, she would have had her fingers crossed behind her back.

'I do feel I need a holiday,' Selma continued, in the same pretend-nonchalant voice. 'I can't remember when I last had one.'

'Grandma, I'd love you to come, but,' she paused, 'well just at the moment, things are a bit difficult at home.'

'Oh, I shouldn't worry,' Selma said cheerfully, 'I'm sure Henry wouldn't mind, he seems such a nice boy.'

Amelia breathed in deeply. She was tired, it had been a difficult day. Then she remembered how all through her life, Selma's door had always been open to her. If it had ever been inconvenient to have Amelia to stay at Ashcombe, Selma and Willoughby had never said so.

'We'd love you to come, of course we would,' she said, firmly. 'I'll arrange a day as

59

soon as I get back home. I'll see you tomorrow before I go, anyway. Mummy's coming too.' And she freed her hand and walked quickly to the door, feeling Selma's gaze on her every step.

*　　*　　*

The next morning at ten, Amelia met Dagmar outside the hotel. 'You're looking well.' Dagmar held Amelia at arms length for a moment, studying her face, then, with a pleased smile, pulled her towards her and gave her a kiss.

'So do you,' Amelia said, smiling back, surprised to find her mother's presence comforting. Dagmar did look well too; tall, blonde and elegant in her grey slacks and navy blazer, it was hard to think she was well over fifty. Constant obsessive worrying must agree with her, Amelia thought.

'It's such a nice day,' she said, 'I don't think we need a taxi.' On the walk, she told Dagmar of the disastrous lunch party and about how confused and unhappy Selma seemed.

'I agree, I agree,' mumbled Dagmar.

'And,' Amelia said, thinking, this will get a reaction from her, 'Robert lied to get her to agree to move to Cherryfield. She still thinks she's got Ashcombe to go back to. He must have used his power of attorney.'

'Dear, oh dear. That's too bad.' She heard

her mother's voice suddenly a little way off. When she turned, she found that Dagmar had stopped a couple of yards further down the hill and was busy checking the soles of her shoes, balancing precariously first on one foot, then on the other.

'What's the matter?' Amelia snapped. 'You haven't walked in anything, if that's what you are worried about. I would have smelt it.' And all the irritation accumulated over years of being her mother's daughter rose up in her, making her cruel. 'Concentrate on something other than yourself for once, will you. You have not stood, walked or sat in dogshit, no passing seagull has relieved himself in your hair...'

'Please darling,' Dagmar interrupted her, 'don't speak to me like that. I just can't help myself, you know that.'

Amelia felt like hitting her. Slap! Right across the cheek. Slap! An angry red mark across that pale, smooth skin. She could not remember a single time when she had had her mother's undivided attention, not had to compete for it with dog's mess, germs, worms and things that need wiping down in the night.

'I'm sorry, tell me again.' Dagmar's reddened hand touched Amelia's arm. And, as always after unpleasantness of any kind, whether with Dagmar, or Gerald, a friend, or the man in the shop who tells her fourteen months is a good innings these days for a washing machine, there lurked, deep under layers of righteous anger, a voice that whispered, 'It's really all your fault, Amelia.' It was a triumphant little voice and Amelia constantly feared it was the voice of reason.

'No, I'm sorry,' she said, and she went on telling her mother of the lunch with Admiral Mallett and Henry.

As the door was opened for them at Cherryfield, Dagmar stood aside to let Amelia pass, then she wiped her feet on the doormat, six times for each foot.

Selma was in the lounge. 'Do sit down, Mrs Lindsay,' Nurse Williams said to Dagmar before breezing out to answer a bell.

Dagmar said no thanks, she felt like stretching her legs, then she bent down low, kissing Selma on the cheek, careful not to touch the armrest of the chair. Dagmar always said that she wasn't worried about germs on her own account, what filled her with panic was the thought of passing them on to others. Amelia thought it might be psychologically sound to point out to her mother that by worrying about getting her hands contaminated by the chair, she risked toppling over and crushing her fragile, old mother. She put her hand under Dagmar's elbow and said, indicating the chair next to Selma, 'Why don't you sit down?'

'Yes darling, do,' Selma insisted. 'You make me feel you are about to go any moment and I do so love having you here.'

Dagmar, looking pained, perched on the armrest. 'You sit,' she said to Amelia. Her voice was light but her look implored Amelia not to argue.

'Has the Admiral been down today?' Amelia asked, doing what she was told.

'What's that darling?' Selma looked politely alert.

'Admiral Mallett, how is he this morning?'

'He wasn't down for breakfast. But of course neither was I.' Selma smiled expansively. 'Oh look, there's your young man,' she nodded towards Henry who had stopped in the doorway. 'Why don't you ask him? He seems to know Admiral Mallett better than any of us.'

'Gerald, is Gerald here?' Dagmar looked pleased. 'That's very sweet of him, coming all this way to see Mummy. Quite unlike him too.'

'Good morning everyone.' Henry joined them.

'That's not Gerald,' Dagmar hissed in Amelia's ear.

Amelia leant her head in her hands.

'Let me get you a chair, Mrs Lindsay.' She heard Henry's voice. 'You can't be very comfortable perched like that.' She looked up to see Henry carting a small chintz-covered armchair across from the other side of the room. Dagmar kept smiling as her eyes homed in on the uneven stain that spread across the

63

rose-patterned seat. Henry too was smiling as he held the chair out, waiting. Slowly, Dagmar sank down on to the seat.

'I saw such a lovely wedding dress in *Vogue* the other day.' Selma looked meaningfully at Amelia. 'Just your sort of thing too, darling. Simple, but beautifully cut.'

'You're about as subtle as a tank,' Amelia said.

'I wonder where the bathroom is,' Dagmar mumbled.

'When are you getting married?' Henry looked at Amelia with interest.

'That's a funny question coming from you?' Selma gave a disapproving little laugh.

Amelia turned to Henry, who was beginning to look confused, and said firmly, 'Not at all as far as I know,' and she felt like shaking her grandmother. Alzheimer's will only protect you so far, she thought furiously. Then her eyes fell on Selma's right hand which, even when resting in the grip of the other, kept on shaking. Like dancing feet on lame legs, she thought. What a swine I am to get angry.

She smiled across at Selma. 'It's my fault, Grandma, I keep changing my mind.'

Dagmar shot up from her chair, rather like someone who had sat with her hosts' farting dog at her feet for about as long as she could stand it. 'Where did you say the loo was, Amelia?' she demanded.

Amelia told her. And her mother would go

there, she knew, not because she needed a pee, but to check her slacks, make sure there was no stain from the chair seat and no smell. Then she would soap her hands, scrubbing right up the wrists, before rinsing them in scalding water, careful all the while not to touch the edges of the basin.

Amelia had seen it all often enough. Dagmar would utter little phrases like 'Oh that bun was sticky,' or 'I don't know why they can't make newsprint that doesn't come off the pages.' People on the whole did not think her behaviour odd. If you were good looking and well dressed, Amelia had come to realize, it took stranger acts than Dagmar's for the world to see that you were mad as a hatter.

Dagmar returned relaxed and smiling, all the tension gone from her body. 'Why don't I take Mummy for a stroll, it's so lovely out there? Coming darling?' She asked Amelia.

Amelia said she'd catch them up. 'I'll just finish my coffee.' A nurse came and helped transfer Selma into her wheelchair. Whilst they shifted and hauled, Amelia chatted all the time with her grandmother, trying to take her mind off the undignified procedure, just like a gynaecologist, she thought.

At last Selma was ready and Dagmar pushed her outside in the wheelchair, gripping the tips of the handlebars gingerly.

Henry leant closer to Amelia. 'Just go ahead and yell.' He smiled encouragingly at her.

65

'Is your father better today?' she asked instead, but she thought Henry very perceptive.

'He's not too bad, thanks, but he's spending today in bed. I left him asleep.'

'Amelia! AMELIA!' Selma was calling from the terrace where she had been parked. 'Darling, I've just had a lovely idea.' She leant forward in her wheelchair, peering at them through the open French windows. Across the path, Dagmar stared dreamily at the blossoming cherry tree. 'I shall give a party for my birthday, like we always used to.' Selma held out her hands for Amelia to come over.

'I'll be home well in time for August. I know it won't be the same without darling Willoughby,' for a moment the pleasure was gone from her face, then she made an effort to smile, 'but life must go on, we have to make an effort.'

Amelia took the handlebars and began slowly pushing the wheelchair along the terrace, and down a wooden ramp on to the lawn. She waved at Henry, who sat flicking through a magazine.

'I'll ask Admiral Mallett. You've met the Admiral, haven't you?' It's the repetitions that get you down in the end, Amelia thought, as Selma went on, 'And we mustn't forget little Mrs Finch, and Sheila and Mark, of course, and Tony Bellamy ...' Dagmar joined them as they rounded the corner back towards the

66

terrace.

'... and then there's Violet. We'd never hear the end of it if we left her out.' Selma was smiling happily.

Through the French doors, Amelia noticed that Henry had disappeared.

Later, as lunch was being served, she said goodbye to Selma and, turning to Dagmar, she said sternly, 'You're staying the day, aren't you Mummy?'

Dagmar nodded, a glint of martyrdom in her eyes.

'I have to get back to Devonport,' Henry came down from his father's room. 'I can give you a lift to the station.'

They drove for a while in silence. It took time always, Amelia thought, to shake off Cherryfield. Then as they turned on to the Plymouth road, she said to Henry, 'Would you mind if I raged against God, just for a minute or two?'

'Dig out.' Henry smiled. He was driving rather fast on the outside lane.

'Seriously though,' Amelia said, feeling hot and pushing her hair from her face, 'it's the way God seems to have of giving with one hand, whilst taking with the other. Just look at life. We're given it, great, hurrah! But there's always a sad ending. I mean, who's ever heard of a happy death?'

Henry said nothing but seemed to be listening as he overtook a stream of heavy lorries swaying along the inside lane.

'You would think that birth, at least, would be a completely happy affair, but oh no. Even these days when it's fairly safe, it's still painful and essentially, humiliating. It makes a mockery of what every nice girl since Eve has been taught. "Keep your fanny to yourself, dear," the cry has echoed through the ages, and then the poor girl has half the world staring at her ...' Amelia stopped. 'I'm doing it again,' she said. 'I'm sorry. I'm just hopelessly coarse.'

'Don't worry. Really.' Henry turned a sharp left where it was signposted, 'Station'. 'You carry on.'

'It's just a small example of course,' she suggested meekly, 'but I feel it would have been helpful if the things we like to keep private and the things that have to be public had been more equally divided between the organs. Not concentrated higgledy-piggledy in one area,' Amelia finished lamely.

'I think,' Henry said, 'that you're a little bit unfair to God. He gave most of us perfectly good, effective, reproductive organs that also happen to take care of other, equally important functions. That's all. So you can hardly blame Him for us losing our innocence and getting all coy and refined, can you now?' He drove up in front of the entrance. 'Anyway,' he said, 'you'd need awfully big ears.' And he walked round and opened the car door for her.

CHAPTER SIX

The neck of a champagne bottle periscoped through the ice that was melting inside a red, plastic bucket. It stood in the middle of the kitchen table and was the first thing Gerald saw as he came in, two hours late from the office. 'What's this in aid of?' He threw his briefcase on a chair and loosened his tie.

'In aid of? Oh, nothing in particular.' Then Amelia smiled and threw her arms round his neck. 'I just felt like celebrating, that's all.'

'I don't expect you've noticed, but there is a recession on. Anyway,' he made his voice patient, 'felt like celebrating what?'

'That we're not old and incontinent—all right so I go to the loo four times a night, but at least I get there—that we've got our own place where we can please ourselves, sit with our feet on the table drinking wine and reading, stay up all night, sleep all day, throw a party.' She flung her arms out. 'Anything.' She put a tall-stemmed glass in front of him.

'Do you realize what a luxury it is just to be able to go into your own kitchen and cook whatever *you* want to eat, maybe bring it into the sitting room in front of the television.'

'You know I hate TV dinners,' Gerald said, sitting down with a sigh.

Amelia tried again. Looking quite serious

now, she said, 'Most importantly of all, we've got each other.'

She hauled the bottle from the bucket, dripping water all over the front of her khaki skirt and white cotton shirt. One of his shirts, Gerald noticed. And he wondered, how does she do it? How does someone as vague, as fragile as Amelia, cling on to an illusion with such strength? Wearily he accepted the glass she handed him, she had over-filled it of course. He sipped the champagne and thought how much he preferred a really first class Chablis.

Earlier in the day, Gerald's father had come into his son's office for a chat. 'Gerald, old chap,' he had begun, touching Gerald's shoulder rather in the manner of someone being told to caress a pet snake, 'I know things have changed since my day, we're in the nineties after all. I mean to say, you can hardly put on the television these days without being reminded of the fact.'

At this Gerald couldn't help enquiring, 'Is that the only reason you know what decade it is, because you've seen it on the box?'

'Oh never mind that.' Norman Forbes slid his middle finger along the inside of his collar. 'What I'm trying to say is; it's time you and Amelia got married, time you had a family too for that matter, although that of course is none of my business. With Amelia having passed the thirty mark though . . .' He caught Gerald's eye and clearing his throat, went on, 'This bohemian bit, it's a phase you go through, like having a crush on a chum, that sort of thing.' For a moment, Norman looked wistful.

Gerald was drumming a little tune on the desk with his fingers.

'Living in sin,' Norman said, 'people expect that sort of thing from an artist, positively good for business I shouldn't wonder. But let's face it, you're a solicitor now, and that makes it all different, well in Hampshire it does, anyway.'

Gerald sighed, 'That's exactly what Amelia keeps saying.'

'Well she's a sensible girl. Now I've told you my opinion, as your father and senior partner in the firm. But of course it's your life and your decision entirely.' And Norman had coughed in an encouraging manner and, looking well pleased with himself, strode from the room.

Gerald had banged his fist against the frame round the closed door, very hard, several times, then he had gone in to Clarissa's small office next door and given her some extra work to keep her late.

Back in his own office, he had sat in the brown leather wingchair he'd inherited from his grandfather and thought of how he agreed with his father and Amelia. It really was time he got married and had a family.

There was one point, however, on which he differed from them; it was not Amelia, but Clarissa he wanted to share this new life with.

71

It was Clarissa he wanted to marry, and to be the mother of his children. Clarissa with her solid good sense and her working girl independence, tempered so nicely, he couldn't help thinking, with a good deal of respect for Gerald himself. Amelia, he thought, is a constant reminder of all those past dreams that crash-landed on impact with reality.

'You're not exactly sparkling company.' Amelia, careful not to sound whining, leant across the kitchen table, smiling at Gerald who sat staring morosely into the huge vase of daffodils. She sniffed the air and sat up straight. 'Your scent clashes with mine.'

'What? Oh.' Gerald cleared his throat. Here was his chance. The moment, handed to him on a plate, to come clean. 'Sorry old girl,' he would say, 'there's someone else. It's her scent, Diorissimo, you can smell on my lapel.'

He drained the almost full glass of champagne. 'Oh that,' he said. 'One of the girls, temp as a matter of fact, spilt a whole bottle of the stuff over a brief I was handling.' And that was that. He'd blown it. 'Quite a nice scent really,' he added pathetically.

Later that evening, Gerald lay, unable to sleep, on his side of the wide brass bed. What kept him awake was the unfairness of everything. How could he rest when the world around him was so utterly unreasonable? After all, here he was, an increasingly popular and successful solicitor of thirty-five, unable to marry the nice, perfectly respectable and above all, reasonable, helpmate that was Clarissa. Unable to marry her because of his mistress.

He threw his part of the duvet aside and sat up, noisily splashing Evian water into a glass from the bottle on the bedside table. 'Mistress' was a dated concept, he knew that. He drank down the water in great gulps. But his mistress was what Amelia was. It would have been nice to add 'kept woman', to 'mistress', but he knew that would not be fair. After all she earned quite a bit from her freelancing and there was the money from the sale of her flat.

But she had the mentality of a kept woman then, he decided angrily as he threw himself back down on to his pillow. Come to think of it, he was surprised that she was as successful as she actually was at her work.

He remembered the first time he'd met her, at the exhibition. 'Will you model for me?' he had asked pretty soon after first being introduced. 'I'm planning a nude,' he'd said, looking deep into her slanted grey eyes. 'A sort of eighties Rubensesque effect; the lusciousness of the past, with the new, more angular woman of today.' He had drained his wine glass, expecting her to either laugh or be offended.

But she'd just smiled and said, 'I'd love to. When?'

All so typical of Amelia, he thought bitterly. That immediate and surprising yes, her turning

73

up all smiles in his studio the next afternoon, as agreed. And then panicking, flatly refusing to place her slender, naked right leg across the arm of the chair in the pose he required.

'I'm sorry, I really am,' she had sobbed, 'but I can only model with my legs together.'

Raising himself on one elbow, Gerald looked down at Amelia sleeping at his side, her wavy, auburn hair spread across the white pillow-case, her cheek with its sprinkling of pale freckles, resting on her hand. For a moment, quite against his will, tenderness replaced anger. He bent down and brushed her cheeks with his lips then, sighing deeply, he rolled on to his back and closed his eyes.

*   *   *

Hitler had been a handwasher, Stalin too, Dagmar had read somewhere.

I'm not keeping very nice company, she thought, and she couldn't help smiling, a sad flash of a smile. She was sitting in bed, wrapped in misery as if it was a second blanket. She was in no doubt that the misery was self inflicted and wholly unnecessary, but that, she thought, was about as much help as knowing that you should never have walked under that bus.

I drove away my husband, worried him away. And I've lost Amelia's respect for ever. Dagmar wiped tears from her eyes and, taking a fresh Kleenex from the box at her side, blew

74

her nose noisily. How could a child ever respect a mother like Dagmar? One who, while all normal mothers fretted over the Cold War and what Mick Jagger's lips might do to their daughter's innocence, spent precious hours and days worrying whether or not a door handle could pass on a deadly disease.

And now I'm fifty-five, she thought, and still worrying about the wrong things. All over the world, women were voicing their concern over nuclear power and Aids, and the safety of hormone replacement therapy. But Dagmar was not amongst them. Her thoughts would often drift towards these topics, hover anxiously, touch down briefly. On the whole the resulting conclusions were sensible, robust even. 'Make him use a condom if you are at all unsure,' she would say to Amelia. 'And cold hearted as it might seem, I would think twice before giving mouth to mouth, especially if there are bleeding gums involved.'

But then these were normal concerns and when you've spent the day disinfecting clothes pegs, there was so little time left for normality.

And now, sitting in the king-sized marital bed she never could make herself throw out, she thought for a moment of all the squandered years, of all the planes that had flown overhead, whilst she was stuck on the ground with her unnecessary luggage. She could only dwell on it for a moment though, any more and the thought of all that waste became unbearable.

She reached for the books on the bedside table. She'd read some Wodehouse, she decided, he never failed to cheer her up. It was a new trade paperback of collected novels, her own copy. She had stopped borrowing from the library after discovering that people really did pick their noses whilst they read.

She opened the book at the start of the second story. She read a few lines but she couldn't concentrate. Her hands needed washing. She told herself there was no reason to wash them. 'Look,' she said to herself, 'look, they're clean, perfectly clean.' But she couldn't enjoy Madeleine Basset's soppy speeches or laugh at Bertie's struggles with his aunts, not whilst her stomach felt as if it was filling up with performing fleas.

Again she stretched her raw hands out in front of her. 'Look you stupid woman, there's nothing on them, can't you see?' She was pleading with herself now, but it didn't work, the fleas were performing a clog dance round her guts by now. Near to tears once more, she put the book down carefully on a pristine part of the bed cover and padded across to the bathroom.

That was the trouble with germs, she sniffed to herself as she soaped and scrubbed her hands under the scalding water, they could not be seen. She wished the little buggers could be. They should wear scarlet sweat-shirts with 'I'm a Harmful Germ' blazoned across the chest.

She got back into bed, stretching her legs out, the fleas were gone for now. Next time, she promised herself as she picked up the book, she really would not give in.

*   *   *

At Cherryfield, Selma too was in bed. She'd been there since nine o'clock. She had slept a while, now she dozed. Her bed was warm and soft, the room dark. Her toe wasn't hurting. When Willoughby came to bed she would tell him. He was worried about her, she knew from the way he looked at her when he thought she didn't notice, half affectionate, half exasperated.

'Go and see Dr Scott, there's a good girl,' he had said as her toe got steadily more painful, as the dark shadow on the skin grew in diameter.

But Selma never visited the doctor and Willoughby, bless him, knew that.

She smiled to herself in the darkness of the room. 'Dear, dear Willoughby,' she mumbled sleepily. How lucky she was to have found him. He had married her when she had felt she had nothing to share but grief. He had been as loving and patient a father to Dagmar as he had been to his own son.

'I came to Sweden to look for iron ore and what did I mine but pure gold,' he would tell anyone who'd listen, anyone who'd ask how he

77

went to Sweden to return with a beautiful, Jewish wife and a small, blonde daughter.

Selma drifted along on her good memories. Then, as her gaze fell on unfamiliar objects, she tried to sit up. Where was the large painted mirror that lived on her dressing-table? And her mother's chaise-longue? Where was Willoughby?

She felt the side of the narrow bed. 'Willoughby!' she screamed.

There were footsteps outside the room, then slowly the door opened, letting in a sliver of light. Shuffling steps approached the bed. Out of the darkness, a hand appeared, groping round the top of the bedside table. Muttering to himself, the Admiral reached into the glass where Selma's teeth lay. Drying them in a perfunctory manner against the silk lapel of his dressing-gown he dropped them into a sponge bag where they clattered on top of the five other sets already gathered up.

'Who's that?' Selma's voice trembled as she searched for the light, her blanket pulled up to her neck. 'Who *is* that? What's going on?'

But the Admiral had retreated.

CHAPTER SEVEN

The next morning Amelia woke feeling hungover and miserable. It was Gerald's fault.

78

She'd been forced to drink almost the whole bottle of champagne herself last night, he'd refused even a second glass. She rested her throbbing temples against the cool palms of her hands. With all his talk of a recession, she thought angrily, how could he expect her not to feel she had to finish the bottle. And now he'd gone off without waking her.

Brushing her teeth, thirty seconds on each one as her dentist had told her (it seemed less of a bother than having to decide what next to do) she looked at her face in the mirror. Not too bad, she thought, wiping the toothpaste from her mouth, considering how rotten she was feeling. She didn't think Gerald really looked at her any more; it was a shame. Soon all those little plump cells would become desiccated and the skin would support her flesh no better than a washed out bra or one of those net shopping bags that expanded downwards with every new pound in weight added.

Arching her back, she wondered idly whether a pencil would still drop to the floor if placed under her breasts. She thought she'd better not put it to the test.

It was not that thirty-one was old, she thought, more that nowadays the streets seemed full of people younger.

She pulled the nightdress over her head and, stepping over it as it lay crumpled on the floor, wandered in under the shower.

Even forty wasn't old, it was just that much

nearer to fifty. She tried unsuccessfully to rub up some lather with the Strawberry Body Shampoo. Life, she thought, was just a rush from one birthday to another. You were born, had a quick dance round the flame, then Cherryfield.

Maybe, she thought as she dried herself with Gerald's towel—hers was still in a heap in the bedroom—maybe he was suffering from the male menopause? Her married friends used the phrase frequently on the subject of their husbands. It was a useful blanket explanation of course, as it covered as many sins as the husbands themselves. Anything from unprovoked bursts of fury, bad tempered remarks like, 'So what, grilled lamb-chops have always been my favourite, they damn well aren't now!' to erratic behaviour in bed.

She dressed and slapped some sun-block on her face while she waited for two aspirin to dissolve in a glass of Gerald's fizzy water. She felt she could understand what these men were going through, not excuse them, but understand. She could see them young and confident, so sure they would matter, believing the world to be a mess just waiting for them to clear up. Then all too soon there they were, knocking on the door to middle-age, powerless to change anything much but their wives.

But Gerald was still young. She looked at his photograph taken the summer before, as she sprayed herself liberally with Shalimar. She

80

liked to wear Shalimar when she gardened, it was so unsuitable. There was still time for him to appear on breakfast television as their legal eagle, or to fight to save the rain forests.

Why was Gerald so discontented? Amelia stabbed at the heavy, black soil with a massive garden fork, attempting to dislodge the last of the season's leeks.

It had rained during the night and the sun refracted through the drops of water collected in the pale green foliage. The fruity scent of the slowly warming soil mixed with the sour smell of the leeks, and a few steps away at the edge of the vegetable garden, the cypress was flowering with tiny pink tips at the end of its coniferous leaves.

Amelia straightened up, holding the trug heavy with soil-laden leeks. Looking around her, she listened to the comforting counterpoint of rumbling traffic and bird song; I love this place, she thought.

On her way inside, the phone rang and, not bothering to take off her boots, she hurried through the kitchen and into the hall.

'It's Henry Mallett.' His voice sounded lighter than she remembered. 'They gave me your number at Cherryfield, I hope you don't mind.'

'Not at all,' Amelia said as she perched on the edge of the hall table, idly watching the mud slide off the sole of her boots and on to the fawn-coloured carpet.

'Sister Morris said she was sure you wouldn't. "You are a man of the cloth, after all, Mr Mallett."' Henry managed a passable imitation of Sister Morris. 'Actually I wondered if you were planning to come down again soon. We might have dinner together?' There was a slight pause. 'It would cheer me up.'

'I'm afraid Gerald takes a pretty dim view of me going down too often,' Amelia said. 'I wasn't planning to go for another week or so.' She paused. 'Is anything wrong that you need cheering up?'

'No, not really. There's been a bit of trouble over my father, nothing much, something to do with dentures. I'll see you next time you're down.' And he said goodbye.

Amelia replaced the handset with the uneasy feeling of having let someone down.

* * *

At just that time, Sister Morris was sitting in the kitchen at Cherryfield, gazing in despair at the heap of dentures that lay before her on the formica-topped table. In the dining room, the residents were getting restless.

'I just don't know how we'll ever work out which belongs to whom.'

'Be Prince Charming.' Nurse Williams breezed in with a couple of empty jugs in her hands.

82

'I beg your pardon.' Sister Morris glared at her.

'You'll just have to go round all the kingdom trying them on.' And Nurse Williams was gone.

'Very droll.' Sister Morris returned her disapproving gaze to the dentures. Shaking her head she said to the cook, 'They'll have to have tapioca, Ruth, there's nothing else for it.'

'No tapioca,' said Ruth, who rationed her words as if they were taken from her own meagre salary. 'Wednesday's All Bran.'

'But what are we to do?' Sister Morris wailed. 'Just think what All Bran will do to their gums.'

'Rather not,' said Ruth.

*   *   *

When Gerald returned from the office that evening, making Amelia run to her typewriter in the bay of the sitting room pretending she had been working all along, he announced, 'I'm taking a week off, to go fishing with Nick and Tom.' He said it rather angrily. As if, Amelia thought studying his face, he was reacting to a fuss not yet made. 'Oh,' was all she said.

'All right, out with it, you're upset.' Glowering, Gerald threw his jacket on the armchair. 'You don't own me you know.'

'I never...'

83

'You really have to develop some independence.'

'. . . said I did.'

'Learn to be on your own a bit.' Gerald picked up the magazine on Amelia's desk, looked at the open page and slammed it down again.

Amelia looked at the page too, it was a perfectly harmless one, she thought, unhappily, on the subject of religious festivals.

There was a fizzing noise as Gerald opened a tonic bottle. Then he swore as the tonic overflowed on to Aunt Edith's rosewood card-table. 'Someone's been shaking the bloody bottle,' Gerald said slowly.

Amelia had had enough. 'That was me,' she said, 'I ran out of maracas. As for you going fishing, you are perfectly entitled to go where ever you like, after all, we're not even married.'

'That's right,' Gerald turned, looking almost pleased, 'bring that up, I knew you would, sooner or later.'

Close to tears, Amelia said, 'It's like speaking to the Red Queen in Alice. I only meant that I agree, I don't own you. And if I do mind you going it's only because I would not want to go on holiday without *you* so maybe I'm just a little disappointed that you don't feel the same.' She wiped her eyes angrily with the sleeve of her sweat-shirt. 'That's all,' she added lamely.

On Sunday, Gerald left for his trip. He had spent most of the two previous days noisily carting rods and tins and boots from various parts of the house into the hall. They hadn't spoken much, other than for the purpose of getting on with daily life. Amelia had nursed the hope that her uncharacteristic silence would come to worry Gerald, but in the end she thought that he either liked it or hadn't noticed. She carried on searching the housing pages of local papers for premises suitable for a tea-shop, and worked on the article on the introduction of multi-cultural assemblies in the local schools. 'I'm particularly well qualified for that one,' she muttered to herself as she watched Gerald search for his copy of *Fly-fishing: Poetry in Motion.* 'Seeing as I'm a half-Swedish, half-English, Anglican Jew, living in an unorthodox relationship with a pig.'

'What was that?' Gerald turned to her with a really friendly smile and Amelia, feeling instantly ashamed, smiled back. 'Nothing, nothing at all.' Possessiveness really is an ugly trait, she thought. So she added, 'I hope the fish bite.'

'Where?' Gerald asked, making her laugh.

His goodbye kiss was surprisingly warm, especially considering he had a suitcase in one hand and two fishing rods in the other. 'Was it

Friday you were going down to Cherryfield?' he asked. 'I like to know where I can reach you.'

'You take care,' he called from the open car window, raising his arm in a salute as he drove off. And it seemed to Amelia, as she stood waving by the front door, that the car leapt out of the drive like a spring lamb sighting green pasture.

CHAPTER EIGHT

Amelia closed the front door behind Gerald, straightened her shoulders and decided to make good use of the time he was away. In fact, she thought as she walked briskly through to her desk, it was no bad thing having a week to herself; she could finish the article, clear out her wardrobe, have lunch with a friend, even visit Selma.

But each evening, as the shadows lengthened in the garden, like ghosts dragging their cloaks across the rose-beds, she felt lonely. It was as if she needed another living body around to assure her that she existed outside her own imagination.

When she first moved with Gerald to Abbotslea she had dreamt of concerned vicars on the prowl for dry sherry and converts, of gossipy post-mistresses and nosy neighbours.

She had always had a soft spot for nosy neighbours; they cared, she thought, but the village had turned out a disappointment. Pretty as a chocolate-box cover it may be, but there was a constant display of For Sale signs, standing like flag-poles, in front of the rose-covered cottages as the younger residents climbed up the housing ladder and the older ones, the nosy, gossipy, church-going ones, died off.

True collectivism, Amelia thought, was to be found, not on a farm in Bulgaria, but amongst the older inhabitants of an English country village; 'I've got a glut of broadbeans this season, you have some and I wouldn't say no to a trug of that tasty looking beetroot.' Signs in the village shop-window saying, 'I'm off to town the first Thursday of every month and will have three spare seats in the car. Any one wanting a lift, stand at the disused bus stop on Main Street at eight-thirty.'

But that was all going. It lay interred in the pretty churchyard on top of Vicarage Hill with the bones of old Mrs Craig, bossy Miss Payne and Major Stapleton, lately of the Royal Fusiliers. Behind them came the new-age villagers, blaming each other for the lack of village life as they boarded the seven-fifteen for London or, to be fair Amelia thought, stayed behind locked doors writing articles for the national press about the dissolution of the village spirit.

87

As she sat on Wednesday evening watching six recorded episodes of *Neighbours*, her supper on a tray in front of her, Amelia thought she really was a true parasite. Without another human to feed off she began to function badly, becoming shrivelled of thought and pale of mind.

She looked at the video, pushing forkfuls of the glutinous, cooling pasta around her plate. There was Cherryfield, beckoning in the distance like an old, painted tart: 'Give me your cash and I'll soon make you comfortable.'

'And this,' she said out loud, 'is how I choose to spend the precious time until her arms close round me.' As she spoke, she saw her words fanning out into the room, beetling along the skirting-board, across the sofa and chairs, searching for a listener, before returning to her in ribbon formation.

That's it, she thought, I'm going to bed.

The next morning she opened her curtains to a sky that looked as if it had been painted by an artist with only one shade of dull, mid-grey at his disposal. After dressing, Amelia put the now-finished article in a brown, A4 envelope and, grabbing her handbag, went off to the village shop.

It had stopped raining but a chill breeze made her button up her washed-out green puffa. She always wore the puffa in Abbotslea, it was a statement: I might live in sin with your family solicitor, it said, but at heart I'm a harmless and conventional creature. It was impossible, Amelia hoped, to be a threat and wear a puffa, both at the same time.

As she reached The Stores, she heard her name called. Approaching from the opposite direction, pushing a pram, came Rosalind Hall, Amelia's closest friend in the village. She was wearing a canary yellow sou'wester and round the huge wheels of the old carriage pram, the water splashed, throwing little glistening spears in every direction.

Amelia waited for her, glad to find someone to chat to, although since the birth of little Ronald, Rosalind's son, their friendship had lost its comfortable quality. Rosalind spent a good deal of the time apologizing for having a baby, whilst Amelia apologized for not having one.

'Lucky you,' Rosalind said now, not meaning it, 'you can just put on your coat and march off. If you knew the time it took to get ready with a tiny.'

Amelia refrained from asking, 'Tiny what?' Instead she told Rosalind sincerely that she longed to have someone holding her up.

'Gerald seems very pleased with himself these days, what are you doing to him?' Rosalind asked for something to say, as she smiled down at Ronald who showed his naked gums in an irresistible grin. 'Who's Mummy's little man then?' she cooed to him as she gently rocked the pram with her gumbooted foot.

Amelia looked pleasantly surprised. 'I didn't think I was doing anything right as far as Gerald's concerned. He's not home at the moment, actually.' Amelia sighed. 'It's ridiculous, he's only away for a week, but I really miss him.' As she spoke she bobbed up and down, trying to keep at eye-level with Rosalind whose head kept disappearing under the hood of the pram.

Rosalind looked up with an indulgent smile. 'If that's what not being married does to a relationship, maybe Chris and I should go for divorce. I mean, London is only an hour away.'

'What do you mean London is only an hour away?'

Rosalind's sou'wester appeared again. 'I mean London is not a long distance away from Abbotslea.' She spoke with the same practised patience she employed when speaking to little Ronald. 'As I saw Gerald across the street from the Royal Academy—and you told me he was away for the week—and as childbirth has not completely addled my razor-sharp brain, I put two and two together and assumed London was where Gerald was. We wanted to see the Monet exhibition.' Rosalind's head darted back under the hood and Amelia heard a muffled, 'Didn't we Ronnikins?'

'Gerald was in London yesterday?' Amelia's main feeling was of stupidity. She saw Rosalind's lips move, she heard the words they spoke, but she was damned if she understood.

90

'Did you speak to him?'

Rosalind was beginning to look impatient. 'No, as a matter of fact, I didn't. We just waved across the street. Yes, Mummy's sausage waved to Mr Forbes, didn't he?'

'You're sure it was Gerald?'

Ronald let out a sudden, anguished wail. Rosalind looked at her watch as she loosened the break on the pram with a kick of the foot. 'I didn't go up to him and ask for his driving licence or genetically fingerprint him or anything, but it looked like Gerald to me. Now I really must get home and give Ronnie his elevenses, the poor little mite is starving.'

For once, as she stepped inside the village shop, Amelia was pleased that it was no longer run by Wing Commander Stephens OBE AFC. He'd been a source of endless amusement to Amelia as he plied his trade, always fearful that in so doing he had come down in the world. His manner was chill towards anyone with a small child, an ice-cream or an address in the wrong part of the village and jovially officious to others. It was a manner that had sent most of the villagers into the anonymous comfort of the supermarket in nearby Alresford. Sometimes, Mrs Stephens would appear in check polyester overalls, and tell Amelia of their days attached to the Embassy in Peru, the glittering parties they gave, and the people they met. In the end though even the weekly Saturday sell-off of out-of-date stock couldn't save the Wing Commander from the realities of supply and demand. When he finally sold up, the view of the village was that it had been only a matter of time until he was closed down by the health inspector anyway.

The Stores had been taken over by a big-thinking young couple from a nearby village who were planning a chain of Mini-Marts. Whilst continuing to carry the usual stock: sweets and biscuits, tinned soups and rice-puddings, speciality cheeses and teas, they added frozen Weight-watcher meals, videos for hire and a sub-Post Office, and employed a girl for the newly installed check-out who displayed much the same attitude to her customers as a gardener to worms; as a breed they were necessary but on a one to one basis they had little to offer.

In the old days, Amelia, who had won favour with the Wing Commander due to her pretty face and connections with the Forbeses and in spite of her short skirts and unorthodox relationship with the Forbes' son, would have had to explain both Gerald's business in being absent and her own glum face. As it was, she posted her envelope and bought her cheese and bread with the minimum communication needed for the transactions.

'First class is it? That'll be thirty-one pence,' at the Post Office counter, and 'Two pounds exactly, thank you,' at the check-out.

The rest of the morning, Amelia tried to

make sense of what Rosalind had told her. She hated mysteries and uncertainties. They sent her into frenzied, ineffective action, like someone with a ceiling leaking in five places but only one bucket. First she called Gerald's office to ask his father where Gerald was. She liked Norman and he was fond of her. She wouldn't mind admitting to him that she had mislaid his son. But Norman was at a meeting and the secretary didn't know where Mr Gerald Forbes could be reached, either. 'Is this Miss Lindsay?'

'No, no it isn't,' Amelia answered, suddenly talking at the front of her mouth, in a feeble attempt to disguise her voice.

Next she telephoned Gerald's friend Tom, who was meant to be on the trip. Only the answering machine was at home and, in the manner of those machines, gave little away other than that, 'Tom can't come to the phone right now . . .'

She couldn't call Nick, she didn't have his number or address. She sat by the phone, trying to calm herself down. Gerald would be in touch. There was bound to be a reasonable explanation of why he'd been seen in the centre of London whilst on a fishing trip to Scotland. Gerald was nice. He didn't lie. Any moment now he'd come through the door explaining that the trip had been cut short.

He didn't come home and there was no word from him that day, nor the next. Furious,

93

fretting, with a feeling in her stomach as if her guts were being twisted like spaghetti round a fork, she sat at the kitchen table breathing deeply: in, out, in and out. She visualized herself as a giant boiling kettle with a cork stuffed down its spout, making it impossible for the steam to escape as the pressure was building (she had once attended relaxation classes with Dagmar). 'Now remove that cork,' she said to herself, her voice taking on a faint American accent. 'Feel the steam just pouring out.'

'Sod it!' she screamed, as the vision was taking on a life of its own, with Amelia straddling the huge kettle, desperately wrestling with the cork. 'Bloody hell, bloody, fucking hell!' She stood up, yelling so her throat hurt, her fists pounding the air.

That did help. Pacing the room, she stopped at the open window and leant out, breathing in the damp air.

'Amelia, is that you?' Mrs Jenkins from next door stood by the low stone wall. She was smiling, but it was rather a tight-lipped smile. 'I thought I heard your voice.'

'Mrs Jenkins, ah, yes . . . I was just rehearsing my lines for . . . for the Cherryfield Home for the Elderly's summer play. They're a pretty modern lot at Cherryfield.' She gave a quick wave and dived out of sight.

Twenty-four hours later, Amelia packed an overnight bag and, leaving a note for Gerald to contact her in case he arrived home before her, set off for Kingsmouth.

CHAPTER NINE

Selma loved plants. At Ashcombe they had surrounded her; green bodyguards in the drawing room, a scented, multi-coloured fence outside. When she had first arrived, holding her small, white-faced daughter by the hand, she had walked outside on to the terrace in the moonlight. The camomile crushed under their feet had filled the air around them with its soporific scent, as she looked across the garden to a glimpse of the sea beyond.

* * *

'Get away from me you bloody fool!' As Amelia approached Cherryfield in the late afternoon, Selma's voice reached her from the open first-floor window. Amelia, shocked at hearing her grandmother yell obscenities in much the same manner as she herself had done earlier that day, ducked to avoid a beige Scholl sandal flying straight at her.

A potted begonia, tracing the path of the sandal, crashed at her feet, having narrowly missed her right temple. She could see no-one at the window until a uniformed arm appeared

95

slamming it shut. Bending down again, she picked up the shoe from amid the soil and bits of shattered clay and brushed it off, before resuming her walk to the front door. She rang the bell, her cheeks reddening in anticipation of the telling off from Sister Morris. 'I'm sure she didn't mean to,' she rehearsed. 'She probably didn't realize the window was open.'

'Cooee! Amelia darling!'

She took a step back to find that Selma had managed to open the window again and was leaning out, pink-cheeked and smiling. 'What a lovely surprise. I'll be right down, if ...' Her voice became laden with reproach as she turned into the room. 'If I'm allowed to.'

As Selma descended sideways in the chairlift, her chubby back straight, Amelia wondered if she should mention at least in passing that she had been almost knocked out by a potted plant, maybe even get Selma to give some kind of explanation that might satisfy the still absent Sister Morris. But her grandmother looked so normal, so happy to see her, that she said nothing.

'If you could pass me that wretched thing,' Selma said, pointing at the walking frame standing at the bottom of the stairs. Slowly, her hands, then her weight, were transferred to the frame, and Amelia followed her grandmother's hesitant shuffling towards the conservatory. Now and then Selma would halt, forgetting to move one foot in front of the

96

other, like a sick baby forgetting to breathe. Then with a little start, the shuffle would continue.

'We're doing ever so well on the frame now.' Nurse Williams smiled approvingly at them as they passed in the lounge. There was no mention of the scene upstairs. 'I told you Mrs M, didn't I tell you, there's no harm in trying, I said.'

Amelia got Selma settled in a wicker armchair. She looked at her grandmother's face, it looked such a small face all of a sudden, unsure, all fury spent. 'Are you eating properly?' she asked.

'I get terribly bored with the food here,' Selma said. 'I much preferred it in the other place.'

Amelia couldn't bring herself to ask, 'What other place?' So she said nothing.

'Of course I can't wait until I'm back in my own kitchen.' From having fussed with her handbag and the position of her sore foot, Selma suddenly looked directly at Amelia, 'Play the game with me, please,' her eyes seemed to say.

'I'm sure you're getting better every day,' Amelia said sidling round the truth.

'I won't get better whilst I'm here,' Selma insisted. She leant over as far as she could towards Amelia. 'It's a funny place. You can't make any plans. You know, I don't think I've had a swim in weeks.' She leant back again,

97

closing her eyes for a moment. 'There are no animals here either.'

Each visit, Amelia had dreaded Selma asking after the cats, but she never did, and it struck Amelia that Selma didn't ask about lots of things because she was too frightened of the answers.

'I only live for the moment when I can go back,' Selma said matter of factly.

Amelia felt her cheeks going hot. It was her turn to lean forward and she took Selma's shaking hand between her own two and forced it still. 'It won't be long, I'm sure it won't.'

'Promise?' Selma smiled.

'Promise,' said Amelia, feeling sick.

Selma closed her eyes, and soon she was asleep, leaving Amelia pondering impossible schemes of how to fulfil that promise. Maybe, she thought tiredly, Selma would forget, like she forgot so much else.

Amelia relaxed. Time, in the overheated room, seemed to float. There had been so many times when she'd sat watching Selma doze off in her chair after lunch. Selma had always been a great one for naps. 'You stay here by me, darling,' she'd say, sitting in the bay of the drawing room at Ashcombe, her chair turned towards the window and the view of the sea. 'I'll just close my eyes for a moment,' and she would lean back and go to sleep in just this way. Selma loved the sea, the constantly changing scene from the window. She seemed

98

to bear it no resentment for taking her first husband, Amelia's real grandfather, away from her.

'I stood on the quayside in Gothenburg, waiting each morning for the ferry that would bring him and his parents and sister back from Germany,' Selma had told Amelia.

'I was like the statue of the Seaman's Wife, looking out over the harbour entrance, hoping, watching. The ferries came and ships too, and there were refugees onboard, but never Daniel or his family. Your grandfather was a brave man; he went back to Germany knowing what might happen.'

Selma never wanted to talk about what followed, but there was the postcard, in a hand quite unlike that in the old love letters from Daniel that Amelia had found in a silk-lined box at the back of Selma's huge walnut closet. The uncertain writing on the card said in German, 'I've been taken to a detention camp for my own safety, and am well and healthy.' But Daniel had died in Belsen, and in a drawer in Selma's desk was the letter from Daniel's mother before she too was taken. Only Selma could read the spindly writing, but they all knew the letter, Tante Magda's last letter in its yellowing envelope. There were some photographs too, snapshots of a long-ago summer holiday. In one, Daniel, tall, auburn-haired like Amelia, smiled into the camera, his arm round Selma's shoulder. In another, Tante

Magda sat in the shade of a parasol with Ella, Daniel's little sister, at her side. Some letters, a few photographs, were all that remained of a family.

Amelia sat at Cherryfield, thinking of her grandfather Daniel who had died when he was younger than she was now, and she knew that against his suffering the mislaying of Gerald weighed less than a feather.

When she was small and feeling sorry for herself, Amelia, like most children, had been told to think of those who were worse off. It had always worried her, this summoning up of images of suffering just so that her infinitely lighter burdens would seem even slighter. What was it other than the exploitation of tragedy? Who was there to ask? Selma, more often that not, averted her eyes and mind from that which disturbed her, homing in instead on what was pleasant, a flower, a pretty face, a swath of material just right for the dining-room chairs. Dagmar, on the other hand, seemed convinced that suffering lay in wait behind every poor dupe engaged in carefree pleasure, so rather than be taken unawares, she would seek trouble out, take it by the hand and invite it into her life. Then of course, she could sit back, relax for a moment even, and say, 'There, I told you, we're none of us safe.'

Amelia turned her chair away from the sun that shone low and straight through the window, making her eyes ache.

'What was that darling?' Selma jerked awake in her chair, gazing sleepy-eyed at Amelia.

'I ought to go soon,' Amelia said. 'It's nearly your supper-time. I'll be here most of tomorrow, maybe we could go down to town.'

'Don't leave yet,' Selma said as she always did. 'There,' she pointed at the glass doors leading in to the lounge. 'There's Admiral Mallett, you must stay and meet him.' She raised herself a little in the chair and waved. Smiling at the Admiral who had spotted them, she mouthed, the smile still in place, 'Poor old Admiral Mallett, he's a dear, sweet man, but, between you and me, I think he's just the slightest bit potty.'

The Admiral, leaning heavily on two sticks, turned to speak to someone and Henry stepped into view, guiding his father through the doors.

Her voice, carrying, gracious, Selma called out, 'Admiral, how are you today? Do come and join us.' She indicated an empty chair with her good hand and, as she moved, Amelia noticed for the first time that the bandage which used to reach Selma's ankle bone was now spiralling its way up the leg like a pale serpent. Amelia shuddered and searched Selma's face for signs of pain, but Selma looked relaxed, smiling at the Admiral.

'I've just promised my grandmother that she'll be back home soon.' Amelia bent close to Henry, speaking in a low voice that could not

101

be heard over Selma's conversation with the Admiral.

'That's nice,' Henry said. 'Why didn't you tell me you were coming?'

'I don't know your telephone number, or your address.'

'Nor you do.' Henry smiled at her.

'The point is,' Amelia paused, irritated by the intense way he was looking at her, as if, she thought, he's expecting me any moment to perform a particularly stunning card trick. 'The point is,' she tried again, 'there *is* no house. It's been sold. Now do you see?'

Henry stopped smiling. 'Yes, I do see.'

'Just don't start preaching to me about the sin of dishonesty,' Amelia snapped. 'I couldn't take it.'

'Now you're being unfair,' Henry corrected her mildly. 'I only preach on Sundays and Wednesdays, anything else would have to be considered overtime. What I was going to say,' he stretched his rather heavy legs out in front of him, 'is that you'd better start working on a plan of action.'

Amelia frowned. 'What do you mean, "Plan of Action"?'

'I mean that you need to work out how you are going to get your grandmother back home.' And he turned to his father who was trying to attract his attention with a series of 'I say old chap'.

Amelia stared for a moment at Henry's

serene profile, the firm, short chin, the slightly stubby nose, and thought he must be very thick.

Selma put her chubby hand on Henry's arm, she'd always needed to touch, to hold on and caress. 'Your father has just promised to come to my little party. You must come too. Amelia will bring you. Now don't you forget, sixteenth of August. You put that in your diary.'

Amelia had to listen to Selma chirruping about her plans interrupted only by the twittering of Miss White, who, on joining them, had immediately secured an invitation by demanding one. 'You get nothing in life if you don't ask.'

'Will you have dinner with me tonight?' Henry's voice was casual, but his eyes, squirrel brown Amelia thought, were fixed on hers.

She was starved of admiration. She felt she was a little like one of her own neglected potplants. That's right, she thought, I'm like that poor African Violet who should be fed with tomato fertilizer once a fortnight but is lucky if it gets a drop or so every other month, its blooms growing fewer and fewer until there's just dense, dull-green foliage.

She smiled and said she'd love to have dinner with him and was rewarded with a huge grin of pleasure and relief.

Amelia too felt grateful. She was saved from an evening waiting for a call from Gerald that would not come, saved from yet another

103

dinner on her own in the small dining room of the hotel. Those lonely mealtimes always reminded her of awful teenage dances she was forced to attend, when cropped red hair and a flat chest had very little appeal when compared to long blond tresses and a size 36D bust. Once, at a party in a village hall, a left behind brochure on woodworm infestation had provided relief. She had sat gazing earnestly at its pages, able to pretend, at least to herself, that the last thing she wanted to do at a dance was dance and that, seeing she was so busy with her brochure, it would be a miracle if one could be fitted in, should anyone ask. She had reached 'The Woodworm and your Heirlooms', when a boy with spreading wet stains under his arms finally asked, by the way of an elegant lead in, what it was she was reading.

'Proust,' Amelia had answered, and she hadn't danced that dance either.

Now at each lonely meal, as she sat engrossed in the wine list and the bit at the bottom of the menu about Cromwell having been there first, she felt she could discern a whiff of pesticide in the air.

With a warm smile, she said to Henry, 'I had planned to wear a sign round my neck tonight, with "I'm eating on my own because I've got leprosy", written on it, and now I won't have to.'

Then it was six o'clock and there was tea or,

as Selma insisted, supper-served-far-too-early, in the dining room.

'We're abandoning them to that.' Amelia standing with Henry in the doorway, pointed at the plates of corned beef and limp lettuce being handed round.

Henry said nothing but, as he turned his face away, she saw his cheeks redden.

Looking out over the tables of old people raising forks to their mouths, stabbing at the food, drinking water from thick, cloudy glasses, she felt as if she was watching a programme with the sound turned off, the room was so quiet. The strain of staying alive another day had taken its toll on the residents of Cherryfield; there was no energy left for conversation.

Amelia and Henry walked through the empty Residents' Lounge and into the hall, guilt padding behind them like a big-eyed mongrel refused a walk.

'I'm afraid I'm crying,' Amelia apologized to Henry as an auxiliary locked the front door behind them. 'But today in particular, I feel life's very sad. "Often sad, but never serious." Who was it who said that?' She dabbed at her eyes with a Swiss, embroidered handkerchief that Selma had given her.

'Winston Churchill, Bernard Shaw, Oscar Wilde?' Henry reeled the names out with a smile, but his voice sounded thick, as if he too was crying.

Amelia tried to say something that would cheer him up. 'What about Jesus, what would he say?'

'Don't make fun of me please,' Henry said quietly as he opened the car door for her. 'Not just now.' And he slammed her door shut and walked round to his side before she had time to answer.

They left the car by the ferry and went for a drink at a pub nearby, before wandering the cobbled streets looking for somewhere to eat.

'Not Wimpy,' Henry said as they passed one, 'or Kentucky Fried Chicken. What we need is something French and pretentious, or Italian and lingering. Italian, I think, with dripping candles stuffed into green bottles.'

But Kingsmouth these days was short on anything lingering and long on anything to do with fast food. '"Tato n'topping",' Henry read on the sign. 'I don't think so.' But as they turned up the hill from the harbour they heard faint piano music coming from further up the dark street.

'That used to be rather a shabby boarding house.' Amelia looked at the floodlit façade of the building, where baskets of geraniums were suspended from wrought-iron hooks. The music had stopped, but inside Henry pointed triumphantly to the round tables, each with a lit candle in a wine bottle placed on the check cloth.

'Perfect,' he sighed happily.

As they sat sipping their wine, a tiny dapper man with unnaturally black hair entered through a back door. Stooping slightly, he made his way across the restaurant with quick steps, past a trolley laden with cakes and puddings, and over to the upright piano in the far corner. He lifted his right hand high in the air, before striking the first chord of 'The Blue Danube'.

'Can one ask for more?' Henry said, sitting back in his chair.

The little man played on as the restaurant filled with people. He played waltzes and polkas and marches while Amelia and Henry ate their whitebait and the Roman pork ('We find there is a certain resistance to veal amongst our British diners,' the head waiter had explained) and, after the final medley, he lifted his hands high in the air once more for a final onslaught on the keys. Then he leapt from the stool with surprising speed and, as Amelia and Henry applauded, acknowledged them with a graceful bow before disappearing out the way he had come.

'Selma would love him,' Amelia said. She paused for a moment, thinking. 'It's funny really that classical music or poetry or pictures are regarded as luxuries when they are actually tremendous equalizers. I mean ...' Finding Henry looking as if he was actually listening to her, she stopped for a moment, giving him a quick smile before continuing, 'You don't need to be able-bodied or employed or even sane to get the same kick out of those things as the rest of us. My grandmother can't produce or nurture, she can't explore. She has no say even in her own life and I very much doubt she would survive on her own for more than a week. But Mozart and Strauss, a poem read aloud, a beautiful painting, can still open the same doors to her as they do to us, give the same peace or elation, the same peek at immortality.' Amelia, feeling she was talking too much, drained her glass of red wine, her cheeks a little pinker than usual.

'Maybe that's why so many men at the front write poetry,' Henry said. 'I hate to talk shop but, as the Bible says, "Consider the lilies of the field, how they grow; they toil not, neither do they spin."' He spoke the words softly, but with an intensity that made Amelia feel sorry when he stopped with an 'etc etc'.

She wished too that he wouldn't assume she knew the rest of the quote; she didn't, not exactly, and she would be too lazy to look it up later. 'All right, so I'm not an original thinker,' she laughed.

The little man returned to the piano and, settling again on the round stool, began to play 'A Rhapsody in Blue'.

Whilst she listened, Amelia looked around her at the other diners. At the table behind Henry, five women were chatting and laughing, constantly and easily. At the other tables sat mostly couples, eating their food in near silence, scattering a word here, a comment there, like Amelia chucking corn at her bantams.

Maybe a good gauge of the dynamism of a love affair was not how often you made love, she thought, but how much you talked to each other in restaurants. It was not so long ago that she had been smugly aware of the wealth of things that Gerald and she would find to talk about when they were out. They'd sit, heads close together, forgetting even to eat at times, but lately, lately they had been more like the silently chewing couples she used to despise.

Sighing, she said suddenly to Henry, 'Gerald, that's who my grandmother thinks you are, Gerald might be having an affair.' And she looked up, astonished at her own words, admitting to him what she hadn't even admitted to herself until then.

Henry did not seem surprised, but just looked thoughtfully at her, his head a little to one side, like an overlarge bird, listening for the song of another.

Amelia smiled weakly, 'It's a bit upsetting actually as I love him with all my heart and that sort of thing.' She looked thoughtful, 'I suppose that to you, to most people, I'm an affair already, so where that leaves his new relationship I don't know. Tell me, Henry, what would the church say? Has a deceived mistress got any rights? Can she in fact ever be deceived or just punished?'

'Never mind that for the moment,' Henry said unexpectedly. 'You must ask him straight out if he's playing around. If he is, leave him.'

Amelia looked at him. 'How old are you?'

'Twenty-six.'

'You're very young.' Amelia touched his cheek. 'Funny how having something strategically placed round your neck, a stethoscope, microphone, dog-collar, makes people expect great wisdom from you.'

'I'm sorry.' Henry looked embarrassed.

Amelia smiled and shook her head. 'No I'm sorry, I was rude. It's very kind of you to listen to me. I feel quite alone sometimes. My mother is fine until something really interesting, like a dog's mess, catches her attention. I adored Willoughby but he's dead. I sometimes feel Selma might as well be.' She looked at Henry. 'What's your view on euthanasia?'

'No,' Henry said.

'But why?'

'Because only God has the right to take a life.'

'God giveth and God taketh away,' Amelia mumbled. Then she said, 'But he doesn't decide on giving life, we do, the man and the woman. It's we who decide whether to have a child or not.'

'God gave you that ability.'

'He's given me the ability to take life too.'

'The ability, yes, but not the right.' Henry's

110

amiable face had taken on a stern look. 'What you can do, what you are doing, is to ease the pain, make what's left of someone's life as bearable as possible.'

'But what you are saying is that you can condone the killing of perfectly healthy young men in a war, or I presume you do as you're in the Navy, but you can't accept the easing of the dying of very old ladies?'

Henry poured what was left of the wine into their glasses. 'You have to stand up to evil. Sometimes, in doing that, you might need to use force. There's St Augustine's Doctrine of the Just War; it may have been conceived to justify Rome's colonial wars, but the idea itself is sound. Humans are imperfect.' He smiled. 'Some are a lot less perfect than others. When Hitler rampaged through Europe, should chaps like me have stood back and said to the men and women risking their lives to put an end to some of the worst suffering in the history of mankind, "Thou shalt not kill"?' Henry shook his head. 'I don't think so. You have to build your life on certain principles but, for mere mortals, I do believe it's a mistake to etch them in stone.'

'Wasn't it George Bernard Shaw who said to a lady sitting next to him at dinner, "Now all we're doing is arguing about the price"?'

Henry looked at her, his face serious. 'No, not at all. What we are arguing about is right or wrong as we perceive it, honestly and in our hearts. I believe and so, I'm sure, do you that it is right to defend a child from a brutal killer, even if that means using force, the minimum force necessary to save the child. But who is your grandmother threatening? Your peace of mind?' Henry leant closer to Amelia, putting his hand over Amelia's. 'If you asked her if she wanted to die, what do you think she'd answer?'

Amelia, looking flushed, snatched her hand away, glaring at Henry as if he was personally responsible for the injustices of the universe. 'And that', she said, 'is just the final little nasty thrown in, the ultimate trap, this absurd instinct of survival that we've got. This pathetic desire to cling on long after we know the party is over. Not that it's often much of a party anyway.'

'Tut, tut,' Henry said. 'What a cynic you are.'

'Not a cynic,' but Amelia couldn't help smiling. He is like a sponge, she thought; any anger thrown at him gets soaked up and dissipated. 'No, not a cynic at all. I'm just possessed of what Selma calls "a black bottom". I think what she means is a melancholy disposition.'

'I prefer black bottom,' said Henry. 'It sounds much more dashing. Don't let it take over though.'

'I won't. I keep it decorously covered most of the time. And I won't kill Selma, however

112

much I love her. In my case, conviction is never matched by courage.'

'Thank God for that,' Henry said simply.

*   *   *

There was no message for Miss Lindsay. 'No, no call from a Mr Gerald Forbes,' the night porter answered, looking up from the sports page of the *Evening Herald.* 'Yes,' he was quite sure.

CHAPTER TEN

Dagmar felt pleased with herself as she parked her car in front of Cherryfield. She had woken that morning feeling strong and positive, ready to fight. She had wasted too much of her life already, but no more. She smiled as she thought of the interesting conversation she'd had with the new visiting professor from the States about the relevance of fiction in society. She had surprised herself as much as him with how much she had to say on the subject.

'No risk, no fun.' She mumbled the phrase her husband had used on the ski-slopes where they first met. 'No risk, no fun.' And she refused to give in to the impulse to wrap the car keys in tissue paper before letting them fall into her handbag.

As she rang the doorbell, Amelia caught up with her. They kissed hello, but before they had a chance to speak the door opened and Selma's voice, carrying her outrage through the rooms, reached them from the Residents' Lounge, 'Murderer, brute, Nazi!'

Dagmar and Amelia looked at each other, then ran towards the commotion, Amelia narrowly avoiding knocking into a nurse carrying a bedpan.

'Stay away from me, do you hear?' They heard Selma's voice again, but it sounded smaller now, trembling. 'How do I know you're not planning to boil me too? I'm old, I'm ill.'

They reached the Lounge to find Selma sitting ashen-faced, as far back in her chair as she could, her fingers gripping the armrest.

'Steady on, Selma my dear, steady on.' Admiral Mallett tried to control his voice, as unreliable as a fourteen-year-old boy's, as he rose with difficulty from his seat by the empty aquarium. 'I must say though, Matron.' He stood facing Sister Morris, leaning heavily on his crutches. 'Boiling the little chaps does seem a bit excessive.'

'What on earth is going on here, Sister Morris?' Dagmar demanded as Amelia knelt by Selma, hugging her.

Sister Morris turned, purple-cheeked and panting with fury. 'A ridiculous fuss over nothing, that's what's going on! And may I tell

114

you, Mrs Lindsay, that it's your mother who's the ringleader as usual.'

'Now I say,' the Admiral tottered on his sticks but his voice was steady, 'you can't call the little fellows nothing. I liked 'em. So did Mrs Merryman here. It's not a question of any ringleader.'

Amelia, still with her arms protectively around Selma, asked gently, 'What is it that has upset you so? Try to explain.'

Selma managed to heave herself half out of the chair and now she pointed an accusing finger at Sister Morris. 'I called into the kitchen to see what foul repast they were preparing, the smell coming from there was disgusting. And I find her,' Selma had fallen back into the chair but she was still pointing, 'her, standing like a witch from *Macbeth* over a steaming pan, lowering the Admiral's little guppies into the fiercely boiling water, one by one. She wasn't actually chanting, but it was a near thing; her lips were moving.'

'That's it. I'm going to my quarters,' Sister Morris spoke with hysterical calm. 'If anyone should feel the need to hear what actually happened, I'll be waiting.' And she marched out, head held high, her wooden slip-ons sucking and letting go of the heels of her feet with every angry step.

*   *   *

115

'I suppose I should feel guilty,' Clarissa tossed the green salad with vigour, 'being here in Amelia's kitchen, using her things.' She gave Gerald a coy glance underneath her thick eyelashes, 'Sleeping with you in her bed.'

'My little Goldilocks.' Gerald ruffled her hair affectionately.

For a second, Clarissa stared blankly at him, then her wide brow cleared and she gave an appreciative little laugh. 'Somehow I don't feel bad about it,' she said, 'that's the thing. It's like I'm in my rightful place, and she is the interloper, you know what I mean?' She licked some oil from her fingers. 'Well, she will be soon anyway. It's not even as if I'm breaking up a marriage.'

A whisper of guilt passed through Gerald's mind, but like a solitary cloud on an otherwise perfect blue sky, it cast no lasting shadow. 'You're so sensible, I like that,' he said.

Placing the salad bowl on the table, Clarissa said, 'You are sure though, aren't you, that she's not coming back until Monday? I mean, why did you make such a thing about putting the car away?' She looked earnestly at him. 'It's just that it's so important to do this right.'

Gerald had a vision of Amelia on an operating table, with him expertly removing her heart with the able assistance of Clarissa. He shook himself, Amelia's fancifulness seemed to be infectious. 'I'm quite sure,' he said firmly. 'She really is very good about her

116

grandmother, I must give her that. Too good,' he added hastily, at the sight of Clarissa's already firm chin, jutting. 'I suppose,' he said, 'that the old girl always was more of a mother to her than poor Dagmar.'

'Is she really mad, the mother I mean?' Clarissa picked a Little Gem lettuce leaf from the bowl and nibbled it.

Gerald considered for a moment, as he uncorked the bottle of Chablis. 'Not actually and certifiably, no; neurotic as hell though. She was quite a promising pianist apparently, as was Selma. But, according to Amelia, she spent so much time disinfecting the piano keys, there was no time left to practise.' He felt a little guilty as he spoke, about betraying Amelia's confidence, but then he reminded himself what a pain Amelia could be. 'Amelia is a bit like that.'

'What? Disinfecting things?'

'Good heavens no, look around you. No, I mean unable to follow anything through. Great ideas, a fair amount of talent, but nothing ever comes to anything.'

'Well as long as she doesn't come here.' Clarissa, delighted with her joke, wound her strong arms round Gerald's neck.

Gerald laughed a little uneasily, remembering Amelia's remark that one could always tell a man in love by the way he laughed at even the most feeble of his loved one's jokes.

At the same time, Henry arrived at Cherryfield. He was worried about his father, he hadn't been himself since that disastrous lunch with Amelia and Mrs Merryman. All the fight seemed to have gone out of him. And then there had been the business with the stolen dentures. Henry sighed, raking his fingers through his hair. He had been told by a past girlfriend that she could always tell when he was upset because of his habit of doing just that. Of course months later when he broke off the relationship, she told him how it had always irritated her. There, he did it again: his fingers pushing through his hair as if they could push his problems away with them, but it was a bad time to go off on exercise, now, when his father needed him most.

He found the Admiral in the Residents' Lounge, sitting miserably by the fish-tank, whilst next to him Selma rocked backwards and forwards in her chair, weeping like a child, tears running unstemmed down her pinched cheeks. Amelia was kneeling by her side, crying herself at her grandmother's distress. The television in the corner by the window added to the confusion with an Australian soap being played out at high volume.

Amelia looked up at Henry, her slanted eyes wide and tearful. 'I'm taking her home to Abbotslea. No-one else cares.'

'But what on earth has happened?' Henry asked gently. He put his hand on his father's shoulder.

The Admiral just shook his head and pointed his stick at the empty fish-tank. Henry turned to Amelia.

'Ask that awful Morris,' she said, standing up.

Henry gave her a long look. 'Right,' he said finally. 'I'll go and find her,' and he stalked off.

'She's in her flat,' Amelia called after him, 'but if I were you, I wouldn't bother.'

Henry found Sister Morris in her quarters on the second floor. As she opened the door to him, the heat from an open coalfire hit him in the face like steam from an engine. Above his head, a bell-rope tinkled.

Sister Morris maintained a dignified silence as she indicated a seat for him on the plump sofa covered in differently shaped and patterned cushions. He sat down, moving a pink heart-shaped one embroidered with 'Home Is Where The Heart Is', to avoid it being crushed.

On the mantelpiece stood a collection of china pigs dressed in the manner of different professions: one wore a tie and bowler, another a nurse's uniform, one was a fireman, and there was even a pig with a dog-collar Henry noticed, amused. Sister Morris herself shared her armchair with a large teddy, a calico cat and a giant, stuffed hedgehog, and on the coffee table stood an open Paddington Bear biscuit tin. She seemed determined to keep at bay the ever-present spectre of old age by cramming her tiny sitting room with childish whimsy. Like a medicine-man, Henry thought, decorating his hut with totems and charms to ward off the evil eye.

He cleared his throat and began, choosing his words carefully. 'There seems to be some sort of problem downstairs. I wondered if you could possibly fill me in.'

Sister Morris's chins quivered with emotion and her cheeks reddened. 'I'm glad that someone sees fit to ask me. Of course you are a man of the cloth,' her voice softened, but just for a moment. 'This whole thing has been blown out of all proportion...'

Five minutes later, Henry returned to the Residents' Lounge. 'Right,' he said, sitting down in the empty chair between his father and Selma, 'there's a perfectly good explanation, nothing to get too concerned about. You see the fish were ill,' he continued, feeling like some grotesque version of *Listen with Mother*, as more residents gathered round like ancient vultures, determined not to miss any morsel of scandal.

'Well, boiling them can't have helped,' Miss White said firmly as she manoeuvred herself into an armchair. 'And if that's Sister's little remedy for the ailing, none of us can sleep soundly in our beds. Not that I'm ever blessed with sound sleep.' Her expression suggested suffering bravely born. 'I toss and I turn, I toss...'

'The vet told Sister Morris that there was nothing he could do for them.' Henry spoke firmly. 'I'm afraid putting them out of their misery was the only option.' He smiled encouragingly at Selma who slumped in her rose-patterned armchair. 'Apparently, immersing the fish in boiling water is the quickest and least painful way of doing it.'

'I had lobster once,' Miss White said. 'Highly overrated I thought.'

A large woman, whom Henry hadn't seen before, leant across, her cheeks pink with excitement, her eyes opened wide, 'I don't care *what* that Sister Morris says, I'm not having those poor little fish for my tea.'

'I'm not either,' a cacophony of voices agreed. 'I won't eat a scrap.'

Henry clenched his teeth, worried and ashamed of his sudden urge to shake them, scream at them all to shut up. He looked into the old faces, sagging, whiskery, toothless, confused, and he saw the humiliation in his father's eyes, how straight he sat in the chair by the empty fish-tank. God forgive me, he thought. Getting up from his chair, he walked across and put his hand on the old man's shoulder. 'What do you say we go for a drive, have a drink at the Anchor?'

Then Amelia came downstairs with a small

121

suitcase, badly packed by the look of the corner of blue material that hung out from the side. She was about to help Selma from the chair when she stopped, looking round for the walking-frame.

'I think you're overreacting.' Henry spoke quietly, but he went over to the television which was still on, bleating out some incidental music from a motionless screen, and brought out the walking-frame that stood in the corner behind. He placed it by Selma's chair, then he turned and said quietly to Amelia, 'You should never make decisions when you're in a state. Get your grandmother upstairs for a rest, sit down yourself and think this over.' He looked from Selma's grey expressionless face to Amelia's bright pink cheeks and moist eyes. 'How will you get her back? How will you cope when you get her home? You're not strong enough to lift her?'

'We'll manage,' Amelia said. She smiled mechanically in his direction. 'It won't be for long, she just needs a break from this place.'

Henry didn't argue further but helped Selma up. 'At least let me drive you to the station,' he said as he held the door for them.

Amelia turned. 'That's very kind of you, but my mother should be arriving back any minute, she'll take us.'

Selma too had stopped in the doorway, and for a moment Henry thought he saw a look of triumph in her eyes. He sighed and went back

122

across the room, sitting down, next to his father, on Selma's empty chair.

'What about you, Pa, do you want to get away from here too?'

The Admiral turned and attempted a smile but his hands, black-bruised and wrinkled, gripped the handles of the sticks at his side. 'I'm fine, dear boy, don't worry about me. It's not this place, it's being old. It's no fun.' He put one hand on Henry's. 'But that's life in a blue suit, and even a chap with your connections can't change it.'

*   *   *

Dagmar drove Selma and Amelia to Plymouth Station.

'It's jolly good of you to have Mummy,' she hissed over her shoulder to Amelia. 'I would have liked to have had her myself of course, but they'd never give me the time off.' She added in her normal voice, 'Well, at least I managed to find you a decent dress, Mummy, rather than that permanent-press monstrosity the woman at Cherryfield picked up for you.'

Amelia had calmed down during the trip. She could feel the heat going out of her cheeks and her pulse rate slowing but, as Dagmar pulled up in front of the station, she began to worry again, but for different reasons. Henry had been right, how would she cope? Then again, hadn't Rosalind felt the same mixture of

123

panic and inadequacy when bringing little Ronnie home from hospital in his flower-sprigged Moses basket? Amelia went through her duties in her head: bathing and dressing, food to prepare that was both nourishing and suitable for dentures. How on earth did one clean dentures? At least she had had the forethought to ask one of the nurses at Cherryfield for Selma's medication. Then there was Gerald. Amelia looked helplessly at her mother, but it was too late to change her mind now.

Dagmar wrote, 'Transporting Invalid', in large letters on a piece of paper and fixed it to the windscreen. Then they walked Selma across the platform to the waiting train. Amelia got on first and, taking Selma's wrists, she began to pull her up. Dagmar, careful not to rub her trouser-leg against the dirty bottom step, heaved at Selma's polycotton-clad bottom. 'Just like Pooh getting stuck in Rabbit's hole,' she called cheerfully. Selma, facing Amelia, pretended not to hear.

A guard strode purposefully past the beached Selma, on his way to help a young mother with a twin push-chair on to the next carriage. The babies smiled their toothless thanks. Little blond cherubs, Amelia thought bitterly, as with a final heave, Selma stood tottering on board the train. She too smiled, out of relief and embarrassment, she too showed her gums. Oh my God, Amelia thought, she's left her teeth behind.

Waving at Dagmar from the window, Amelia thought how unfairly arranged it all was. Babies' toothlessness was sweet, their chubbiness, cuddly. They dribble their food, they burp and sick up, lacking all control over their bodily functions, but the package came wrapped in such irresistible cuteness that few people failed to coddle and assist. After all, Amelia thought, how may Residential Homes for the Active Infant did you see dotted along leafy, small-town streets?

She turned away from the window and sat down opposite Selma. So what about old people, why was it made so easy for us to want to abandon them? Amelia felt a pity that was almost painful when she looked across at her grandmother slumped in her seat, unlovely, her dress riding up over her thick knees, an uncertain smile on her pinched, grey face. No, it wasn't fair.

She handed Selma a copy of *Good Housekeeping*. Selma said, 'How lovely,' and leafed through it happily. She had always had *Good Housekeeping* reserved for her at the newsagent in Kingsmouth, even after Willoughby's retirement when economies had to be made.

Does she know, really know, Amelia wondered, as she sits avidly reading those recipes that she will never again prepare a meal?

125

'I need to spend a penny.' Selma put the magazine down.

Amelia's back hurt as she pulled Selma up from her seat. For a moment, they stood facing each other, Amelia bent, Selma tottering, their hands clasped together. Amelia wondered what to do next. Dagmar had helped tow Selma to her seat, as the aisle was too narrow for the walking-frame.

'We have to turn,' Amelia said finally. 'The loo is that way.' She pointed over Selma's shoulder. Still holding hands, they circled slowly round, an unmatched pair in a bizarre dance.

At Ashcombe, Dagmar had played the piano with the sun pouring through the half drawn blinds, as Selma grasped Amelia's small hands in hers. '*Dansa min docka*,' she had sung in Swedish, 'Dance my doll, dance whilst you're young, soon you'll be old and heavy.' Round and round they had danced, across the pattern of sunbeams on the oak floor.

The train jolted to a stop. Selma lurched towards Amelia who managed to stay upright, stopping them both from collapsing on the floor. 'I can't go now,' Selma whispered, 'we're at a station.'

'I'll just take you through now. It's easier to move when the train is standing still.'

Walking backwards, step after careful step, Amelia lead Selma through the carriage. People looked up at them only to immediately

126

avert their eyes in embarrassment, a couple of children giggled. Selma's eyes were blank as she stared ahead.

'You sit here.' Amelia placed Selma on an empty seat at the end of the carriage whilst she pulled at the heavy, sliding doors. She pushed her bottom against one, to hold it open; at the same time she leant forward to help Selma up and through. My vertebrae are going to crack, I'm going to spend the rest of my life a helpless cripple, Amelia thought, biting her bottom lip. As the train was about to pull out, she jerked Selma from her seat and helped her out into the corridor. Sideways like crabs they manoeuvred themselves in front of the door marked WC and Amelia began propelling her grandmother inside.

Selma stalled. There had been an English setter at Ashcombe who used to dig his paws in, just like that, when asked to go for a walk in the rain.

'Don't you want to go?' Amelia asked her gently.

Selma looked helplessly at her. 'I don't need to now.'

Amelia stared somewhere in the direction of Selma's good leg. She thought, I'd rather be dead, if I was her, I'd rather be dead. But making her voice matter of fact, Sister Morris-like, she said, 'No problem,' and, with a smile fixed determinedly on her face, she began helping Selma back to her seat.

On the taxi-ride from Basingstoke, Selma brightened, chatting happily, enjoying the drive through the rain-washed streets of Alresford. She knew the town from childhood visits to an aunt, and her memories were all of those visits long ago. When the car stopped at a red light, an old woman, her thick legs disappearing inside dumpy suede boots, a plastic rain cover tied round her whispy grey hair, hastened across.

'Goodness me, some people are hideous,' Selma remarked cheerfully. She sat there, whiskery-chinned, and missing her teeth, her cardigan spotted with stains, and yet she looked at the woman at the crossing with gleeful disapproval. Selma had been beautiful. Thank God, Amelia thought, that in her mind she still is.

The taxi pulled up in front of the Old Rectory and the driver got out to help extract Selma from the passenger seat. As she was hauled from the car, Selma farted loudly. For a second no-one moved. It was as if the driver's eyes and Amelia's were fencing in embarrassed attempts to avoid a meeting, darting here and there, up, down, right, left. Finally, they both spoke at once, the driver inspecting his fingernails, Amelia investigating the contents of her purse. 'How much do I owe you?'

'That'll be nine pounds eighty, love.'

'No dear, let me.' Selma, looking as if the little incident had nothing to do with her, leant heavily against the car as her hand scrabbled round the inside of her handbag. She handed a five pound note to the driver before bringing out some loose change which she counted out carefully, her hand shaking, 'One, two, three, four pound coins,' she smiled at the driver, 'and two fifties. Keep the change,' she added graciously.

Amelia hadn't cancelled the papers and she picked out the bulky bundle from the box on the gate. She frowned at the study window. 'I must have left the light on,' she said.

She helped Selma inside the house and left her in the armchair in the sitting room before getting the bags from outside. 'I'll bring you a cup of tea.' She smiled encouragingly.

The room seemed to Selma, as she waited, like a half-remembered face. There was something familiar about its square shape and regular features, but to whom did it belong? She sat miserably searching her mind, which seemed to her increasingly like a treasure chest to which she had lost the key.

As she heard murmurings from the room next door she grew restless. She had arrived here with Amelia, but where was here?

The sounds from next door grew louder, worrying sounds: muffled, agonized, oddly familiar. Where was Amelia? Selma tried to get up from the deep chair, but, like a woman drowning, each time she managed painfully to rise to the surface, the soft hold of the chair reclaimed her.

At last Amelia returned. She appeared smiling in the doorway, a tray in her hands, just as from the other room a name was called, then repeated over and over again. 'Gerry, oh Gerry, Gerry, Gerry!'

Amelia stood motionless, listening, then, with the smile still on her face like a hand held in a wave to someone already gone, she walked across the room. Her cheeks were bright pink as she carefully placed the tray on the table in front of Selma.

A few more steps, quicker now, and she reached the study door and flung it open.

The tall back of Gerald's swivel chair rocked, two thick legs hung over the arm-rests, the toes of the small feet curling and straightening in ecstasy.

The chair swivelled round and she saw Gerald, his face contorted, a girl straddling him, her skirt hitched up over her naked buttocks.

'Hello, Gerald,' Amelia said, 'I didn't realize you were home.'

130

CHAPTER ELEVEN

Watching Gerald's attempt to leap from the chair with Clarissa still straddling his waist, gave Amelia a few seconds of intense enjoyment. Slapping her hand across her mouth, she bent over laughing until the sound of Gerald's voice stopped her.

'Get off darling,' he hissed. It was the 'darling', that alerted Amelia's attention.

'I'm doing my best,' Clarissa groaned as, swinging herself round on her bare bottom, she managed to stand up. Her skirt slid down over her hips and covered her as she balanced on one foot, threading the other through the leg of her knickers.

Amelia stood silent, looking at the heavily built young woman whose fine blond hair hung in damp tendrils over a square-shaped face that was turning ice-cream pink as she wriggled and tugged at her pants through the fine floral skirt. Amelia looked away.

Gerald stood by the desk. He had pulled his trousers on, but through the half-open fly peeked a corner of his blue-and-white-striped shirt. The one that took absolutely ages to iron; the thought flew through Amelia's mind, as appropriate as a paper aeroplane at a funeral. 'Who is this girl? It's Clarissa isn't it?' Amelia answered her own question in a quiet, level voice. Stay calm, she told herself, and any moment now he'll cross the floor to me. He'll say how very sorry he is, how it should never have happened. Soon that solid girl with her unremarkably pretty face, will be escorted to the front door and I can begin to deal with all of this. At least now she knew who it was that had squirted lemon into the cream of her existence. Figments of the imagination were notoriously difficult to fight; young women with lank hair and pink-flushed bottoms, should be easier.

'Of course it's Clarissa,' Gerald snapped. 'I'm sorry,' his voice softened, 'I forgot you haven't met.'

He's behaving as if we're at some slightly awkward drinks party, Amelia thought. Next, this Clarissa will be telling me she feels as if she's known me for absolutely ages. She bit her lip, waiting for Gerald to revert to script.

'Look, old thing.' Now Gerald did take a step towards her, but what followed was all wrong. 'I'm really sorry you had to find out like this, it's the last thing we wanted to happen. But you see I've been meaning to tell you for weeks. You're so bloody unsuspecting.' He flung his arms out helplessly, glancing over to Clarissa for support.

'I feel absolutely awful.' Clarissa, in control again now that she had her knickers on, spoke with a Perspex-voice, clear and brittle. Gerald moved closer to her and put his arms round her shoulders.

The quiet gesture of realignment hit Amelia like a punch in the solar plexus. Sitting down in the hard chair by the door she doubled over, trying to stop herself from being sick.

'Amelia darling, won't you introduce me to our hosts?' Selma stood in the doorway, having got herself across the sitting room by walking sideways, transferring her hands and weight from one piece of furniture to the next. 'Amelia, are you all right?'

Amelia sat up slowly. 'Yes, of course. Fine, absolutely fine.' She gazed helplessly at Gerald who looked away.

Amelia stood up. 'Grandma, you remember Gerald. And this is Gerald's ... friend, Clarissa.'

Selma looked pleased with the introduction, saying in a rather grand voice, 'How very nice to meet you both. It's most kind of you to have my granddaughter and me to stay.' She wobbled on her feet and clung on to the moving door. She looked as if she was about to fall but Amelia grabbed the chair and pushed it under her just in time. Selma collapsed on to it with a little thud.

Gerald shot her a worried glance. 'I think we'd better go.'

'You can come back later, Gerald, when we've all had a chance to calm down,' Clarissa said with quiet authority.

'Let her go Gerald, but *you* can't, surely you

133

must see that. You can't just leave like this.' Amelia's voice rose and then, bang! Her fist slammed into the shelf of the bookcase.

The colour rose again on Clarissa's cheeks, like bright pink dye washing over shiny paper. 'Gerald, you are not sending me home like some ... some trollop!'

At the familiar old-fashioned word, Selma grew alert. 'Now don't you fight children,' she said from her chair.

'Oh can't you see this is hopeless, trying to talk like this?' Gerald said. 'You can stay here for the present Amelia. Your grandmother too, of course.' He gave a little nod in Selma's direction. 'And I'll be over in the next day or two.'

Before Amelia could think of anything to stop him, he was at the front door. 'Really, I mean it. There's no hurry for you to move out, I can stay at Clarissa's for now.' He looked at her and raised his arm, touching her cheek with his index finger in a quick caress. Then he hurried off, following Clarissa down the short path to the gate. As she stood watching after them, Amelia imagined a shadowy image of herself separating like a film from her body and popping up between Gerald and Clarissa, slipping its wafer-thin arms into theirs. Shuddering, she slowly closed the front door behind them and wandered into the sitting room. Her gaze fell on Selma sitting crumpled in the armchair. She felt utterly alone.

134

'You have to keep going, for the children's sake.' How many times had she read that phrase in a magazine, or heard it spoken by an acquaintance or some sad, faded figure in a television interview? By that evening Amelia knew just what these people meant. She couldn't throw herself on the bed and weep, she couldn't rant and rave or shred Gerald's cashmere sweater. She couldn't even get drunk on his most expensive wine, not now she had Selma. So, two hours after Gerald had walked out she was cooking onions and carrots which she blended into a thick, smooth soup: easy to swallow, teeth not essential. Then there was the broken china to clear up, after Selma had dropped the plates she was trying to bring over to the sink. Selma had looked down surprised at the blue and white chips scattered at her feet. 'I seem to be all fingers and thumbs these days. Mind you I've never liked working in someone else's kitchen.'

By nine o'clock, Selma was asleep in the armchair. Amelia woke her an hour later. 'Bedtime don't you think?' she said, working a smile across her lips.

The walking-frame had to be abandoned at the bottom of the stairs. Amelia began the climb backwards pulling Selma along by both hands, coaxing her up step by step. Halfway up they stopped for a rest and Amelia burst into tears.

Selma stared at her and her face crumpled. 'Don't cry Amelia. Please stop it. I can't bear it when you cry.'

Amelia took a deep breath and tried another bright smile. 'I'm sorry. I'm just a bit tired. Silly me.'

She helped Selma undress, peeling off layers of foundation garments that lent shape to the sagging, grey-toned flesh. Arching her aching back she said, 'Let's not bother with a bath tonight.'

At last Selma was in bed. Propped up against two pillows she looked expectantly at Amelia. After a moment she said, 'You know I think I might just go downstairs and make myself a mug of warm milk.'

'I'll do it.' Amelia came downstairs slamming each foot down so hard on the wooden steps that it hurt. She heated the milk, muttering all the while into the saucepan. When she thought she heard Selma calling, she hurried to the door only to come back to find the milk rising above the rim of the saucepan, flooding down on to the hob. When finally she got back upstairs, Selma was fast asleep on her back.

*   *   *

Three days after Gerald walked out with Clarissa, he returned on his own. He had telephoned to see if Amelia would be in, and now he sat in his usual place at the large kitchen table. Amelia sat opposite him, elbows on the table, her chin resting on the upturned palms of her hands.

'You all right?' he asked as if he didn't know the answer was no.

Amelia looked into the face she knew so well, the long chin and the large grey eyes, not unlike her own in colour, the small white scar on the upper lip. She knew now, she thought, how people in those science-fiction films felt when their loved-ones' minds were taken over by aliens. The man sitting opposite her at the table looked like Gerald, rubbed his eyes with his knuckles like Gerald, had a voice like Gerald's, but inside she had no doubt, the little green men had taken over.

'I miss you,' she said.

Gerald looked mildly irritated. 'Well, there we are.' He cleared his throat, drumming his fingers surreptitiously against the edge of the table.

I wonder what he would do if I walked over to him and put my hand down his trousers? Amelia tilted her head a little to one side as she continued to gaze across at him. This man, she thought, has lain naked and vulnerable in my arms several times a week for two years. Suddenly, he is a prohibited area; if I put out my hand and touch his cheek, I'm trespassing.

Trying to sound business-like, rather than

137

pleading, she asked, 'There is really nothing I can do or say to make you come back?'

'No Amelia, there isn't.' Gerald's voice was patient, commiserating even, in an impersonal way. It was the voice he used, she thought, when telling Mrs Smith that all avenues had been exhausted in the firm's attempts to stop Mrs Smith's neighbour blocking her access with his lawnmower.

Gerald leant across the table towards her. 'I really am sorry you had to find out the way you did. It's the last thing Clarissa and I wanted. But it can't have come as a complete shock. If you were honest with yourself you must have known that things weren't right between us.'

'I wasn't.'

'What?' Gerald pulled back in his chair. 'What do you mean?' Again that awful irritation crept in, making Amelia blink hard to stop embarrassing tears.

'I mean that I wasn't honest.'

Gerald sighed. 'Can't you see we're too different? It's no-one's fault, but to be truthful...'

'Truthful and Honest,' Amelia thought, two paragons often used to prop up the most cruel constructions.

'... I don't understand you. Everything you do seems like a game, something to occupy you whilst you drift around waiting for life to start. I take you one way and you come meekly enough, but all the time I have the feeling that
138

you're floating off in the opposite direction looking for goodness knows what.' Gerald spoke with sudden passion. 'I needed someone ... someone substantial.' He looked at Amelia, pleading for understanding.

Amelia stared back at him, horrified. She had given him her love, shared his life for two years, and that was how he saw her: insubstantial, floating, not quite normal. She blinked and swallowed, reeling from his latest punch, seeing Gerald before her again in the chair with Clarissa. Looking helplessly at him, shrugging her shoulders, she said, 'Clarissa is certainly substantial.' It was all she could find to say.

'For Christ's sake! You're just hopelessly immature.' Gerald, his cheeks reddening, slammed his fist on the table. 'Faced with a serious situation, the best you can do is come up with a juvenile crack like that.'

'I'm sorry,' Amelia said but she felt a curious sense of relief; after all she was hopeless, shiftless, nothing was expected of her now.

'Would you like a drink?' She stood up from the table.

'Thanks,' he nodded, mollified.

Amelia brought a bottle of Chablis from the fridge. The cork fragmented as she drove in the corkscrew just off centre.

'Here, let me do it,' Gerald said, as he always did, taking the bottle from her. Then, as if he had only just then remembered Selma's existence, he asked, 'Where is your grandmother?'

Amelia pointed to the lawn where Selma sat, her back turned, an emerald green, gold-tasselled shawl wrapped around her shoulders. 'I brought her walking-frame back inside with me.' She gave a little smile. 'It was the only way we could get some privacy.'

Leaving Cherryfield had shaken what was left of Selma's sense of place. Like a young child who had moved too often, she kept close to her granddaughter, the one constant in her life. So now, wherever Amelia went, she would hear behind her the sound of the wooden legs of the walking-frame, bashing against doors and furniture as Selma, swearing and muttering, shuffled in her wake.

Gerald turned the bottle round in his hand. 'A bit excessive, a 1983 Chablis?'

'No,' Amelia said simply.

Gerald sighed and changed the subject. 'You might not think you have any reason to like Clarissa, but she suggested I let you stay on here until the end of the summer, to give you plenty of time to sort out a place of your own.'

He really needs to bring her into his conversation, Amelia thought. Like a speaker in a television debate taking sips from the glass of water by his side, Gerald refreshes himself with little gulps of her name.

'She's a real brick, is Clarissa,' she said. 'I don't know where I'd be without her. Have some more wine.'

'No thanks, I'm driving.'

'You could always stay the night,' Amelia offered, watching Gerald make up his mind whether she was being helpful or provocative. He settled on the fence and said in a neutral voice, 'It's only half past six.'

Amelia glanced unnecessarily at her watch. 'So it is.' She smiled brightly across the table at him. 'What a lot of time we've got to chat.'

Ten minutes later Gerald stood up to leave. 'I'll come over again,' he said. 'There's still the matter of how to divide up all the stuff.' He patted her cheek with the quick, embarrassed gesture she had begun to hate. 'I'll always be your friend, Amelia. If there's anything you need you only have to ask.'

'Actually,' Amelia said, 'there is something.'

Gerald turned on the doorstep. 'Yes?'

'I could do with a good solicitor.'

'Very funny.' Gerald's mouth turned up at the corners in something that could pass for a smile, Amelia thought, if one wasn't very fussy.

She went round the house to the lawn where Selma was asleep in the soft-cushioned chair under the apple tree. Quietly she sat down on the dry grass, leaning back against the tree trunk. The evening sun spread a golden tint through the air and, by the shrubbery, rabbits were appearing, cautiously at first, then as nothing moved they got braver, grazing on the uncut grass.

141

God! I love this garden, she thought, then she buried her face in the crook of her arm. Until Gerald's visit she had found it impossible to extinguish completely a belief in her power over him. Now he pranced before her closed eyes like a pied piper, taking her life with him; home, garden, her hopes of children. She lifted her head and in front of her, hedging the terrace, were the beds of Bourbon roses she had planted when they first moved in. Souvenir De La Malmaison, Honorine de Brabant, Mme Isaac Pereire, Louise Odier: now all those richly scented, extravagantly painted granddames would give their autumn encore to Clarissa.

Amelia flinched as she felt a hand on her shoulder.

'Are you all right, darling? You're looking a bit peeky.' Selma was peering down at her, concerned.

Selma, with Amelia's Indian shawl draped round her shoulders and her hair brushed smooth, looked so much like her old pre-Cherryfield self that Amelia was aching to tell her all about Gerald and Clarissa. For years she had come to her grandmother with her problems, confided in her and no-one else, and Selma had listened, plucking out the troubles as if they were thorns, advised and made better.

Oh no, Amelia thought, straightened up against the warm tree trunk. Don't even try it now. It's a mirage, this familiar Selma, tempting your words towards her into nothing.

'Come on, darling something's up, I can tell.'

She'll look at me, Amelia thought, and she'll tell me none of it would have happened if I'd stopped sucking my thumb or she'll ask me to go to fetch her game of ludo. But Selma's gaze was on her, steady and alert.

'It's Gerald, he's left me. I still love him and this place,' she gesticulated out at the garden. 'Now I'll have to leave here too, start again somewhere else.' It wasn't until she was halfway through the sentence that she realized how that might sound to Selma, whose only option was Cherryfield.

'I am sorry darling, this, this . . . what did you say his name was?'

'Gerald.'

'Gerald, yes of course. I don't know why, but I keep on thinking his name is Henry. I'm sorry you and he aren't friends any more.' She put her hand out to Amelia who took it, keeping it still. 'I know it's not much comfort now, but you'll find someone else. You forget about him and concentrate on finding yourself a nice place to live; your own home is the most important thing.'

Amelia looked up at her with tears in her eyes. If her grandmother had leapt from the deck-chair and torn a rubber mask from her face revealing her old self, wise, serene, and beautiful, she could not have surprised Amelia any more than she had just done by speaking

143

perfect sense. With a deep sigh of contentment Amelia edged closer to her.

'Anyway,' Selma pursed her lips. 'It really was very naughty of him to leave so early when you'd gone through all that trouble.'

CHAPTER TWELVE

'I felt rather hurt,' Amelia said and, as she said it, she wondered why she always seemed to oscillate between understatement and exaggeration without ever settling comfortably in between.

'Yes?' Rosalind, sitting at the kitchen table, stopped gazing adoringly at Ronald and looked instead, in a waiting way, at Amelia.

'Oh sorry.' Amelia started again. 'It was him saying I was vague and drifting. It was so unfair. I mean I might not be a constantly focused mapper-out of every detail of my life, but I did have plans. Not very fashionable plans maybe. I admit that articles in *Cosmopolitan* about young women attempting to emulate Maria in *The Sound of Music* are rare...'

Rosalind looked faintly surprised. 'I didn't know you sang.'

'... better her in fact; I was going to have all the children myself.' She looked up from her coffee mug at Rosalind. 'Sang? No I don't.'

144

She frowned. 'It was the big happy warm family bit I was after. I dreamt of being an inspirational mother. Jam making, huge teas, animals and homework jumbled up all over the kitchen, picnics in the garden. I even thought of turning Aunt Edith's sitting-room curtains into children's clothes.'

Rosalind leant across the table saying in a quiet concerned voice, 'Are you very short of cash?'

It was Amelia's turn to look surprised. 'No, not really. I mean I've still got most of the money from the flat invested and the freelancing brings in quite a bit. Of course I lived rent free, there was no mortgage. The deal was that I should look after everything here, grow our own vegetables, keep the hens, all that. He would support us with his painting.' With what she felt was unusual clear-sightedness she said, 'It was a kind of reversed trendiness, it made him feel original, a bit of a rebel. There I'd be, floating around in long frocks, the very model of a good old-fashioned artist's muse.' She rubbed her eyes. 'I suppose that, to him, I was just a phase, like his painting, but he was my whole life.'

'But isn't this Clarissa woman a clerk at his office?' Rosalind asked. 'I mean she's a career girl.'

Amelia sighed. 'I know. I think giving people what they want is a very dangerous thing.' She bent down and stroked Ronald's satin cheek. He jumbled up his features and produced a beaming smile.

'So what are you going to do? Are you moving back to London?'

'I really don't know. I can't think yet. And London is so ...' She shrugged her shoulders helplessly. 'Well, so big.'

Rosalind picked Ronald up from his rug on the floor and stood up. Draped across his mother's shoulder he looked sideways at Amelia, attempting another smile, his large head bobbing like a peony on a weak stem.

'Well, come for coffee next week anyway,' Rosalind said. 'That'll be something planned. I have to dash, Ronnie needs his bottle and a rest.'

'I better start Grandma's lunch too,' Amelia said seeing Rosalind and Ronnie out. 'She's having a nap but she's always ravenous when she wakes up.'

*   *   *

Flushed from the heat of the stove, Amelia flung open the kitchen windows to let in a breeze. She stayed for a moment, enjoying the air on her face and the sound of the housemartins nesting under the eaves.

'Lentils?' Selma, already seated at the table, said in an affronted voice. 'Lentils in June?'

Reluctantly, Amelia turned round. 'I'm sorry, but I felt you needed the protein, and I

146

couldn't think of anything else to make; for soup I mean. I do wish those teeth would hurry up and come. I bet Sister Morris is being deliberately slow in sending them.' She sat down opposite Selma and smiled encouragingly as she put the spoon into her own bowl. 'Mmmm,' she said, 'I make quite a good lentil soup.'

'If you say so, darling,' Selma said, both eyebrows raised. She lifted the spoon to her mouth, snatching at it as her shaking hand kept pulling it away from her lips. Splashing it back down into the bowl she said, 'You know, I haven't been for a swim for ages. I'm sure that's why I'm feeling so stiff.'

Amelia swallowed a mouthful of soup, wondering how to respond. 'Rosalind's parents have a pool,' she said finally. 'They live just outside the village.' She smiled suddenly. 'I'm sure they wouldn't mind us having a dip.'

Rosalind's mother was delighted for Amelia and her grandmother to use the pool. 'She even offered you the loan of a costume,' Amelia told Selma as they waited for a taxi. Luckily, she thought, Mrs Rowlands was a large woman.

The pool was separated from the main garden by a crumbling brick wall covered in clematis and pink roses. The walking-frame did not move well on crazy-paving, but slowly Amelia managed to get Selma across to the small gate that was kept locked in case of visiting grandchildren. Mrs Rowlands arrived, all smiles and easy chatter, clutching a monstrous bathing-costume in shocking pink. Amelia took Selma in to the changing hut.

'Here,' she pulled out a plastic freezer bag and a rubber-band from her bag. 'For your foot.'

The water was warm and Selma lay on her back, holding the stair-rail with one hand, letting the water carry her weight. Her eyes were closed and she was smiling. Amelia swam up and down the widths of the pool, careful not to take her eyes off Selma for long. 'Lovely water, doesn't make my eyes sting or anything,' she called up to Mrs Rowlands who sat knitting in a candy-striped deck-chair.

'It's because we use hardly any chlorine, thanks to the dye,' Mrs Rowlands called back.

Amelia swam to the edge and heaved herself up on her elbows. 'The dye?'

'We won't pour in masses of chemicals, Ambrose can't stand it, so we've got this completely harmless dye you see. If any of the grandchildren do a wee, the water turns bright purple all around them. They don't do it again I can tell you.' Mrs Rowlands laughed uproariously.

'Excuse me.' Amelia dropped back into the pool and swam over to Selma. 'I'm getting cold, shall we get up?'

Selma, still floating on her back, her hand on the rail, opened her eyes. 'You get out darling. I'm not in the least bit cold.' And she closed her eyes and continued to float pleasurably on the sweet clear water.

'What about your toe?' Amelia tried again. This time Selma opened just one eye, it looked displeased. 'My toe is fine.'

Amelia swam around in little fretful circles, her neck craned, watching for any signs of bright purple dye. It isn't fair, she thought, it just isn't fair. She stopped and trod water.

'It's getting pretty late. I asked the taxi to pick us up at half past three, it's ten minutes past now.'

From the poolside, Mrs Rowlands gave a little wave. 'There's no need for you to feel you have to keep us company,' Amelia called. 'I'm sure you're terribly busy.'

'Never too busy for you Amelia. We haven't seen enough of you since little Ronnie was born. Rosalind never seems to have time for anyone else any more.' Mrs Rowlands finished a row and put the knitting down. 'Ronnie is much too young to swim, of course, we don't hold with this water-baby thing you know. Ambrose thinks it's terribly unhygienic.' She had come up to the edge of the pool, and now she stood looking down at Amelia, a dimply smile on her large moon face. 'I said to him, "They don't understand shame at two months."'

Amelia grabbed Selma under both arms. 'I'm getting you out now,' she hissed, hauling her up on to the first step. A whirling snake of

149

purple dye uncoiled in the water round Selma's knees. As she looked up, Amelia's eyes met Mrs Rowland's across the width of the pool. Pushing her dripping hair from her forehead, she smiled nervously. 'Well well, time to get up.'

'I'm sure you're right Amelia.' Mrs Rowlands didn't smile back as she picked up her knitting from the chair. 'Don't put the cover back on please. There are things . . .' Here she paused, looking pointedly at Selma's plump and crumpled figure on the steps and at the whirl of purple fading to pale pink at its outer edge. 'Things we have to do.' And she turned and hurried back up towards the house with outraged little steps that seemed to tap out against the paving, 'Wait till Ambrose sees, wait till Ambrose sees.'

* * *

When Amelia came in with a mug of hot milk to Selma's room later that night, she found her already asleep, flat on her back, snoring. Amelia stood looking down at her, a reluctant mother gazing at her monstrous child. Then she turned and walked down to her desk in the sitting-room alcove. Half an hour later she switched off the light and went to bed; it was as she had always suspected, suffering did not necessarily make you a better poet.

150

Two sets of square white sheets and pillow-cases from Selma's double bed flapped on the washing-line, adding to Amelia's sensation of being a Lilliputian nanny landed with a Brobdingnagian baby. As she added a pair of panelled knickers to the line, the telephone rang. It was Dagmar again, wanting to know how Selma was.

'All right,' Amelia said, listening for the slamming and clanking that would herald Selma's appearance. 'No real problems,' she added.

'And you?' Dagmar sounded concerned.

Amelia wanted to tell Dagmar about Gerald, but she knew that the instant she did, she would regret it. Confiding in Dagmar was as comforting as putting your head in a lion's mouth; she would tear at your problem, worry it and gnaw it, leaving you with the chewed over remains. Then again on other days, bloated with her own worries, she would have no energy left for Amelia at all.

'We're all fine,' Amelia said mechanically.

'That's good. Amelia, you won't believe this but I've met this wonderful man. He's a visiting professor of North American literature, about my age, divorced. Oh darling, I really think something may come of this.'

'That's lovely,' Amelia said and meant it.

'You must make the effort to come over to

151

Exeter to meet him, when you bring Mummy back.' There was a pause. 'When is she coming back?'

Amelia leapt backwards to avoid the passage door being smashed in her face by Selma's sudden entrance. Selma found the push-open doors of the Old Rectory very helpful as she could shove them open with the legs of the walking-frame whilst steadying herself against the door-frame.

'Here's Grandma now,' Amelia said pointedly. 'Do you want a word?' She handed the phone to Selma. As she left the room she heard her say, 'I'm very well, thank you, apart from this wretched toe playing up. I haven't been able to play tennis once. I had a lovely swim though. No, not this morning, last week I think,' she said guessing wildly.

Last week, Amelia thought as she wandered back into the garden, was when I still believed I could have a future here. Gerald used to accuse her of being negative. She knew that was not true. She was in fact as rosy-edged, as reality-bashing an optimist ever to protect her most precious visions of heaven under a cloak of pessimism. Too much happiness had always made her feel insecure though, like a trapeze artist reaching the highest platform, the one nearest the ceiling of the circus tent. Too much happiness might tempt God, the God who felt that Job needed to be taught a lesson.

Nothing to be frightened of now, she

thought, and looking heavenwards through the garnet-red leaves of the copper beech she called, 'You didn't surprise me, you know that God!' Then she continued to peg out the washing.

On her way back to the house she stopped at the vegetable garden and pulled out a large weed from the soil in one satisfactory movement, leaving no roots behind. Why do I bother? she sighed. I should hire a plane to fly over the garden showering it with Weedol.

Back inside, there was a smell of burning. She ran through the passage and into the kitchen. A saucepan stood on the ceramic hob, boiling dry as spirals of stinking smoke rose from the black puddles on the side of the hot-plate. Amelia grabbed the saucepan handle only to pull her hand away, swearing. She grabbed an oven cloth and removed the pan before putting her burnt palm under running cold water.

'What a dreadful smell.' Selma's walking-frame bashed into the kitchen door, causing her to stop abruptly, doubling over the top of the frame. Recovering her balance she added helpfully, 'Something burning I wouldn't be surprised.'

'I think you left a saucepan of milk on the stove,' Amelia said, shoving her irritation to the pit of her stomach where it was left to fester. 'I'm going in to town for some shopping, do you want to come? We have to take the bus I'm afraid, but I'll book a taxi for coming back.'

*   *   *

Selma got through the main doors of the supermarket, but got stuck in the trolley turnstile. A small queue of shoppers formed behind whilst Amelia unwedged her. They manoeuvred themselves through the crowded aisles, Selma catching ankles with the legs of the frame and Amelia smiling nervously as apologies rolled off her tongue like sweets off a conveyor belt. Near to tears, she looked enviously at the young mothers whose babies fitted so conveniently into the trolley-seats. Then she looked at Selma who stood gazing expectantly at her, a packet of smoked kippers in her hand. All those years, she thought as she gently removed the package from Selma's grip and replaced them in the chill cabinet, dreaming of children and family life and this is what I got. It was as if God had read her heart's desire, but through a mirror, and given her Selma.

'Let's carry on shall we.' She smiled encouragingly whilst before her eyes was a vision of her grandmother stuffed into the child-seat of the trolley, her cone-shaped legs sticking out through the gap in the bars.

Wandering round the shelves like a robot programmed at random, Amelia picked a packet of peas here, some butter there, lentils, tins of tuna. It was probably silly to expect something as easy as a child to love and nurture, she thought. History after all was full of women whose youth had been spent in tandem with age and decline. She returned a leaking Mr Muscle bottle to the shelf, then thinking it anti-social to leave it for the next shopper, she promptly removed it again, giving it to a passing supervisor.

'All right?' she asked Selma who looked small and tired from the halting progress through an hostile environment.

I will campaign for especially designed old people's trolleys in every supermarket, she thought, demand large plastic-covered chairs in every restaurant. Why not old people's crèches at the workplace? Why not, why bloody not? All those mothers had chosen to have babies, or at least acquired them through a careless act of pleasure. But Amelia had not sat down one day, misty-eyed, saying, 'What about it darling, shall we have our own, our very own shaking, muddled, incontinent human remnant?' Nor was Selma the product of a moment of abandoned pleasure, well not Amelia's anyhow.

She parked Selma in a chair by the Ten Pence a Ride plastic camel and queued up at the check-out. Looking at her watch she saw that the taxi would already be waiting, so when it was her turn she didn't bother to pack her shopping but threw the tins and packages willy nilly back into the trolley. Picking up Selma again on the way out she had to push herself forward to stop the automatic doors clamping the walking-frame. The taxi was waiting outside, its meter running, and the driver stood by impatiently while Amelia loaded her shopping into the boot.

'You know, I'd love some chocolates. Did we get any?' Selma asked from her seat in the front.

'No.'

'Would you be so good as to help me out?' Selma asked the driver. Then she tried to turn round towards Amelia. 'I won't be a moment darling.' She grabbed on to the walking-frame parked by the car door, and began shuffling towards the store entrance.

'I've got another pick-up in twenty minutes,' the driver grumbled.

'There isn't time!' Amelia called, her head appearing from the boot.

Selma turned and looked at her incensed. 'Really darling, don't fuss. I'm just getting some sweets. I'll get you some too.' And helped through the doors by another shopper who shot Amelia a disapproving look, Selma disappeared inside.

Ten minutes later the taxi driver invited Amelia to unload her shopping from his car. He drove off revving his engine, leaving Amelia to find another trolley before going off

156

in search of Selma.

She did not find her at 'Pick'n Mix' nor by 'Chilled Produce, Dairy or Household Goods'. Surely no-one kidnapped old ladies? Was there a back entrance through which she could have wandered? Amelia hurried through the aisles finally reaching 'Tobacco and Spirits' at the back.

'There you are, darling. We wondered where you could have got to.' Selma was sitting at the tobacco counter attended by a young man in the red uniform of the supermarket staff, in her left hand was an unlit cigarette. She waved it in Amelia's direction.

'Yes, madam.' The young man with a sparse moustache nestling amongst his spots, made the 'madam' sound like an insult. 'To leave Granny like this. She was in quite a state when I found her I can tell you.'

Selma took a poor view normally of people other than Amelia calling her Granny, but today she joined the young man in looking reproachfully at Amelia.

Then with a pointed 'You take care now' to Selma, the assistant was off. Selma smiled fondly after him. 'What a dear little man,' she said.

'You don't smoke,' Amelia said coldly.

'Of course I smoke.' Selma looked at Amelia as if she thought she had gone quite mad. 'But not in here, apparently you're not allowed to. Cullen's never had silly rules like that.'

157

Amelia narrowed her eyes at her grandmother but felt it would be unsporting to point out that Selma hadn't smoked since 1959, the year Amelia was born in fact. Instead, she helped Selma up and again manoeuvred her back out on to the pavement.

'Excuse me Madam, do you possess a receipt for these goods?'

Amelia looked up to meet the pebble stare of a middle-aged man in a black leather jacket. He flashed an ID in front of her face.

'What do you mean?' Then her brow cleared and she smiled. 'Oh I see, you think that because I walked out from the shop without going through the check-out ...' The man crossed arms shaped like legs of lamb, heavy at the top, narrow little tubes at the bottom, and pushed his chin out. Amelia stopped smiling. 'What I'm trying to say is that I paid once but then I lost my grandmother who had gone back in to buy some sweets...'

'Where is the car, darling? I'm feeling rather tired,' Selma said in a small voice.

'Just show me the receipt, madam, would you? Then you'll be free to go.'

'The receipt.' Amelia riffled through her handbag.

'A credit card receipt or check stub will do,' the man said, scenting blood.

Amelia knelt down and tipped the contents of her bag on the pavement: house-keys, tampax, lipstick, brush, a photo of Gerald.

'It isn't there, is it madam?'

'You don't have to sound so bloody pleased about it,' Amelia snapped, as she caught sight of Selma's white face. She began emptying the trolley hoping the receipt would be hiding somewhere amongst the mound of groceries. In the end her shopping was all around her on the pavement but there was still no sign of the receipt.

'If you would be so good as to come with me now, madam.' It seemed hard for the man to hide his satisfaction and Amelia wondered when she was last called 'madam' by someone not intent on crushing her.

I definitely shouldn't have sworn at him, Amelia thought as he remained with his arms folded across his chest while she re-loaded the trolley. When she had finished, he grabbed the handle and began pushing it towards the shop with one hand, the other he kept at Amelia's elbow.

'I assure you, I have paid.' Amelia stopped by the doors. 'Just ask the check-out girl.'

'Which check-out would that be?'

'How the he ... How should I know?' Amelia said resignedly.

The man gave her a little nudge through the door, then kept it open for Selma who stopped halfway inside, blocking the entrance. 'Why are we going in here?' she asked.

'It seems your ... granddaughter is it, left the shop without paying.'

'Amelia? Nonsense.'

The man ignored her and marched Amelia to the supervisor's desk, pulpit-like in front of the vast picture windows of the store. Picking up the intercom he announced, 'If any member of staff remembers taking money from this lady, could he or she proceed to the manager's office.'

'Can someone please tell me what's happening.' Selma, her face grey and pinched, wobbled on her feet.

'I'm sorry but I really must get my grandmother home,' Amelia said.

The man looked from Selma to Amelia. 'I'll get the police to drive her. She can wait in the office with you until they come, there's a seat there.'

As she was marched through the shop, at a pace slow enough for Selma to keep up with, Amelia felt the looks of the other shoppers: hostile, embarrassed, amused. She didn't look away but returned their gaze, stony-faced. Suddenly overcome with loathing for every one of her fellow men, she felt sure it was moments like these that made people fire machine-guns into crowded places.

'Now I've seen it all,' an outraged voice declared. It was Selma's friend from the tobacco counter. 'That woman is not fit to look after a cat.'

The police arrived at the small upstairs office and Selma was taken home by a sympathetic policewoman. No-one turned up to say that they had taken Amelia's money. The policeman perched on the manager's desk.

'Now are you sure you didn't just think you had paid? It can't be easy with the old lady to keep an eye on as well.'

'I didn't, and it isn't,' Amelia said tiredly.

*   *   *

She took the bus home. The girl at check-out number five remembered Amelia paying, but she had been at lunch when the store detective made his announcement. 'Lucky the supervisor asked me,' the girl said with a pleased smile, helping to pack Amelia's groceries in plastic carriers.

'Keep the receipt next time,' the policeman called cheerfully.

Amelia had wandered out from the shop, slouching, leaving a trail of multicoloured ice-cream dripping from the air-hole of one of the bags. As she hurled it into the Victorian reproduction rubbish-bin by the bus-stop, she wanted to sit down on the cobbled pavement and scream, give all the shoppers something worth gawping at as she was carried off to a nice, peaceful asylum. She stood there, fists clenched, mouth open and ready to howl. Nothing happened. A nervous breakdown, she thought, obviously didn't come cheap. Then the bus arrived.

Back home, Selma was watching the World Cup. She sat leaning back in the armchair, her bad foot stretched out in front of her. In her hand was a lit cigarette tipped with a long snout of ashes. As she turned to greet Amelia, the ashes crumbled on to the floor.

'Listen,' she said, taking Amelia's hand when Luciano Pavarotti began to sing at the end of the transmission. As the last notes of 'Nessun Dorma' faded she sighed, and there were tears in her eyes. 'Rugby might be the game for gentlemen, but the music isn't half as good.'

In the night, Amelia woke from a dream where Gerald had insisted they light a fire although it was a hot summer's day. She forced heavy eyelids open and sat up, sniffing the stale bedroom air into which flowed the raw smell of burning. She threw off the duvet and ran from the room. On the landing the smell got stronger and as she hurried along, her bare feet thudding against the worn, green carpet, a broken vale of smoke floated towards her from Selma's room.

CHAPTER THIRTEEN

'I won't keep you a moment Alan,' Dagmar called anxiously from the bathroom. He was taking her to the best restaurant in Devon and now she was making them late. Alan abhorred unpunctuality. Dagmar did not know him well, but she did know that, so she had been sitting waiting in the armchair by the window a good ten minutes before he was due.

She had dressed with even more care than usual: was there not a flavour of 'mutton dressed as lamb' about the black lace dress? It would look lovely on Amelia, she thought with an irritated sigh as she slipped it off. She brought out a blue check suit. The sort of suit that turned her into just another middle-aged woman, a background person past whom the indifferent eyes of shop assistants and waiters swept on the way to something worth while. She chucked it on the bed.

Finally she had appeared in the sitting room wearing a translucent cornflower-blue skirt that billowed round her ankles when she walked, and a bright yellow blouse. Alan was fond of Matisse. Lounging in the emerald-green armchair, she thought she'd remind him of one of the painter's languid ladies reclining.

While she had waited, craning her neck to see if his car had arrived in the street below, she felt a smell. Not a strong smell, more a faint discord mingling with the rose and lily of the valley of her scent. Tilting her head, sniffing the air like a setter scenting a bird, she decided it must be her shirt. She wasn't absolutely sure it had been to the cleaners. Even if it had been they seemed to throw everything in together

163

these days, bundles of stained trousers, dirty macs and fine silk blouses, all into those great troughs by the counter. She looked at her watch and hurried off to her bedroom, tearing off the shirt and pulling one she didn't like quite as much off its hanger. Nothing was going to be allowed to spoil her evening. She was going to be as pristine as a library book, just unboxed.

The door bell rang as she buttoned the last button. 'Come in.' She had flung the door open. 'Nervous pee.' She flashed Alan an apologetic smile as she dashed off to the bathroom.

'I won't keep you a moment Alan,' she called again as she washed her hands and straightened her skirt, checking her face in the mirror. Parting her lips in a fake smile to check there were no pink lipstick smears on her teeth, she picked a comb off the shelf. It slipped from her fingers, landing on the floor behind the basin. 'Bugger,' she murmured softly to herself as she bent down groping for the comb.

'I'm coming,' she called again, but her hands had begun to shake and her heart thumped hard; she feared the undersides of things, the unseen surfaces, like others feared a dark cellar. Her fingers touched the plastic of the comb and she pulled it out between her forefinger and thumb and put it under the tap, rinsing, soaping, and rinsing again. Then it was the turn of her hands. She washed them like a surgeon would before an operation, scrubbing between the fingers and high up on the wrists. The soap foamed round the shirt cuffs leaving transparent patches on the silk. Last she washed her yellow and white metal watch in case it too had rubbed against the back of the basin. When she dried it the strap left little grey oxidization marks on the pale-yellow towel.

'There you are. I sure hope they'll keep that table.' Alan, amiable normally to the point of placidity, frowned at Dagmar as she draped a flowery chiffon shawl round her shoulders.

Dagmar hurried down the stairs behind him, her chafed hands stinging from the hot water. She really would have to stop all this nonsense she told herself sternly. She smiled up at Alan as he held the car door open. I won't waste you, she thought. Not you.

As they drove out of town, she chatted ceaselessly, drowning her lurking fears in great rivers of words. Now and then she glanced sideways at Alan to make sure she still amused him.

The restaurant was small and the crowded tables so close that, to sit down, Dagmar had to slide her bottom along the top of the next door table. The smell of cooking food, grilled and sautéed, steeped in garlic mingled with tobacco fumes in a warm haze above the rustic oak furniture. On each table stood a vase of pinks and lavender and a Dartington glass candle stick with a pink candle.

165

'Hey, not bad.' Alan reached across the table for Dagmar's hand. 'I'm sorry I snapped at you back there. I suppose I've got something of an obsession with punctuality.'

I wish people wouldn't use that word 'obsession' so lightly, Dagmar thought as she smiled back, giving Alan's hand a little squeeze. When her friend Claudia didn't care to leave her warm bed on a raw Monday morning, she suffered from exhaustion. When Penny had a weeping attack after three weeks of building works at her house, she suffered depression. What did Alan know about obsession, the tiger that gripped Dagmar between its claws day and night even in her dreams.

'I do understand,' she lied easily. 'There's nothing more irritating than being kept waiting.' She warmed to the subject. 'I mean it's a kind of arrogance, assuming that other people's time is less precious than one's own.'

'Now that's exactly it!' Alan emphasized his agreement, banging his fist on the table. 'And Imogen, my ex-wife, she never saw that, she was just late all the time.' He scanned the menu. 'The snails here come recommended.'

Dagmar, who disliked snails, said she'd love to try some. Her cheeks glowed and her laugh, as she arched her long white neck, was a little loud.

'If you prefer,' the waitress said at her elbow, 'we do a mock escargot.'

'I don't think I like the sound of that.' Dagmar laughed again. 'How is your mock turtle?'

The waitress registered polite confusion.

'Now don't tell me you're a fan of Alice too?' Alan leant across the table.

'But of course,' Dagmar lied. She had always been uncomfortable with *Alice in Wonderland*.

Alan talked about his favourite writers and Dagmar followed like a practised dancing partner. He thinks I'm wonderful, she thought jubilantly. Her next thought, snapping at the heels of the first, was: Dear God, let it last, let me stay in control.

'You'd love the Cape.' Alan pushed his plate away, and leant back in his chair contentedly. 'My home is pretty small, but it's in a real nice part of town, all clapboard and wisteria.'

Dagmar had made sure to place her handbag on a shiny, stain-free part of the floor and now the waitress coming to clear the plates caught her foot on the strap. Losing her balance for a moment she put her other foot flat on to Dagmar's bag. As Alan spoke of his home town Dagmar stared at the brown mark on the toe-cap of the waitress's sturdy shoe.

'I've always wanted to go to the States, especially New England.' Dagmar dragged her gaze from the floor, looking up at Alan with an uneven smile.

'Christmas back home is glorious,' Alan said. 'Snowdrifts like candy floss, coloured

167

lights on the trees in the yard...'

The girl could have stepped in something. There was enough dogmess on the quaint streets outside the restaurant to render it a faeces minefield. Dagmar nodded and smiled across the table as her thoughts rampaged. It was like the test of coordination Robert had set her when they were children, rubbing your tummy with one hand while you patted your head with the other. She would smile and talk while all the time her mind was engaged in a quite different dialogue.

'I've always loved a white Christmas,' she said, but the constant performing of the trick made her weary. She could almost feel her mind being drained of sparkle and enthusiasm, leaving her conversation stale. She tried hard to plug the leak.

'One year when I was a little girl in Sweden during the war, we had what we call a real Wolves' Winter ...' Her voice trailed off as she kept sneaking glances at the floor, checking the bag for marks. She thought she could see a tiny smear by the clasp. 'It was Christmas ...' she began again but the gloss had worn off her story like glitter off an old bauble. She had wanted to tell Alan about the huge Christmas tree her Jewish grandparents insisted on decorating so that she would not feel left out from the fun of her friends. She wanted to tell him of the night when she had crept up on the deep window-sill and peeked through a gap in the black-out curtain at the snowdrifts glistening in the starlight. By the time Selma came and led her away, she had decided that God must be rather careless to let all that light through the black sky.

But she said nothing of this to Alan. Instead she picked up the bag from the floor, searching the tan leather for dirt whilst pretending to have difficulties with the clasp. 'Got something in my eye.' She brought a powder compact out and pulled at her eyelid.

Alan chatted on but after a while his conversation too grew less animated. They finished their pears in port wine sauce with the odd routine sentence interrupting their eating.

'You're tired, aren't you?' Alan put his hand over hers. 'I'll take you straight home.'

Back in her flat, Dagmar tilted her face up for a good night peck on the cheek, and closed the door behind him. She stood for a moment, her back against the door, thinking of how the charm had been squeezed from their evening by that great, spreading tumour of anxiety. With a little moan of distress she held the handbag up to her face. Then she shook it hard, tipping its contents on the floor, before running whitefaced into the kitchen, smashing the bag into the bin, kicking the bin-lid shut.

Later she sat in bed with a mug of tea and a plate of chocolate biscuits trying to repaint the evening in more pleasing shades. The telephone rang. She grabbed the receiver hoping for a miracle, for it to be Alan saying what a truly lovely evening it had been.

It was Amelia. 'I'm at the hospital,' she told Dagmar. 'It's Selma. I'm afraid she set fire to herself.'

CHAPTER FOURTEEN

Amelia spent most of the night staring at Selma who slept sedated at the hospital in Basingstoke. Rasping breaths were forced from her smoke-damaged lungs, a curtain had been drawn round her as it had been round Willoughby. Amelia felt she was in a capsule floating through space. Now and then sounds would reach them from faraway earth, muted clatter of heels on vinyl, whispers.

The curtains opened and a nurse told her to go home and get some rest.

*   *   *

At the Old Rectory, Gerald slept in the wing-chair in front of a flickering television screen. Gingerly Amelia picked the remote control from his lap and pressed 'Off'. She stood for a while just looking at him. She felt like a cannibal feasting on his youth and wholesomeness, listening to his breath that pulsed lightly and easily from his parted lips.

She knelt by him, putting her cheek close to his face, feeling the warm breath against her skin. Gerald stirred and she got up quickly.

'You looked so, so ... unsinged.' She smiled, embarrassed.

'I heard about the fire.' Gerald sat up straight, brushing the hair from his eyes. 'When Mrs Jenkins called, I came immediately. I've checked the damage upstairs.' To her surprise he smiled. 'It could be worse.' Crossing one long leg over the other he asked, 'What about your grandmother, how is she?'

'I don't really know.' Out of habit Amelia perched on the arm of his chair. 'She was smoking in bed; I should have thought of that one. But she's hanging on, and the hospital doesn't think she's in any immediate danger. Whether she will recover fully or not is another matter.' She spoke calmly, then suddenly she bashed her forehead against the palms of her clenched fists. When she looked up again, there were tears in her eyes. 'God help me Gerald, I don't even know if I want her to.'

Gerald pulled her down on to his knee and put his arm round her shoulders. He made little comforting noises to stop her crying. 'It's the shock,' he mumbled, 'it's the shock.'

The worry and guilt that had been like a grinding fist in her stomach began to ease and she was almost asleep when she felt Gerald's arm pull away from behind her back.

171

'Blast! It's five o'clock, I have to get home.'
Nudging her off his knee, he sprang from the
chair.

Amelia looked at him sleepily. 'I thought
you'd come back.'

Gerald sighed. 'You have to accept it's over
between us.' He took a step back towards her.
'God, Amelia, I didn't mean to give you the
wrong idea.' He looked pityingly at her. 'I'm
sorry, I really am.' He patted her cheek.

She shied away, drawing in a long, shivering
breath. She could see him back at Clarissa's
place. 'Poor old Amelia,' he'd say. 'It's pathetic
really the way she clings on.'

If my head split open this moment she
thought, hot anger would spew out and drown
us like the great flood. She clenched her fists,
staring after Gerald who was walking towards
the door, stiff-backed, eyes ahead as if he
believed one backward glance would turn him
into salt. I'll give Selma a blow torch next time,
she thought. But before I die, I'll hang that
big-assed Sloane by her thick ankles and choke
her with her own Laura Ashley skirt.

'No, no I'm sorry,' she called after him. 'I
can't think what got over me. It's the shock as
you said.' She forced a smile to her lips and left
it to fight with the expression in her eyes.

*   *   *

Selma surprised everyone but Amelia by

remaining alive. A week after setting fire to her continental quilt she was still coughing painfully from the smoke and her legs were covered in weeping burns, but she was alive and her heart stayed strong; it seemed to have marched to a different tune from the rest of her used-up body.

The hospital needed her bed.

Amelia phoned Cherryfield and asked to be put through to Sister Morris.

'And who shall I say is calling?'

'Judas,' Amelia mumbled. 'I mean to say, it's Miss Lindsay.'

'Sister Morris here.'

Amelia had sprung Selma from Cherryfield and now, on the eve of recapture, she was actually finding the voice of the Chief Warden comforting. Sister Morris told her that there would be no problem having Mrs Merryman back as the payments had been kept up.

'I feel so responsible.' Amelia humbled herself. 'She had taken up smoking again, I think she'd forgotten she ever gave it up. But I never thought ... It was awful. There she was like one of those toadstools, you know they look like an upside-down skittle and give out puffs of smoke. She wore her hairnet too.' The picture was vivid before Amelia's eyes and somehow the hairnet added to the horror, she wasn't quite sure why. 'There's no doubt she needs better care than I can give her. It's all my fault, I should never have taken her away.'

In victory, Sister Morris was magnanimous. 'Don't be too hard on yourself Miss Lindsay, you did what you thought best. Although, as we professionals know only too well, with our elderly that's seldom enough. Now if you could give me the name of the doctor in charge of your grandmother.'

*   *   *

'I can't wait to get out of here. I do so detest hospitals.' Selma greeted the news on Saturday morning that she was being discharged, with a self-congratulatory little smile. 'I've had far worse burns than these,' she gesticulated in the direction of her bandaged legs, 'so I really don't see what all the fuss is about.'

She raised her arms out obediently for the nurse to dress her, and Amelia stared at the bones that seemed like a giant clothes hanger holding up the sagging flesh. She glanced at her own arms, bare in a short-sleeved T-shirt, as if making sure of their firm roundness and the honey-tone of the skin before turning away guiltily.

Gerald's Citroën was parked outside the hospital. When he came around to measure up the spare room for wallpaper, Amelia had asked to borrow it for the trip down to Cherryfield.

'I'm sure Clarissa has a Fiat Uno or something to take you around in, and I bet she calls it Algie,' she had added ungratefully.

'Hughie actually.' Gerald had smiled briefly before remembering where his loyalties lay.

Now Selma was installed in the front seat of his car, padded legs stretched out in front of her, the seat pushed back as far as it would go. Amelia waved her thanks to the orderly as she drove out of the hospital car park.

'I hate hospitals,' Selma said again, then she coughed, a racking cough that wrenched mucus from her nose and eyes, a cough that doubled her over and sucked the energy from her so that when it finished she sat back, grey faced, moist eyes staring, and said nothing for a long time.

Amelia suffered with her, driving along on the motorway, unable to stop the car and put her arms round her to comfort. Chopin had died playing his 'Polonaise', coughing blood until there seemed to be more over the ivory of the piano than inside his own frail body, or so Selma had told her once. Maybe, Amelia thought, that was a better death; a great fountain of agony in the midst of life and beauty? It had to be better than what Selma was going through; having life sucked from her in little painful spurts.

They were on the A303 driving west, when Selma spoke again. 'I thought I was going home with you. We seem to have been driving for an awfully long time.'

'Do you need the loo?'

175

'No, darling, I said we seem to have been...'

'Cherryfield,' Amelia interrupted, pity and shame making her brusque. 'We're going to Cherryfield. You need looking after properly and it's a lot better than a hospital. You're lucky to be alive.' The phrase slipped out and they both considered it in silence.

'I suppose I am,' Selma said finally to Amelia's astonishment. Was it an automatic response, or did she actually mean it? Amelia glanced at Selma's profile. Did she really feel lucky to be alive? Did she even remember Cherryfield?

'Admiral Mallett will be pleased to see you,' Amelia tried. Selma didn't seem to have heard.

Gerald's mother had said once that she wanted Gerald to put her down if she ever got senile. 'Put her down,' that was the phrase she had used and she had spoken in earnest. Amelia had asked Gerald later, 'Why are people so scared of becoming senile? After all you yourself, are the one person who won't know. There you'll be making everyone else's life a misery, but *you* won't know or care.' A senile mind, she had imagined, was like a wiped-clean video, all gone, blank. She had been so wrong. The film was still there, but with scenes cut out at random, replaced out of sequence, rendering the whole senseless. Familiar faces turned up in strange places, flashbacks made more sense than the dislocated present. No, senility offered no

176

escape. She put her foot down on the accelerator, watching the speedometer rise to eighty. You were condemned to stay snatching at bits of reality as tantalizing as sunbeams and as hard to hold.

'I know Admiral Mallett, nice man,' Selma said, answering suddenly.

Amelia looked out at the rape fields and the rich green meadows, bright as a flea-market picture, as if it was her journeys through the English summer landscape that were numbered, not Selma's.

'You do remember Cherryfield?' she asked quietly.

Again there was a pause, as if they were communicating by satellite.

'Of course I remember it, awful place. Robert tried to persuade me to move there for good.' Selma turned to look at Amelia. 'Where is Robert? I don't seem to have seen him for ages.'

'Brazil, he lives there now ...' She was about to add, remember? But she said instead, 'He knows about the accident. He'll phone as soon as you're back.'

'I must go over and visit him,' Selma declared.

*   *   *

At Cherryfield, Sister Morris greeted them in front of the house, a large, ginger-haired man

177

in tow.

'Welcome back, Mrs Merryman,' Sister Morris smiled, her lips moving not up, but horizontally before springing back to their usual defensive position clamped across her teeth. 'This is Mr Jones, he's joined us in your absence to help behind the scenes: fetching, carrying, that sort of thing.'

Amelia looked at the hefty, grinning Mr Jones and imagined him bounding up and down the passages and stairs of Cherryfield on all fours, old people dangling like wounded birds from his jaws. But he was gentle as he eased Selma from her seat, transferring her to the wheelchair parked on the grass verge.

Amelia hauled a small case from the car boot. 'I left most of her clothes here. They should all be in her room still.' She started to walk towards the house.

'She's not in her old room.' Sister Morris, to Amelia's surprise, coloured, lowering her gaze like a guilty child. Any moment now, Amelia thought, she'll be scuffing her white lace-ups against the gravel.

'Is there a good reason for moving her?' Amelia asked.

Sister Morris looked up as Selma was wheeled past by Mr Jones. 'At this present moment in time,' the round-about phrase gave Sister Morris time to recover her breezy confidence, 'we feel Mrs Merryman would benefit from a higher degree of care. So we put her in Honeysuckle.' She added the last sentence speedily as if to race through any objections Amelia might have.

'But that's the Annexe.' Amelia was horrified. She felt like a mother who having persuaded her child to have a verruca removed finds the surgeon poised for an amputation. 'You can't do that, she couldn't take it.' And as Sister Morris started towards the door she called after her, 'She calls it Death Row you know!'

Sister Morris continued inside. 'And that's not a helpful attitude, not at all.' She chucked the words over her shoulder at Amelia. 'We are only doing what we think best for our residents. If I may remind you, it's that kind of emotional response which got your grandmother into this sorry state in the first place.'

It was Amelia's turn to hang her head. Sister Morris was right. It had been a panic withdrawal, removing Selma from Cherryfield. It had done only harm.

'My room is upstairs.' Selma tried to look over her shoulder at Mr Jones. 'I'm sure of it. Amelia are you there? Could you please tell this man that my room is upstairs.'

Again, Amelia thought how easy it would be to cruise along on Selma's senility, to say with absolute conviction that she was mistaken yet again, that her room was, and always had been, in the Annexe; as easy as pulling the lifebelt

179

from a drowning man.

Mr Jones had stopped at the bottom of the stairs with a helpless glance at Sister Morris. Amelia hurried up to Selma and knelt at her side.

'It's all right Grandma, it's just for a little while.'

'What is?' Selma's voice rose to a squeak.

Amelia looked up reproachfully at Sister Morris, then she put her hand on Selma's. 'They're moving you into the Annexe just while your burns heal. It's not an age thing, nothing like that. It's only because of this nasty accident. I mean, if it was I who had got burnt, I'd be in a hospital ward now.'

'So why am I not? Why am I not in hospital?'

Amelia had tears in her eyes when she looked at Selma. 'Please,' she whispered, 'I'm trying.'

'I want to go home.' Selma snatched her hand away. 'I want to go to Ashcombe. I miss the cats.' She looked hard at Amelia. 'Where are the cats?'

Amelia stood up. And what do I say now? Do I look her in the eyes and say: Ashcombe is sold. Your things are in storage waiting for you to die so they can be divided up between your children. And the cats? They were put down. We tried to find a new home for them but they were too old and smelly, no-one wanted them. Was that what she was meant to say? She sighed. 'Let's get you settled in your room shall

180

we?'

'Amelia.' Selma grabbed her elbow, looking at her as if there was no-one else in the world. 'I know I won't get home for my birthday, not now I've had this stupid accident.'

She's giving up, Amelia thought, distressed, relinquishing hope.

'But Christmas, darling,' Selma continued, 'that's altogether different. I'll be one hundred per cent by then.' She put her hand on Amelia's arm and whispered, 'I couldn't bear not having Christmas at home.'

Amelia just stared after her as Mr Jones began to push the wheelchair towards the Annexe.

'Amelia!' Selma sounded terrified now.

'Yes, of course,' Amelia said quickly, 'of course you'll be home for Christmas.' And merry little devils danced through her mind chanting, 'Liar, liar, pants on fire.'

She followed Mr Jones through the double swing doors at the end of the long passage. A stocky young nurse, her starched cap perched on spiky black hair, hurried towards them with a big smile. 'We haven't met,' she said to Amelia, putting out her hand. 'I'm Nurse Scott.' Then she bent down over the wheelchair, putting her face close to Selma's. 'We'll look after you, Mrs Merryman. There's nothing for you to worry about.'

'Oh bugger off,' Selma said.

The nurse pretended not to hear. She took

the wheelchair from the silent Mr Jones and pushed it inside a brightly lit, sparsely furnished room. As she took Selma past the first bed, she said, pointing, 'That's Mrs Ambrose. Her husband's over in the main house. They're new this week, in fact.' She parked Selma at the foot of the second bed by the small window.

The table by Mrs Ambrose's bed was cluttered; there were several photographs, unframed ones, leaning against the carafe of water and against the small vase of roses, and two in silver frames of the same young man in an RAF cap. A Bible lay nearest the bed and a rosary of milky beads rippled across the leather cover. Over the bed was pinned a drawing of a matchstick boy with an enormous head, playing on a beach, and written across the bottom was 'To deerest Grany, from Joe'.

Amelia took a step closer, peering down at the bed. But where was Mrs Ambrose? She had an image of a skeleton in a frilly nightie jumping up from under the smooth pink counterpane crying, surprise, surprise!

'I don't think she's here.' Amelia turned to Nurse Scott. 'Mrs Ambrose, she seems to have disappeared.'

Nurse Scott turned briefly from undressing Selma, who seemed for the moment to have stopped protesting. 'She's in the Lounge, visiting Mr Ambrose. Now, while I do Mrs Merryman's legs, why don't you have a nice walk round the garden. Come back in fifteen minutes or so.'

*　　*　　*

From the open door of his room, Admiral Mallett watched the girl in her pale blue and white uniform collect Mrs Merryman's clothes. The bundle, three patterned summer dresses, a couple of cardigans, a gabardine mac that had ceased to be beige in favour of motley grey, hung over the girl's sturdy freckled arm as she clip-clopped along the landing.

'What's going on, Nurse? Mrs Merryman is coming back, isn't she?' In his mind his voice was firm, the words casual. What he heard was an old man's croak pleading for assurance. People kept leaving, dying, and he could do nothing to stop it.

The nurse didn't answer so he called out again, 'Nurse!'

Now she turned. 'Admiral Mallett, I didn't see you there. Yes Mrs Merryman is back, we're moving her across to Honeysuckle.' And she was off, brisk heels across polished boards.

Poor little Mrs Merryman. An old man's tears, quick to appear, welled up in his eyes. How she will hate it. He turned and stuttered across to the huge mahogany chest of drawers brought from home. The keys to the Rover lay in the top right drawer. He slipped them into his trouser pocket and, refusing the chair-lift, laboured downstairs holding the banister tight with both hands, moving crab-like down the steps.

In the hall, Sister Morris stood by the large vase on the refectory table, subjugating a bunch of gladioli.

'I'm off for a drive,' the Admiral said airily as he passed.

Sister Morris turned, a rebellious bloom in hand. 'Really Admiral, is that wise?'

'Entirely,' he replied. 'I possess a valid licence.'

'But Admiral...'

'Now I mustn't keep you, Sister. Good day.'

He hadn't driven the car himself since he moved to the wretched place, when was that now? Late April, three months already. Silly not to have done so, he thought, as he reversed the car from the Cherryfield parking lot. His reactions might not be as quick as they were, but he made up for that with experience. Experience did still count for something, he told himself as he drove out from the drive and on to a clear road. At the next junction a tractor pulled out in front. Admiral Mallett didn't mind, he was in no hurry. It was good to have a reason to slow down in fact. Henry had been clever persuading him to get an automatic, saved the hip. Leaning forward a little in his seat, he flicked his eyes over to the left, enjoying the sight of the three large oak trees that stood in the centre of the vast field, defying the farmer's wish for uncluttered progress.

A flash of red screeched past the Admiral's Rover, swaying back to the left side of the road ahead of the tractor before disappearing round the twist in the road. 'Bloody fool,' the Admiral muttered to himself.

A few hundred yards down the road the tractor turned left. The Admiral slammed on the brakes. The man hadn't indicated, he could have sworn it. Behind him the Volvo Estate stopped inches from the back of the Rover. The front of a white Audi, nosing the rear of the Volvo, folded like a fan as it clanked into the metallic-blue boot.

The Admiral saw the crash in his rear-view mirror and pulled on to the verge. Pushing the door open, he heaved his legs on to the ground. He grabbed his stick and got to his feet. Peering at a passing car he stepped across to the site of the accident. By the side of the Volvo a woman stood crying, clutching a small girl by the hand. The Audi driver, a young man, the sleeves of his white shirt rolled up, stared red-faced at the folded front of his car.

Wobbling on his feet, the Admiral shook his head and tut-tutted sympathetically. Turning to the weeping woman, he cooed, 'There, there, young lady, it's not so bad, no-one's hurt. Worse things happen at sea eh?' He smiled at the little girl who smiled back, a small smile.

The young man glared. 'You know,' the
185

Admiral jabbed the stick at him, 'this is what comes of not keeping your distance.' He turned back to the woman. 'Are you sure you're all right, madam? Would you not like me to drive you to a doctor. And the little girl?' Taking a couple of steps towards them he smiled again, competent, in charge; that was service training for you.

'You silly old fart.' The words came slowly, steeped in contempt, making him turn around, stooping over his stick, cheeks colouring. 'Stupid old sod, you shouldn't be allowed on the road.' The young man with his heavy arms crossed over his chest was shouting at him. Somehow this all appeared to be his fault; the crying woman and white-faced child, the concertinaed car, were all his fault. The Admiral blinked and swallowed hard.

'Don't speak to him like that.' The woman had stopped crying and now she glared at the Audi driver. She took a step towards the Admiral and said soothingly, 'There's no great harm done as you said, no-one's hurt.'

'No harm done, you silly cow, what do you think this is?' The young man aimed a kick at the smashed-in front of his car. 'It's all right for you in that bloody tank but what about this? "No harm done."' He mimicked her voice.

That young man should not be allowed to speak to her like that. I should stop him, the Admiral fretted. But he was frightened, just a frightened old man who was no use to anyone.

For the second time that day he felt close to tears.

'Don't you worry.' It was the woman comforting him once again. 'It's difficult sometimes to see the indicator in this bright light.' She turned to the young man who had sat down in the passenger seat of his car, his feet on the road, his head in his hands. Now he looked up miserably.

'It's a new car. My own too, not the firm's.' He sighed, not even bothering to look at the Admiral. 'Tell the old fart to piss off and let us get on with it. You are insured, aren't you?' he asked the woman.

She nodded, then took the Admiral by the arm. 'You just drive on home,' she said, escorting him back to the Rover. 'We'll be fine.'

'We'll be fine,' the child echoed, speaking for the first time. 'But you should go home. My daddy says old people shouldn't be on the roads.'

The Admiral drove off. He could still hear the level-toned insults spouted at him by the Audi driver, wounding words lobbed at him with the indifference of a kick aimed at a stray dog. And the little girl, 'Daddy says old people shouldn't be on the roads.' In the eyes of those young people he, Rear-Admiral John Mallett DSO, DSC, was an alien life form. As if on entering his eighth decade he had simultaneously exited the human race. Could they really not see that he was just like them, only a few years on? After all, he had not entered this earth a scraggy, trembling old man.

He passed two teenage boys on their bicycles, rucksacks slung over one shoulder. They were calling to each other, laughing. I'm your future don't you see! he wanted to cry out after them. You're my past. That's all it is.

He turned off the main Totnes road on to the quiet lane leading to Harbertonford. There was no-one behind him, no-one in front. He dared take his eyes off the road to feast them on the lush greens and bright yellows of the fields. He took a double bend expertly.

'Not so fast, Johnnie.' He heard a soft voice, half scared, half excited, in his ear. Lydia, the girl who had become Henry's mother, had clung to him like a soft baby vine on that first drive together. A London child, dressed for the country in a cotton shift dress and with a white floppy hat on her long, straight hair, she had found the Devon lanes wild, she told him.

'Wild,' he had repeated smiling down at her. 'I never thought of them as that.'

He was forty-nine and an Admiral already. She was twenty-four and liked the Beatles.

'You must have been in the war?' she had asked at the London drinks party where they met.

'Which one, the big one or Korea?'

'You mean you were in both?' Her huge,

188

black-fringed eyes had gazed blue at him. 'Crikey!'

She had chatted and laughed on that drive to Devonport, and he, quiet as always, hadn't tired of hearing her voice, small and breathless, fluttering in his ears like puffs of dandelion seeds. She had touched the dark hair on his forearm with her pink-frosted nails. 'I love your arms. They're so reassuring. Boys my age are all such weeds.' Her skinny shoulders heaved in a sigh. He could feel her look on him. 'You're sexy.'

The car had jerked to the right.

'You don't mind me being honest, do you? I think if one feels something positive about another person, one might as well tell them. Don't you?'

Heart beating faster, mouth twitching into a smile, he had said, 'I think I do.'

The lorry looming in the rearview mirror brought him back to now with angry hooting. He glanced at the speedometer and saw the needle at twenty. Putting his hand out of the open window he gave a little wave as if to say, 'Sorry, old chap, I'll get on with it.' He put his foot down. The lorry stayed close up. He pressed his foot harder on the accelerator, went faster than was comfortable, but the lorry was always there, its cab in the rear-view mirror almost on top of the Rover.

Round the next bend was the crossroads. He had to turn right on to the main road to get back to Kingsmouth. The light was fading. He edged the car out to get a better view past the tall hedges. The cars ran in a steady stream from both directions. Opposite, somebody was waiting too. The chap wasn't signalling so he'd be wanting to cross straight over: his right of way. The Admiral leant far over the wheel, eyes right, eyes left, right again as if he was watching a tennis match. There was a gap. He stood back for the other car to cross. The lorry hooted. 'All right, all right,' the Admiral muttered, but he was fretting. The car had crossed but there was another one now. No more gaps in the traffic either, just a road like a conveyor belt, pushing out car after car. The lorry driver put his fingers on the horn and kept them there. The Admiral glanced in the rear-view mirror, then stretched further over the wheel, heart pumping, eyes flicking from side to side and across. His mouth tasted sour. He ran his tongue across his cracked lips. He needed a pee too.

The lorry driver had stopped sounding his horn. The Admiral sat back a little and some of the tension left his neck and shoulders.

'No need to panic old boy,' he told himself. Bound to get across eventually. The blighter will just have to wait.

'Beeeep!' It started up again, and now others joined in, a chorus straight from hell. The shock sent tears to his eyes. His eyes darted from side to side as he jerked the car out on to the main road. Another horn made him look right. He saw the open mouth of the driver of the van. This is it, he thought, and everything was sound: crashing, splitting, shattering. Then silence.

CHAPTER FIFTEEN

Henry Mallett stood in the garden at Cherryfield, his back to the French windows. He stood quite still under the cherry tree, his head slightly raised. Talking to God maybe, Amelia thought as she came up quietly behind him. He turned and, when he saw her, a slow smile of pleasure softened his face. Amelia thought it must have taken a lot of effort to find a shirt as awful as the one he was wearing—turquoise with an asymmetric pattern in black and lime-green.

Henry looked as if he was about to kiss her cheek, then thinking the better of it, he took her hand instead in a firm handshake.

'Pleased to meet you I'm sure,' Amelia simpered but he ignored her and said, 'I heard about the fire. Thank God you're both OK.'

Amelia stopped simpering. 'I'm OK, Selma is in Death Row.'

'I heard that too. I'm sorry. How is she taking it?' He waited for her answer in that way he had of cocking his head slightly towards you as if he couldn't bear to miss a word you said. It always made her feel she ought to reward his attentiveness with a comment of earth-shattering profundity.

'Badly,' she said.

Still, Henry's attentive silence, as they wandered across the lawn, seemed to suck thoughts from her she hadn't even admitted to herself.

'I wish she was dead.' She looked up at him, half expecting him to raise a condemnatory finger with a flash of Old Testament fire. But he didn't. He just kept listening, so she went on talking.

'Selma's the only person left whom I really love and who loves me back, and still I wish her dead. That's how badly she's taking it.' She flung herself down on the dry grass. 'I might be wrong of course.' She turned to him as he sat down next to her. 'Of course she might have taken one look at the Annexe and thought, "This is the place for me, I'm happy," but somehow when a person sits slumped in a wheelchair, tears trickling down their face, their poor, useless hand jerking and dancing on the end of the arm like a badly managed puppet, I reckon they're not so happy after all.' She glared at him. He smiled back at her. She stopped glaring and asked, 'Is your father well?'

'Not too bad. He's out for a drive apparently. It's good news that, I think. He's

not been out on his own since coming here.'
Henry changed tack seamlessly. 'Your mother,
don't you love her?'

As she thought about it, Amelia pulled a tuft
of grass from the lawn and scattered it over her
legs. 'Maybe, I suppose so. But it's like sunlight
trying to penetrate so many layers of
atmosphere that, when it finally arrives, it's
weak. Selma was life enhancing. My mother is
life denying. I worry that I might be like her.'

'Your poor mother, she must be very
unhappy,' Henry said.

Amelia gave him a dirty look. 'And this time
I promised Selma she'd be home for
Christmas.' She made it sound like a challenge
to him: so what does someone like you, with
your faith and your energy, do with someone
like me, so shiftless and feeble?

'How long are you going to go on lying to
her?'

Amelia had no fight left in her. 'Oh Henry, I
don't know. It's like paying off one credit card
with another; sooner or later it will end in
tears.'

'But what are you going to do about it?'
Henry insisted.

'I don't know what I'm going to do,' she
whined. 'You always say, "What are you going
to do about it?" in that revoltingly energetic
way. But I'm tired.' Her voice rose in pitch.
'I'm tired of worrying about Selma, tired of
feeling sorry for her. It's not fair.' She finished

pulling the petals off a daisy and looked up at him. 'Isn't it the Bible that says, "For everything there is a time"? Well, this is the time for me to be concerned with three months colic and the aluminium content in baby formula. Or at least to be left in peace to get on with being a self-centred thirtysomething minding my brilliant career. Instead, pity for Selma rides my back like a witch whose claws dig deeper into my shoulders each time I try to shake her off.'

Henry cleared his throat and Amelia added quickly, 'And please don't tell me to get my pleasures from helping others and to look forward to an absolutely stunning afterlife. I couldn't take it just at the moment. I've got a dreadful headache.' The face she raised to him was pallid in the strong light, each gold-brown freckle showing against the white skin.

'It's obvious you haven't been to church for some time if that's your idea of preaching,' Henry said dryly, but he looked concerned.

I could cover his nice, firm mouth with passionate kisses, Amelia thought. That would make him run off and leave me alone.

'I was actually about to offer some constructive advice,' he continued.

'I don't want that either. I just want to be left alone to get on with my life.'

'Get on with dreaming about how to get on with your life, you mean. Waiting for Gerald to marry you. Waiting for children to be born who can do everything you never had the guts and energy to do yourself.'

Amelia didn't even bother to look offended. 'Gerald's left me for an independent career woman, the sort, in fact, that I was before I gave it all up for him.' She added thoughtfully, 'Of course I was better looking.'

'Are better looking,' Henry surprisingly corrected her. Then he mumbled dutifully, 'I'm sorry to hear it though,' before allowing his normal expression of barely harnessed eagerness to return. 'But now it's happened, take the opportunity to do something positive with your life. Take charge. See that witch on your back as a jockey spurring you on. Cherryfield is not that far away from any of us, so get on with life. Grab it by the neck, wrestle it to the ground and say "I'm on top".' Henry's bright brown eyes were round as he looked intently at her.

'That's the Naval part of the Chaplain speaking, is it?' Amelia couldn't help smiling. She scratched her right knee thoughtfully; her tights were itching in the heat but she refused to go barelegged. When Gerald had asked her why she seemed to be the only female still wearing tights in the summer she had said, 'Blue-tinged, freckled legs just aren't nice.' Of course stockings were cooler, she thought now as she scratched on absent-mindedly, but the suspender belt kept slipping down over her hips, making the stockings wrinkle. Hold-ups

195

were positively dangerous, she was sure of it, the way they gripped the flesh part of your thighs like a tourniquet.

'Penny for them?' Amelia looked up to find Henry gazing at her.

She stopped scratching and smiled suddenly. 'Would you believe: stockings and suspenders?'

He grinned back. 'As it's you, yes.'

'I do have something planned you know,' she said, serious now. 'I want to open a café. The old-fashioned continental kind. Somewhere where elderly matrons can catch their breath after a hard day's shopping for darning needles and corn plasters. Somewhere where they can slam down their copious shopping baskets on the table with a sigh of contentment as they order fattening pastries. I picture them wearing hats,' she said. 'I find the hats important you see, because it takes a person in control of their life to wear one regularly.' She looked at Henry with a little smile. 'I don't suppose that's the sort of thing you mean.'

Henry looked a little taken aback. Amused, Amelia noticed that he was trying hard not to look at her legs.

'What about your journalism?' he asked.

She shrugged her shoulders. 'I should never have left the paper. It's not easy to break back in, particularly in the present climate. It's almost all dead men's shoes. I could try the provincials of course, but it would be a step back.' Hoping to impress him a little she added, 'About the café; I thought of arranging poetry recitals, that sort of thing, and there'll be the antiquarian books. I want people to be able to look at them while they eat. I'd have to be careful about stains, of course.'

Whilst she spoke, Henry was looking intently at her and she paused, as always a little disconcerted to find herself listened to. 'I can't see my matrons buying many books really, they prefer the library, but younger people, the kind who think old ladies are trendy ...' She fell silent, looking out over the garden. It was only July but the soft mist that rolled in from the sea, settling across the beech hedges, belonged to autumn. She liked autumn; no hot days demanding you made the most of them.

'Why don't you open your café down here?' Henry asked. 'You'd be near your mother and grandmother. And me.'

'Maybe.' She smiled up at him. 'I like London, but I didn't enjoy living there much. I prefer little nosy places.'

'Well get on with it then. Go down to the estate agents in town and see what they've got.'

I'm so weak, Amelia thought, that I will even turn decisive on someone else's say so. She looked him in the eyes. 'OK, I will. I'll check on Selma and then I'll go.' She stood up and brushed the grass from her skirt.

Henry got up too. 'I wonder where my father

is?' Glancing at his watch, he frowned. 'He should have come back by now.'

*　　*　　*

While Amelia wandered around the estate agents by the harbour being shown details of houses with shopfronts, houses with sub-Post Offices and houses with permission to erect twenty-five dog kennels, Henry was told of his father's death.

A woman police constable came to Cherryfield to inform Sister Morris of the accident. 'I was told I might find the son, the Reverend Mallett, here,' she said.

Out in the garden the mist had cleared, giving way to evening sunlight. 'Did he die instantly?' Henry asked, bending double as if he was going to be sick.

Everyone asked that, the policewoman thought. 'Not instantly, no,' she said softly, adding quickly what she knew he wanted to hear, 'but he didn't suffer. He died in the ambulance, put up a real fight they told me, but he didn't suffer. He's in the hospital now if you'd like to see him.'

'I don't think he fought to stay alive. I think he fought to die,' Henry said, his fingers raking through his hair.

The policewoman thought it a funny thing for a Reverend to say. From the shadow of the cherry tree Sister Morris cleared her throat.

198

'Now why should you think that, Mr Mallett? Your father was quite happy here you know.'

'I'm sure he was,' the policewoman mumbled soothingly as she prepared to leave. She thought the Reverend Mallett had an almost wild look in his eyes as he got up to follow her. 'I'm sure he didn't suffer,' she said again, trying to comfort.

*   *   *

It was the unexpectedness of his death that made Amelia burst into tears when Sister Morris told her of the Admiral's accident. She had returned from town with a bundle of prospectuses to show Henry, finding Selma still asleep and the Residents' Lounge a nest of lustily growing rumours. The Admiral had had a stroke. He'd been run down by a lorry. He'd collided with a tractor.

But Miss White felt sure she had the real answer to what had happened. 'It's the KGB.' She shook her head. 'That Blake has a lot to answer for.'

Then Sister Morris came in and explained to everyone what had happened.

Miss White nodded wisely. 'That's right dear. It's always known as a car crash when the KGB have done their dirty work.' She added thoughtfully, 'One would have thought they'd have come up with something new by now.'

'The Russians are our friends now, Miss White,' the old man in the next door armchair corrected her mildly.

'They might be your friends Mr Ambrose,' Miss White snapped, 'but they're certainly not mine.'

Amelia fled.

*   *   *

She called the Naval Barracks at Devonport from the hotel, asking to speak to Henry. While she waited, she practised little suitable phrases of commiseration and comfort. I'm thinking of you at this difficult time: too formal. It was all for the best: too cold hearted. Anything, anything at all I can do: so bland. Then before she had a chance to stop it, the worst thought of all broke loose from its harness of decency and bolted through her mind: You're free. Henry you're free. She shuddered and blushed, changing the receiver from her left to her right ear. Finally the exchange came back, informing her that Henry was nowhere to be found.

She called Dagmar, but something in her mother's voice, a kind of honeyed impatience, took Amelia back instantly to her childhood when it was never quite the right moment or there wasn't enough time. Her desire to tell was replaced by a sullen desire to withhold, and, in the end, all she said was, 'We're back.'

'Alan and I are planning to come over tomorrow,' Dagmar said. 'I'll bring the puppy. Did I tell you I've bought a puppy. Alan adores dogs.'

*　　*　　*

Amelia went for a walk after dinner. Away from the harbour, the narrow streets were empty. There was a full moon in the dark-blue sky and the evening breeze was Mediterranean in its warmth. A little out of breath she stopped at the top of the hill and looked towards Ashcombe. A light came on in the sitting room, then the curtains were drawn.

In Selma's childhood home, at the Jewish New Year, glasses would be raised in the toast of the Diaspora: Next Year in Jerusalem! Ashcombe had become Selma's Jerusalem now. It had held everything she wanted in life: husband, children, calm, flower-filled rooms and a sitting room with a grand piano and windows looking out at the sea.

At Cherryfield there was Sister Morris and Miss White, nourishing pilchards for tea, music from the television and a vista of ornamental cherries. Selma never did like ornamental cherries. 'Next Year in Jerusalem,' Amelia sing-songed to herself before turning around and walking back to the hotel. And how on earth am I meant to achieve that?

It was two in the morning when Amelia was woken by a knock on her hotel-room door. At first the noise seemed part of her dream where she pushed Selma in a supermarket trolley round a small town full of glass-fronted houses. But Selma kept shaking her head and saying, 'No darling, that's not Jerusalem either.' Amelia knocked on yet another door, louder and louder, and then she woke up. She rolled over in bed and, half asleep still, put her feet on the floor. She padded across to the door and asked, without opening, 'Who is it?'

'Night porter, Miss Lindsay. Sorry to disturb you at such an hour but I've got a priest for you downstairs. He won't go away. Says his name's Mallett.'

Amelia opened the door. 'Send him up, would you please?'

The night porter had obviously been in as deep a sleep as Amelia. His sparse sandy hair rose in a coxcomb and his eyes were bloodshot. Now he opened them wide, taking in Amelia's short nightshirt and the amount of naked leg appearing below it. 'Up here Miss?'

'He is a priest. A priest in need of comfort.'

'I thought they were the ones meant to give comfort,' the porter muttered.

'Well this one operates both ways.' Impatiently, Amelia took a step past him out on to the landing.

202

'I'll get him,' the porter said quickly, obviously deciding his boss would prefer sin to be contained within four walls rather than wandering the hotel at will.

Amelia stayed in the open doorway listening. She heard mumbled voices, then heavy steps hurrying up the wooden stairs.

'Amelia, I'm sorry about this.' Henry almost fell into her arms and she backed inside the room, still holding him. He was crying, she could feel it. She moved her hand up carefully, stroking his hair, patting him, mumbling small phrases of comfort. She felt him shivering and, just as she was beginning to think her back would break, he released her.

'I'm sorry,' he said again, throwing himself down on the pink boudoir chair by the window.

'I'm glad you came. I've tried to reach you all evening.'

'I know. Thank you.' He wasn't looking at her. 'He's better off where he is now. Grief is just selfish.' He sobbed and tried to pass it off as a cough.

Amelia knelt by the chair and took his hands. 'And none the worse for that,' she whispered. 'You're a chaplain, not a saint. You loved him.'

Henry looked up at her with a small smile. 'It was always just him and I, and Winter of course. My mother died when I was one. I don't remember her at all.'

'I don't remember much about my father, other than that he had bright blue eyes and no interest in his daughter. "Irish eyes," my mother has a tendency to mutter and that's all the answer I get.' Amelia fell silent, trying to weigh up how much idle chit-chat was appropriate.

Henry seemed calmer now as he sat gazing intently at her. Squeezed into the small, pink-upholstered chair, he reminded her of Willoughby's boxer who all his life had nurtured a hopeless ambition to fit on to the plate-size silk cushion belonging to Selma's Siamese. 'Who is Winter?' she asked gently.

'Winter.' Again that quick smile. 'He was my father's PO steward. When he retired from the Navy he stayed on working for us. He helped bring me up until I went away to school. Then he went off to run a pub in Modbury. We kept in touch until he died five years ago. I loved him.'

Amelia sighed. 'There are times,' she said, 'when there seems to be more death than life in life, if you see what I mean.'

Henry laughed miserably. 'At least Winter died a happy man. His doctor told him he'd have to cut out beer or at least switch to the low alcohol stuff. He died of a ruptured bladder while trying to get the old kick from Kaliber.' Henry laughed again, unsuitably and loudly and for so long that Amelia got worried. Then he sobbed, a snorting embarrassed kind of sob.

'I just miss my father so much already. You see I never mourned my mother; I was too young. Of course I missed the idea of a mother, all that soft indulgence ...' He looked wide eyed at Amelia. 'What other children had and took for granted. But losing my father; it's a bit as if all your life you've been in this warm, cosy room and suddenly the walls collapse around you and you're standing there exposed to the world.'

He gripped Amelia's hand. 'I just hope he wasn't scared. He was one of the bravest men I knew and the thought of him being scared and alone...'

He just wants his father back, Amelia thought. How can you ever hope to help a person who is grieving when the one person really able to comfort them is the one they've lost? A phrase appeared in her head, one she'd heard Selma use. 'Say not in grief that he is no more, but in thankfulness that he was,' she mumbled more to herself than to Henry.

Henry smiled at her and she sat back, leaning her shoulder against his knees. 'Tell me about your father.' She had always found it strange how there seemed to exist a conspiracy of silence around someone grieving, as if his friends were attempting, out of sheer embarrassment, to kill even the memory of the dead.

They talked about the Admiral for a long time and then Amelia stood up and put her hand out to Henry. 'Shall we go to bed?' The moment she spoke she regretted it. Tasteless, that's what it was. She felt her face go hot as Henry sat back and looked at her. Like a guilty child she said quickly, 'I didn't really mean it.'

'I wish you had,' he smiled and pulled her down on his knee. 'Although I would have had to say no, I'm not a chaplain just for the pretty uniform.' He kissed her hand lightly. 'It was a very nice thought. Thank you.'

It was five o'clock when he left. Amelia stood at the window watching him walk off towards the car park as the sun rose over the sea beyond.

CHAPTER SIXTEEN

'Mrs Merryman has had a good night,' Nurse Williams said as she opened the door for Amelia later that morning. 'She insisted on waiting for you in the Lounge. We really felt it would be better for her to rest in her room, but she can be quite determined when she wants to, your gran.'

'I know,' Amelia said. 'It's excellent that she knows what she wants, isn't it?'

Sister Morris busied past them with an anxious looking middle-aged couple in tow. 'And this is our Residents' Lounge.' There was a pause. 'Normally, of course, we have a waiting list but what with the cold spell in March and Number Two suddenly becoming available ...' They disappeared upstairs.

Before Amelia had got out of the hall the bell rang and Dagmar stood in the doorway together with a tall man who was holding the lead to a struggling black puppy that looked like a labrador.

'Darling.' Dagmar's lips brushed against Amelia's cheek, Dagmar's smile radiated across the hall. 'And this is Alan.' Her eyes darted between Amelia and Alan, the words rushed from her lips. Alan took a step inside and almost fell over as the puppy entwined its lead round his legs.

'Admiral Mallett died yesterday,' Amelia whispered as they approached the Lounge. 'I expect Grandma will be pretty upset.'

'There'll be wailing and gnashing of dentures,' Dagmar said and laughed out loud. She stopped suddenly. 'Oh I'm sorry, darling, he was a dear old boy. It's just that it's all so awful.' Her voice rose shrilly and Amelia stiffened and glanced at Alan. She couldn't bear her mother making a fool of herself.

'He looked so fit, I always thought,' Dagmar said in a normal voice now. 'How old was he?'

When you're old and you die, no-one thinks to ask how it happened, Amelia thought. It's just assumed that you expired by the rules, quietly, without fuss.

'He was a bit of a devil in the car. He

crashed,' she said, hoping she'd done right by the Admiral.

'He was a dear friend of yours?' Alan stood back to let her go through the door first. He had a nice voice; quiet with a soft New England accent.

'I was fond of him, and I've got to know his son quite well,' Amelia said, raising her arm to wave at Selma who was slumped in a chair by the television. The seat by the fish-tank was empty. A sad son and an empty space by a fish-tank, were those all the traces left from the Admiral's moment on earth? Amelia wondered, shuddering.

Selma stared blankly at them as they approached. Her tightly bandaged legs rested on a small stool and she was dressed in a shapeless, yellow dress that accentuated the greyness of her skin. When Dagmar bent down and kissed her she smiled suddenly. 'Hello, darling.' She snatched at Dagmar's hand. 'You know for a moment there I didn't recognize you. Have you changed your hair?'

Dagmar had worn her hair in the same glossy bob for twenty years. 'No, Mummy.' Dagmar winked at Alan as she straightened up. 'Mummy this is Professor Blake, he insisted on meeting you,' she announced, smiling proudly.

Amelia thought she might as well have thrown her arms out wide, announcing, 'And now for my next trick and without a safety-net,

208

I will introduce my mother.'

Alan extended his free hand to Selma, who received it suspiciously. 'A great pleasure to meet you, ma'am.' Selma looked stonily at him; she had never been keen on conspicuously good manners.

The puppy had been licking his scrotum absorbedly, but now he lifted his face, alert, ears pricked. He got up and took a little leap at Dagmar before settling down to licking her legs in their shiny tights, with the same rapt attention.

Alan offered a chair to Dagmar who refused, saying she needed to stretch her legs after the journey.

With a 'May I?' to Selma, Alan sat down himself. 'Cute little fellow isn't he?' He pointed at the puppy. 'You know I never would have guessed the countrywoman in your daughter. Of course, I've always loved animals, nature, feeling the dirt under my fingers, that kind of thing. Now Dagmar here comes and tells me that's the life for her as well.' He brought a pipe from his pocket and crossed one long leg over the other. 'Of course that comes as no surprise to her mother.'

Selma opened her mouth to speak.

'That's enough now.' Dagmar, speaking between clenched teeth, was doing a little dance to avoid the long pink tongue of the puppy.

'Simon, you little rascal ... That's enough.

Simon! Do you hear me? That's enough I said.' Dagmar's eyes darted across to Alan to make sure he wasn't looking, then she gave the puppy a shove with the point of her shoe. 'Get him off me, will you, Amelia?' she hissed. 'Did you see where he had his tongue just now? All over his you know what.'

Amelia squatted down on the carpet and put her hands out. Simon, stubby tail wagging, threw himself towards her to investigate.

'Why don't you sit down, dear?' Alan asked again.

Dagmar smiled nervously at him and rushed a tissue from her pocket, dropping it across the seat of the chair before sitting down.

Leaning down towards Amelia she hissed, 'Puppies are worm-infested. It doesn't matter what you do about it.' Then she forgot to whisper. 'How am I supposed to enjoy the rest of the day with these filthy tights on?'

Alan turned around and looked at her, one bushy eyebrow raised.

'There are no worms on your legs,' Amelia said. She hadn't meant to sound so sharp.

'Shuss.' Dagmar glanced nervously at Alan who was once more in conversation with Selma. 'Anyway,' she whispered, 'it's the eggs that are dangerous. They get stuck everywhere. You can't see them, and even the strongest disinfectant can't get rid of them.' It almost sounded, Amelia thought, as if she was making a commercial on behalf of the wretched worms.

She whispered back to Dagmar, 'I don't know how to break it to Grandma about Admiral Mallett. It doesn't seem as if she's been told.'

'Oh, don't you think so?' Dagmar stretched her right leg out in front of her, twisting it to check the back of the glossy tights. 'Did you know a child could go blind if he ingested those eggs?'

'I hardly think some little cherub will dive out of the woodwork and begin to lick your legs. Not here. Not at Cherryfield.' Incensed by Dagmar's inability to think of anyone but herself even for a minute, Amelia ignored Dagmar's hurt look and moved her chair closer to Selma's.

Alan was saying how he too loved Jane Austen, and when there was a pause, a long one waiting for Selma to fill it with a reply, Amelia broke in.

'Any news? All well around here?' She made her voice light but she looked intently at her grandmother. She was aware that Miss White, sitting by herself a few yards away, was listening, an expectant smile on her lips, head cocked as if waiting for an opportunity to pounce on the conversation. Now she seized her chance with the ease of a trained hijacker.

'I hear you're one of our American cousins.' She leant so far towards Alan that Amelia feared she might topple from her chair any

211

moment. Alan turned with a polite smile. Selma looked furious and did not introduce them.

'You will agree with me that it would almost certainly be the KGB?'

'Pardon me, ma'am.' Alan looking confused, turned in vain to Dagmar for help, but she was staring out across the room with the faraway look that intrigued strangers but Amelia knew meant she was wondering how to remove her tights without seeming odd.

'Admiral Mallett.' Miss White sounded impatient.

Amelia sat up in her chair, ready with a comforting hand for Selma.

'They're burying him tomorrow I'm told. Bury 'em quickly if you want to stop tongues wagging, they say.'

Well they failed miserably with you, you old crow. Amelia glared at Miss White. She turned to Selma with soothing words ready to fire and found that her grandmother's expression of sullen confusion had not changed by a flicker. She still hasn't taken it in, Amelia thought, taking Selma's hand. As she prepared her speech she could feel the hand trembling in hers like a frightened heart.

'I meant to tell you yesterday but you were asleep.' She spoke softly. 'The Admiral was involved in a car crash. They say he didn't...'

'I know,' Selma interrupted. 'Poor old boy. Awful shame. We shall miss him.' But she directed her next remark at Alan, eager to snatch back the conversation from Miss White. 'Of course it's her endings I find a little disappointing.'

Amelia had let go of Selma's hand and now she stared at her open-mouthed.

'Shut your mouth, darling,' Dagmar said unnecessarily, as she moved her shoe away from Simon who lay prostrate on the carpet, his adoring gaze following her every move.

Amelia kept looking at Selma. Was this another display of dignity and a stiff upper lip from a member of the generation that lived through a world war, or had senility blanked out compassion and affection too? Maybe Selma spoke so little of her grief for Willoughby not because she was brave, but because she didn't really feel any? Had age blunted love and loss like waves blunting bits of glass on the shore, until they were smooth and round, unable to hurt you?

Selma was taking a lot of trouble to ignore Miss White, arranging her lips into a supercilious half smile every time the little woman spoke.

Maybe you can't love me any more either, Amelia thought, and she sniffed and blinked away a tear. Oh my grandmother, what have you become?

'My God he stinks!' Dagmar leapt from the chair and pointed at Simon who placed his plump behind on her shoe, looking up adoringly, the tip of his tail wagging slowly, expectantly, like a snake sizing up its prey. The two old women stopped glaring at each other and stared instead at Dagmar, loose-mouthed. As the room fell silent, Dagmar's cheeks turned slowly pink.

'What's the matter, dear?' Alan asked, his voice chilly.

Amelia couldn't smell a thing but she chipped in hurriedly, 'He does stink a bit.' Dagmar's addiction was to fear rather than drugs or alcohol but Amelia was, all the same, an addict's child; her mother might drive her to despair, irritate her more than a sackful of red ants, but it was Amelia's job to make sure no-one else got to share those feelings. 'It sort of hits you in wafts,' she added for good measure.

Alan bent down and, putting his hand out, called Simon over. 'Hi there fellow. What's all this about you making smells?' He sniffed the puppy's neck. Simon, snout lifted, black gums stretched back, grinned at him. Then Alan slid his hand under Simon's collar before smelling his fingers. 'I'd say he's had a bit of a roll. Must have been when he ran loose from the car,' he said to Dagmar. 'You, little fellow, will get into the tub when we get home.'

'By car?' Dagmar looked near to tears.

'Well, you don't expect the little fellow to walk to Exeter do you?' Alan laughed up at her.

214

'I'm sure there's a tap outside,' Selma said. 'Why don't you wash him off there?' Dagmar and Amelia looked at Selma, shocked by the sense of her suggestion.

Alan said, 'It's OK, thanks but we'll...'

'I'll do it straight away.' Dagmar was up from the chair already, a too bright smile on her lips. She grabbed the lead from Alan giving it a little jerk. 'Come on, Simon darling.' Her voice was so tense, Amelia thought, you could shoot arrows from it.

Simon remained sitting.

'He doesn't want to come,' Miss White said.

'Oh do shut up.' Selma frowned.

'Mrs Merryman really!' Miss White looked around her with relish as if to say, 'There did I not tell you she's a naughty girl.'

'Dagmar for God's sake, can't we just forget about Simon for a minute. We're upsetting the good folks here.' Alan glared under thick eyebrows.

Dagmar ignored him, but regretfully, as if she wished she didn't have to. 'Come on Simon, we're off.' Dagmar gave the lead such a tug that Simon, still sitting, slid on his bottom across several yards of high-gloss floor, the collar riding up over the folds in his fat little neck and up across his ears. Then suddenly he got up and trotted out of the room behind Dagmar as if that's what he'd intended all along.

'Temper, temper,' chirruped Miss White.

215

Old age makes you evil, Amelia thought.

They sat in silence as a nurse brought a middle-aged woman to see Mr Ambrose, who had melted chameleon-like into the taupe cover of his armchair, a little away from their group.

'I'll go and give my mother a hand with Simon.' Amelia got up.

* * *

'Stand still! Stand still I tell you.' Dagmar stood, feet wide apart, clutching a gushing hose in one hand and the puppy's lead in the other. Simon was making little leaps in all directions to avoid the sharp jet of cold water. The whites of his eyes were showing but his tail was attempting a wag.

'If you move away once more...'

With a squeal of terror the puppy hid from the jet behind Dagmar's legs. 'Go away! You little bastard, go away, do you hear me!' Dagmar grabbed the end of the lead, lashing the puppy over and over across his chubby back. Simon screamed and, pulling loose, tore past Amelia on her way out.

Dagmar, red-faced and panting, looked up to see Alan staring at her from the terrace. 'You beat that little dog,' he said and strode off after Simon.

CHAPTER SEVENTEEN

For a child, the unpredictability of a neurotic parent was terror in an apron. Even now, at thirty-one, Amelia was shaking as she led her sobbing mother to the bathroom. Her heart was still racing, her windpipe still felt as if it had shrunk two sizes, as she sat on the edge of the bath, watching Dagmar wipe the smudges of mascara from her cheeks.

Dabbing at the paper-thin skin under her eyes with the corner of a rough towel Dagmar turned her streaky face to Amelia. 'I didn't mean to hit Simon. I just don't know what came over me.' Sobbing, she leant against the wall, burying her face in the crook of her arm.

The usual I expect, Amelia thought. She felt only a little pity for Dagmar, little and highly diluted by pity for Simon and for herself. One day, she thought as she waited for Dagmar to stop crying, I'll tell Henry what it's been like. 'How would you feel,' I'll say to him, 'if your God suddenly started hurling bricks at you as you stood chatting to him by the altar? What would it do to your confidence if he returned your prayers with a string of four letter words? Because that's how it feels for a child having the grown-up in her life go mad.'

With a deep sigh she got up and walked across to Dagmar. 'It's all right,' she said,

217

putting her arm round her mother's thin shoulders that were so like her own. 'It's all right.'

Alan waited unsmiling in the hall with the puppy, wet and shiny, curled up at his feet. As Dagmar came down the stairs he said nothing, but looked pointedly at his watch. Simon unscrambled himself and padded up towards Dagmar, a questioning little wag to his tail. Looking up at Alan, she kneeled and put her hand out and Simon stretched out his fat neck towards it, sniffing it as if it was hot.

'Let's go shall we?' Alan's voice was cold. 'I've said goodbye to your ma.'

'I haven't yet. I won't keep you a moment.' She almost ran from the hall, knees a little bent.

'Well it was nice meeting you.' Alan put his hand out to Amelia with a smile big enough to be polite but too tight to be warm.

'I'll see you again soon I expect.' Amelia poked at his anger, testing it.

Alan shrugged his shoulders and said, 'Maybe.'

Dagmar returned to the hall so flattened by what she had done that she might have been her own shadow slinking through the doorway. When she kissed Amelia goodbye she held her cold cheek against hers for a long moment.

'We had planned for you to join us for lunch in town, but I think under the circumstances maybe not,' she whispered. In the doorway she

218

turned and shrugged her shoulders with a little smile before going off after Alan.

Alan held the door of the estate car open for Dagmar, before lifting Simon into the back and walking round to the driver's seat. She's done it again, Amelia thought sadly, she's seen an opportunity for happiness, grasped it with both hands ... and throttled it. She gave a little wave to the departing car and closed the door.

*　　*　　*

Back in the Residents' Lounge a tiny woman sat in a wheelchair next to Mr Ambrose, head flopping as if it was too great a burden for the thin neck. Now she got a kiss from her visitor. 'You take care, Mother. See you next month as usual.' The Ambroses' daughter-in-law nodded and smiled at Miss White who sat engrossed in a holiday programme on television, then she made for the door with such hurried little steps that she almost bumped in to Amelia.

'So sorry,' the woman mumbled but there was no hiding the relief in her face: it was over for this time.

What could one do when old, Amelia wondered, to avoid putting such an expression on a loved one's face? Tell jokes, tap-dance, hand out large sums of money?

Slumped in her wheelchair, Mrs Ambrose's lips moved ceaselessly, churning out mumbled,

219

jumbled phrases; words without end, Amen, Amelia thought as she stepped over the woman's twig-like legs to get across to Selma who slept in the chair by the French windows.

'Don't trample me.' The voice was strong and firm. 'What I'm saying is: you don't pay all this money to sit here being trampled on.'

Startled, Amelia turned to look into Mrs Ambrose's lifted face. Her eyes, large and sky-blue, were smiling.

'I'm so sorry,' Amelia mumbled.

Mr Ambrose looked up from his crossword puzzle. Taking his wife's hand he said, 'It's all right Dorothy, you're quite safe,' and once more Mrs Ambrose's head dropped down on to her chest, like a wind-up doll who had sprung alive, done its turn, then fallen still.

Would Gerald have become her comforter when she got old and made no sense? Amelia wondered as she sat down next to Selma. She didn't think so. He had often said, with the air of one confessing to an endearing quirk in their personality, 'I know it's silly but I'm just no use at a sick bed.' Not many men were, she had noticed. He'd probably be safe with Clarissa though, it was difficult not to feel she would be as crisply put together at ninety as she was now.

Selma slept on. Amelia wondered if Dagmar had been forgiven. Maybe this very moment they were making up in bed. Amelia, though pleased at the thought, blushed. Teenagers

220

refused to contemplate that their parents' sexual organs were there for anything other than show, rather like a false pocket or a button without a button hole, once they themselves had been achieved. At thirty-one you knew better, but that didn't mean you had to like it. Amelia looked surreptitiously at the Ambroses. And when did it stop anyway? Was it sudden or gradual? A situation reached multilaterally or unilaterally?

Just then Mrs Ambrose raised her head, giving Amelia the uncomfortable feeling she might have spoken the question aloud, but Dorothy Ambrose just gazed at her husband with huge, clear eyes. Mr Ambrose seemed to feel his wife's eyes on him and, looking up from his paper, he took her hand once more, giving it a little squeeze.

Amelia, feeling moved by the little scene, smiled, just as Mrs Ambrose, her eyes fixed on her husband's face, bared her teeth, good teeth still, and sunk them into the fleshy part of his palm.

Miss White was bored with the television. Mr Ambrose's small cry of pain and Amelia's sharp intake of breath provided a welcome break. She prodded Amelia with her stick as Mr Ambrose, quite composed again, gently released his hand from his wife's teeth. 'Mrs Ambrose bites I'm afraid,' she explained in a loud whisper. 'I don't know why.'

Mrs Ambrose smiled cheerfully at her

husband. 'Silly old fart,' she said.

Selma had woken up and now Miss White turned to her with a self-important air. 'I said, I don't know why Mrs Ambrose bites.'

Amelia made herself small, avoiding looking at Mr Ambrose, but Selma didn't seem surprised. She nodded, her faded eyes grave. 'They're the worst,' she said. 'Human bites are the worst.'

* * *

For the first few miles of their journey back to Exeter, Dagmar thought there was a chance that Alan might forgive her. He chatted amiably enough, complimenting her on Selma and Amelia as if, Dagmar thought, I could take credit for either. But she smiled modestly and said she had tried her best.

'It hasn't been easy, being a single parent.' Growing in confidence she carried on, 'I used to read these books about beautiful women hurling themselves off cliffs and under trains rather than living with their lover's betrayal. At the time it seemed rather a good option, but then I looked at this chubby red-haired little thing, my daughter, and thought it would be the worst betrayal of all.' She laughed as she always did when talking about what was serious.

When Alan neither looked at her nor spoke, Dagmar knew she had lost him. For the rest of the journey she might as well have been appearing on a television set with the sound turned off; her lips moved, she sang her heart out, but not a sound reached through to her audience.

They drove up in front of Dagmar's block of flats and Alan, as always, dashed around to open the car door for her. 'Here we are.'

He makes the little phrase seem so final, Dagmar thought, like a coach driver in a Hammer horror pulling up outside the Castle of Doom. 'Here we are Miss.' Dagmar burst into loud giggles.

Alan didn't bother to ask why, but walked around the back to let Simon out from the boot, handing her the lead.

Dagmar pulled her hand away and shook her head. 'You take him, please.' Simon tried to lift his leg against the porch and lost his balance.

Alan nodded but he was looking pityingly into her eyes as if he had already broken the bad news. 'Goodbye Dagmar.' He pronounced her name as he always did, with the emphasis on the 'r'. 'You take care now.'

Shall I scream, she thought, throw myself at his feet and beg, cling to his legs as he walks away? 'Goodbye then,' she said.

Alan walked off to the car and started the engine.

*   *   *

Dagmar looked around her at the sitting room: tables shining with beeswax, spotless carpet, clear-surfaced ornaments, dust-free picture frames. Lots of people chose the colours for their home according to how easily they showed the dirt. Dagmar knew she was different in as much as she picked the ones, dove greys, pinks and yellows, that showed it most. That way she could identify the enemy. At the furniture store she had shuddered at the golden-brown carpet—God only knows what could be lurking in there—and shaken her head at the practical chintzes.

She wandered through into the kitchen where the kitchen cupboards dazzled white. She made herself a pot of tea and sat down at the high-gloss table. 'There,' she said out loud, clanking the teaspoon down on the saucer. 'I've managed to drive away everyone I've ever cared for, but through it all I've kept my flat clean.' Then she threw the cup across the room.

*   *   *

As soon as Amelia entered the lobby she heard the playing.

The more she had thought, as she sat in the Lounge at Cherryfield, the surer she had become that Alan would be giving Dagmar a hard time. 'If he even bothered to do that,' she muttered as she dialled her mother's number. Someone the other end had lifted the receiver and then hung up immediately. Amelia had worried some more and then got into Gerald's car and driven off to Exeter.

Now she hurried up the stairs, wondering briefly why steps always seemed constructed for someone with a natural one-and-a-half-step stride, when she noticed the difference in the playing from upstairs. Dagmar's music tended towards the ladylike; there was no excess in the playing. But the notes now echoing down the stairwell seemed to be hounded from the instrument, fleeing, stumbling.

Out of breath, she reached the second floor and rang the bell but the playing continued. She rang again, but as there was still no answer she tried the door and finding it unlocked, stepped inside. At the entrance to the sitting room she stopped dead.

Dagmar sat crouched over the piano keyboard like a bird of prey. Mould seemed to be growing from her head and shoulders, the blue-grey spores covering her hair and hanging in furry threads from her arms as she lifted them before letting her hands crash down for the final crescendo.

'Oh my God.' Amelia rushed over to Dagmar who merely swivelled around slowly, a sweet smile on her lips.

'There you see,' she said, opening her eyes wide. 'It really doesn't matter being dirty.'

CHAPTER EIGHTEEN

It was a remark in the Kingsmouth Post Office a week later that had caused Amelia to sit as she did now, crouched in the shrubbery that sheltered Ashcombe from the lane running past the front of the house.

'Those Hamiltons, no sooner have they got that house than they are off on holiday. "And while I'm about it," she says, "cancel the papers for the Christmas period too, we're off to our little place in Antigua."' Mrs Hodges, the newsagent, made a passable imitation of Doreen Hamilton for the benefit of her customers.

'They're away over Christmas too, are they?' Amelia paid for Selma's *Good Housekeeping*.

Mrs Hodges nodded and pursed her lips. 'Three whole weeks. They're always moving house those Hamiltons but they never seem to take much pleasure in what they get. Not like your grandmother. She loved that place, she did.'

'She loved that place, she did,' Amelia repeated to herself as, knees aching, she watched Doreen Hamilton lock the front door on her way out. By the look of the large, old-fashioned key in her hand the locks hadn't been changed.

As Doreen click-clacked down the hill in her

high-heeled sandals, a wicker basket dangling from the crook of her arm, Amelia emerged from behind an oleander shrub and ran through the heavy wooden portal that led into the main garden. Looking around to make sure she was on her own, she walked up to the French windows and pressed her nose against the glass, framing her face with her spread-out fingers. She stood for a while peering into the sitting room before stepping back and pulling a small black notebook and a pencil from the back pocket of her jeans. She wrote intently in the book for a minute or two, looked into the room again before checking her notes, then, putting the book and pencil back in her pocket, she hurried back on to the road.

After five minutes she reached the start of a footpath. She turned left on to it and, when she found a large flat rock, she sat down, stretching her legs out in front of her. Looking across town to the green terraced hill and Cherryfield, she thought how soft the light was in Devon, as if the rain never quite left but only hung back a little distance, filtering the sunlight, ready for its next appearance. She rested her elbows against the warm rock and closed her eyes; it had been a bad week and she was tired.

*   *   *

Dagmar, sitting at the piano, had seemed surprised at Amelia's distress but she had allowed herself to be led into the bathroom. Amelia had found the ripped and empty hoover bag behind the sofa and the fluff and dust had insinuated itself into every cranny of the room so that with each step they took it rose on the air like a fountain.

'Being clean causes so much misery,' Dagmar said reasonably as Amelia stripped her down to bra and pants and pushed her towards the bath-tub.

Amelia tipped half a bottle of Apricot bubble-bath into the hot water and, having watched the foam rise, she turned the taps off. 'I'll leave you to it then,' she said in a small voice.

She had found the number of Dagmar's GP. 'There's no chance of an appointment today I'm afraid, none at all.' The receptionist spoke with quiet satisfaction at an obstacle well placed.

'But this is an emergency. My mother is insane.'

'Could you hold please, there's a call on the other line.'

Amelia listened for sounds from the bathroom and as there were none she had visions of Dagmar floating in the bath like an elderly Ophelia, grey tentacles of fluff instead of flowers trailing from her hair. 'Come on, come on,' she muttered into the phone.

'Yes?' the receptionist had returned, and sounded as if she had hoped Amelia would have given up.

'My mother; she's gone mad.' Some people lied in times of stress, Amelia always got an urge to be truthful, flawlessly exact. She added, 'More accurately; she's gone madder.' She paused again. 'A lot more mad.'

The doctor came. By then Dagmar was sleeping, warm and clean, in her bed. 'In there.' Amelia opened the bedroom door gently to let him in. Outside she paced the sitting room like an expectant father in a fifties comedy.

'What do you think?' She pounced as Dr Norland reappeared.

'She's quite calm now.' The doctor, young and tweed-clad, perched on the arm of the nearest chair.

'Quite calm now.' Amelia had visions of a raging ape, bellowing and rattling the bars of its cage before sinking to its haunches, silent, hands still clinging on to the bars. 'Quite calm now.'

'I'll admit her to the psychiatric unit overnight, for observation. I don't hold with doling out pills willy-nilly but see she takes these for the next month, just to help her over the acute stage of her problem.' Dr Norland held out a prescription.

Amelia remained standing. If she settled down in a chair it might scare him off, make him think she was going to keep him there talking for a long time.

'There's a question I've wanted answered all

my life,' she said. 'What exactly is my mother's problem?'

Dr Norland closed his bag and stood up. 'Not all that much. She's an obsessive of course. Today's incident was an extreme reaction to stress. I doubt it will recur.' He moved towards the front door.

'But Dr Norland.'

He stopped and turned. 'Yes.'

'This whatever it is, this obsessiveness has blighted her life, and mine. Today she tipped the contents of a hoover bag over her head whilst playing the "Warsaw Concerto". How can you say it's nothing much?'

'Because in a way it isn't.' He smiled and shrugged his shoulders. 'Anxiety is natural. We need it to survive. Our forefathers were busy doing just that, surviving, but increasingly the every-day threats, the ones we could see and hear and identify, have been removed from our lives, leaving us free to worry about remoter and vaguer issues that are almost always beyond our control. The anxiety increases, but its focus is blurred. That in itself induces stress. Your mother is a naturally anxious person, probably with low self-esteem, and her unfocused anxieties have been allowed to take over. In due course some sessions with a therapist would not be a bad idea.' He opened the door but turned on the threshold. 'You've heard of rebels without a cause. Well, my surgery is full of worriers without a worry.'

230

With a quick smile he was off, running down the stairs.

Amelia had expected some cataclysmic change in her mother, whether for better or for worse she didn't know, but surely no-one could go through such turmoil and come out the same? But Dagmar, returning from hospital, was quiet but otherwise how she had always been; a little distracted, a little irritable, busy worrying away at her worries.

Amelia stayed on though, just in case. In case of precisely what she didn't know but, when she set off for the Admiral's funeral on the Wednesday, she kept thinking of those films where people clear away ropes and sharp instruments from the suicidal and she wondered briefly if maybe she should hide the hoover.

Henry had assisted the vicar of Kingsmouth at the funeral service. He had looked pale but he had smiled at Amelia when she entered the church and he had read the lesson with a steady voice. It was only when he had stood up again to speak those lines by Tennyson, that his voice had faltered.

Lying on the warm rock, looking at the clouds appearing over the hills, Amelia said them to herself: '"Sunset and evening star, And one clear call for me! And may there be no moaning of the bar When I put out to sea."'

Then the vicar had led the mourners into the churchyard, and a high wind had driven the rain into their faces like a shower of tacks. At Willoughby's funeral the sun had been shining from a high February sky. Amelia remembered thinking it almost an insult, like giving a painting as a birthday present to a blind man. No, Amelia had approved of the rain and the wind as she followed the vicar, watching his huge black cloak dance round his ankles with the prematurely fallen leaves. There it goes, she had thought as the coffin was lowered into the ground, the universe according to John Mallett.

*　　*　　*

It was Sunday now, a week exactly since Dagmar's breakdown. 'Breakdown,' Amelia mouthed the word to herself as she got up from the rock, it makes her sound like a beat-up old mini. She checked her back pocket for the notebook and began the walk down to the ferry where Gerald's car was parked. Dagmar was as able to cope now as she had ever been, so there was no reason not to go back to the Old Rectory: it was still her home for another two weeks.

*　　*　　*

'Five Warden-Assisted Bungalows—Buy Now, Pay later.' Was that really what it said? Driving into Abbotslea, she turned and looked over her shoulder, 'Five Warden-Assisted Bungalows, For Sale,' she read on the large sign by the new development she had just passed. Then, as she slowed down for the blind corner at the crossroads, she thought quite calmly, I'm going mad. She found herself relax at the thought. After all Selma was going mad slowly, through old age. Dagmar had simply gone mad. If some Biblical curse or, if that was being pretentious, maybe a more ordinary gypsy one, had been lobbed in the direction of her family why not just give in? No more responsibilities; now there was a nice thought.

She slammed on the brakes, narrowly avoiding Old Mike Aylard wandering round in the middle of the street with his deer-stalker and his wife's fox collar to keep him warm in the July sunshine. Far from getting a sense of fellow feeling, she had a sudden urge to run him down. Maybe it's the competition, she thought. She could stay in Abbotslea, buy herself a little place, but would there be room for two afflicted in the village? Could she hope to oust Old Mike from his position as village fool?

She saw Rosalind and Ronnie coming out of the stores and gave them a cheery wave.

Now Mrs Wetherburn-Pryce, for example, had never invited Amelia to one of her coffee mornings. Amelia had never wanted to go to one, but she resented not being asked. There were no real gentry in Abbotslea so the

233

Wetherburn-Pryces, residing at The Poplars, the largest house in the village, and possessing a double-barrelled name, were commonly agreed to be the next best thing. Rosalind had explained as tactfully as she could to Amelia, when she had first moved in with Gerald, that it wasn't that dear old Janet didn't like her, more that Amelia confused her, refusing to be placed.

'She feels you are People Like Us, really,' Rosalind had mumbled the phrase a little shamefacedly, 'but she can't cope with the thought of you living with Gerald and not being married. She was very fond of his aunt.'

Now, on the other hand, Amelia thought cheerfully as she drove up outside the Old Rectory, I might well get her racing over with an invitation, just by strewing ashes in my hair and ambling through the village dressed in a dustbin liner; thereby qualifying as A Worthy Cause. In fact, by the simple task of going completely mad, I might achieve the social acceptance that has so far eluded me. She yanked the hand-brake tight and got out of the car.

There was a note for her on the hall table: 'Please return car immediately. Love, Gerald'.

She crumpled the white paper and left it on the table. It was nice to be in possession again of something he desired. She sniffed the air, scenting the prickly smell of wet paint. Had Gerald had the spare room redecorated

234

already? She passed the sitting-room door and the smell got suddenly stronger. Opening the door carefully, as if expecting to see a rotting corpse on the hearth rug, she stopped, looking in amazement at the strange room she had entered. Gone was the slightly shabby creamy-yellow of the walls. Instead they had been ragged or dragged, she wasn't sure which, with a vivid shade of coral that seemed to prise her eyes open as she looked at them. And the books, where were they? And the bookcases on either side of the fireplace? Amelia took quick steps into the room, looking around, bending over and peering down as if she hoped to find them hiding behind the sofa. Then she saw the second note, written on the same thick paper as the one in the hall and placed on a green china plate in the shape of a flattened cabbage. Clarissa's plate she thought as she picked the paper up and read: 'Thought that as you weren't coming back for a while we might as well do the sitting room too. Books in the garage. Love, Gerald'.

She stared at the note as she sank down into the old armchair that was as vast as a two-seater sofa and blessedly familiar. 'Books in the garage. Love, Gerald.'

That was it. It really was all over. Deep down in the small, steel-enforced compartment of her mind where the really big dreams were stored, she had kept the hope of Gerald returning. Those words blew it open as if they were gelignite, and out hope hobbled, gasped and died.

'It's your loss Gerald Forbes,' she said out loud. 'You're stuck for ever now with a woman who came into this world wearing a calf-length pleated skirt.' Then she cried.

After a while, when her crying had made the sides of her face ache, and the light outside was going, she pressed her mind gingerly for a beautiful phrase; surely all this sadness could result in one decent line of poetry. She wiped her nose on the back of her hand and got up to find a notepad and pen. At least they had left her desk untouched.

In Swedish, she thought, heart and pain obligingly rhymed, a God-send for bad poets. But no lines, bad or good, came to her, only the memory of the evening shortly after they had moved into the Old Rectory when Gerald and she had unpacked the tea-chests with their respective books, comparing taste and showing off with heavy titles.

'I enjoy Proust tremendously,' she remembered saying as Gerald picked up her unbroken copy of *Swann's Way*, 'it's just that once I put him down, I find it rather difficult to pick him up again.'

She thought of the evenings they had sat a little self-consciously in front of the fire reading aloud to each other from novels as dense as German bread and finding they actually enjoyed them. Amelia sighed and scribbled on

236

her pad.

'Heart ...? Fart. Although you are a great big fart your name is engraved all over my heart.'

The telephone rang. It was Henry.

'Thank you again for coming to the funeral, it meant a lot.' He was silent for a moment. 'Anyway, how are things?'

'Gerald and Clarissa have just turned my home into a bookless mixture of Laura Ashley and a tart's boudoir.'

'That's bad luck,' Henry said. 'Actually I called to say I've seen this place for sale in Kingsmouth that might do for your café. It used to be a dairy.'

'Is it the one by the harbour?'

'That's it.'

'I don't know,' Amelia said unsatisfactorily, waiting for Henry to say, 'What do you mean you don't know?'

Instead, he said, 'At my father's funeral, in the middle of all the sadness, the thought went through my mind that you look really good in black. I feel pretty awful about that.'

'Well, you shouldn't, and you know that. Anyway, your father liked me, why would he mind that you thought I looked nice at his funeral?' There was no answer so she asked, 'Henry, how are you coping?'

She could hear him swallow hard. 'When someone you love, dies,' he said, 'it's as if they leave you with half shares of your life together.

The person you were in their eyes dies with them.' He paused, and just as Amelia was trying hard to think of something to say that was comforting and not commonplace, Henry went on, 'I just miss him. Anyway, I thought I'd let you know about the dairy.' He hung up so quickly Amelia hardly had time to say goodbye.

Amelia spent the evening packing. She put her clothes in three suitcases and two dustbin liners. She put the bin liners and one of the suitcases in the garage where the books lay in neat stacks. Then she fixed little stick-on labels, marked with a large red A, on everything in the Old Rectory that belonged to her: two Swedish oil paintings given to her by Selma, three English watercolours she had bought herself, a couple of small tables, some chairs, ornaments, kitchen utensils. On things they had bought together or been given as a couple, she stuck labels with a question mark. By ten o'clock it was all ready and she wandered up to the bedroom wondering how many times Clarissa and Gerald had made love in the bed.

'They can't always want to use the chair,' she said trying to cheer herself up. Before turning off the light, she phoned Dagmar who answered in a polite, detached little voice and said that all was well.

How nice it would be, Amelia thought after ringing off, if she had had a mother to whom she could say 'I've arrived back at my home to find it in the process of metamorphosing into someone else's. In the sitting room and in the spare room the transformation is almost complete, and I daren't go to sleep for fear of waking up in a mock-virginal chamber with frilly dressing-table and ruched blinds at the windows.'

She lay for a long time flat on her back staring at the shadows on the ceiling, then she threw off the duvet and ran downstairs. She switched the light on in the sitting room and went across to the French windows, unlocking them and flinging them open so that they hit right back against the wall of the house. She stood for a moment breathing in the cool night air before hurrying out on to the terrace in the path made by the beam of light from inside. Shivering in her short nightshirt, she ran round to the front of the house and got in to the car, starting the engine. With the headlights full on she mounted the lawn and continued through the opening between the yew-hedge and the house, back towards the terrace, scratching the paint of the car as she forced it through the narrow gap. The wheels ran smoothly across the lawn and she lined the Citroën up opposite the wide-open French windows. For a second the wheels lost their grip and slithered as she forced them up the low verge, then she was up and edging through into the sitting room, stopping neatly in front of the fireplace. She tightened the hand-brake and switched off the engine before letting herself out.

She was shivering as she got back into bed but she pulled the duvet up close and within minutes she was asleep.

The next morning she called a taxi and walked out of the Old Rectory for the last time. On the hall table was a note. 'Car's in the sitting room. Love, Amelia.'

CHAPTER NINETEEN

Amelia went to stay with an old colleague in London. Her friendship with Kate had been a mostly apologetic affair over the telephone since she moved away to the country, but when you're fleeing, Amelia thought, there's no time for pride. She stayed with Kate for two weeks, helping her with some research and writing a feature on 'The New English Novel' for a Swedish magazine. She had posed the question, 'What is the New English Novel?' in the article and counted herself lucky that no-one seemed to expect an answer. It had brought her a cheque for two hundred and fifty pounds. Then she had gone to Dagmar, home to mother, telling herself she was doing Dagmar a favour.

Dagmar told her the burns on Selma's legs were healing. They had stopped weeping and had kept dry for a whole week, enough of an improvement for Amelia to ask Sister Morris if it wasn't possible to move her back to her old room in the main part of Cherryfield.

'She hates being sidelined,' Amelia explained, keeping up with Sister Morris's brisk step along the glossy corridor. 'It's important for her to feel the pulse of life. However weak. Sister Morris, please, I hate talking to a moving object.'

Sister Morris stopped and turned, her hand on the kitchen door.

'Sister Morris, my grandmother doesn't feel she belongs in a nursing home at all...'

'Few people do Miss Lindsay.'

'... let alone in Honeysuckle. She thinks she only gave up tennis because of her injuries in the fire.'

Nurse Williams came bustling out from a Staff Only room, wanting to know if Sister Morris knew where Thursday's clean sheets had got to.

'Maybe someone is trying to escape,' Amelia suggested.

'Very droll,' Sister Morris said. 'If you'll excuse me for just one moment.' She started down the corridor.

'You'll have her back in a sec,' Nurse Williams called as she followed behind.

Amelia was staying at The Anchor. She was meeting Henry for dinner and the next morning she had an appointment to look over the dairy. She sighed. She didn't want the dairy, she wanted her home. All those things she had wrongly thought of as hers, my home, my car, my Gerald, my stuff all!

It was getting expensive too, this staying in hotels. She had taken on writing verses for a greetings cards company to eke out her income, but she took so long over each one that she never earned much. Every week it seemed she was writing out a cheque for forty pounds or more to the indifferent receptionist who was so at odds with the old world charm of the oak-panelled reception of the inn. The thought of the money had even kept her awake at night. Cheque after cheque floated past her inner eye. It was worse even than counting sheep, something she had always hated.

'Count sheep, darling,' Dagmar used to say when some particularly virulent childhood monster had kept sleep at bay. Obediently, because Amelia had been an obedient child, she had closed her eyes and soon become entangled in the problems of sheep. Sheep that crowded over the fence, shoving each other out of the way in their fight to reach the greener pasture at the other side. And always there had been the lamb. A little white lamb with a black patch who got left behind, bleating pathetically, leaving Amelia to try and retrieve its errant mother who had been amongst the first to jump the fence.

Amelia was deep in her own thoughts when Sister Morris returned with a throwaway apology before picking up the conversation where they had dropped it.

'... Gangrene,' she said. 'We fear the foot is gangrenous. So you see, moving her in that condition...'

Amelia stared at her. 'But that's not possible. Gangrene I mean. It's the sort of thing people got in *Gone with the Wind*, in that dreadful field hospital. You know the bit where Scarlett goes looking for Ashley?'

Take a grip on yourself, she thought explaining, 'What I mean is, I didn't think it was something that was allowed to happen these days.'

'It's not a question of allowing it to happen Miss Lindsay, I assure you. I'm afraid that even with the best care in the world,' Sister Morris emphasized best, 'it does still occur, especially in our elderly. Her foot was quite bad already when she came here you know.'

'But what are you doing about it?'

'Everything that can be done, I assure you. But you can see that it's quite out of the question moving your grandmother. Now you must excuse me.' Sister Morris hurried off.

Selma was sleeping in her wheelchair. Have wheelchair, won't travel, Amelia thought sadly as she bent over and kissed Selma's forehead. Selma's skin felt clammy and it took longer than usual for her to wake. When she did open her eyes, she looked at Amelia as if she had seen her only moments earlier.

'I'm sorry, darling, I must have dozed off. You should have woken me.'

The curl had gradually gone from Selma's hair and it was the flat grey of wire wool, an unfamiliar shade on Selma, but of course her natural one. She was wearing a haphazardly-patterned polyester dress that rode up over her knees, straining round the thighs. Amelia began to understand the sense of having no mirrors in the rooms in Honeysuckle, other than a tiny one above the basin. When Sister Morris had asked Amelia to buy some more easy-care dresses for Selma, Amelia wanted to know what was wrong with the clothes her grandmother had brought with her to Cherryfield. 'My grandmother hates man-made fibres,' she had explained, 'and I do think it's important to let her keep some dislikes.'

Just listening to Sister Morris's explanation of why precisely Selma should wear easy-care dresses seemed a betrayal though, an unacceptable intrusion into her privacy, so Amelia had nodded agreement halfway through and rushed down to the town to find what little there was to choose from in Wash'n Dry, size eighteen.

As she wheeled Selma through into the conservatory, Selma said, 'There's a woman here who keeps a rabbit in a box. Very strange.'

'A real rabbit?' Amelia asked, feeling stupid.

'Must be, she keeps taking it greens, or tries to.'

Amelia parked the chair at the far end of the room. 'I've brought you something.' She bent down and picked a package from her bag. 'A Disc-man.'

'A what, dear?'

'A Disc-man. It's like a record player only better and you have little earphones so you won't disturb anyone else. It will stop you hearing that blasted television too. I've got you some discs as well: Bach's "Concerto for Two Violins", Lars-Erik Larsson's "Pastoral", "Finlandia" and ...'

'There's that Hudd woman, the one with the rabbit.' Selma pointed to a tall woman entering the conservatory with the aid of two sticks. Her limbs were long and bony and her large face was crowned by a thick white plait wound round the top of her head. As she searched for a chair she liked the look of, she spotted Amelia and hastened across the tiled floor.

'I wonder, would you mind getting some oats? Porridge oats will do.' Her voice was deep and her eyes flickered nervously from Amelia to the door as she spoke. 'Some carrots too.' And, groping round the pocket of her long cardigan, she pulled out a pound coin.

Poor old soul, Amelia thought but she took the coin and nodded, 'Of course, no problem.' She wondered if she should collude in the madness and ask after the rabbit's health and happiness.

'I've never had much truck with pets,' the

woman said. 'Cats huh, vicious smelly things. But rabbits, they're different. There's no malice in a rabbit.' She shuffled off.

'Silly fool,' Selma hissed.

*   *   *

China that matched, Henry thought: cups, saucers, plates, all matching in some cheerful pattern and no chipped edges, was one of the things his children would grow up with. He fingered the ashtray as he waited for Amelia in the bar of The Anchor Inn.

Would she be upset, he wondered, when he told her they were sailing soon? He took a deep gulp from his vodka and tonic. Lately he had felt something dangerously close to excitement at the thought of war; so he had prayed with more fervour than ever for peace and the other night he had stayed in the chapel until morning. He had thought of the people in the squadron, his people, and had wanted to beg their forgiveness. He kept asking God's. It was the thought of being needed that caused that shameful excitement. In a war, people would be faced with the most basic reality; you stay alive or you don't, and he would be able to help. All the years of work and preparation would be put to use as never before. He sighed, his thoughts were as ill-disciplined as a street full of urchins, racing through his mind unbidden and unwanted, upturning ideas and scattering the contents all over his mind. He rubbed his eyes with his knuckles, hard, relishing the pain as the bones pressed against the eyeballs; he could almost hear the veins popping.

When he looked up again, he saw Amelia coming through the doors. As he stood up to greet her he wondered at how pale she still was after a whole hot summer. *She* needed him, she might not know it yet, but she did, he thought, as he watched her cross the floor. It was always a surprise to him to see how straight backed she walked; he suspected that mentally she wandered through life with an apologetic stoop. He smiled to himself; at heart he was just a frustrated big brother. There had been no little sisters or brothers at home, not even a dog or a cat, just two large, well-meaning, preoccupied men.

Amelia looked hard at him before kissing him hello. 'Your eyes look a bit red. Are you all right?'

'Me?' He smiled. 'I'm absolutely fine.' He went over to the bar to get her whisky and water, and when he got back he asked, 'Have you looked at the dairy yet?'

'Not yet,' Amelia said, feeling her glance crawling around shiftily somewhere at floor level. 'I'm not really so sure now about this café idea, or rather I'm worried that Kingsmouth isn't quite the place for it.' She sipped her drink and felt irritated by her own habit of adding little unnecessary 'actuallys', 'not sos' and 'quites' to any unpopular statement she made, as if trying to dilute what she was saying to an acceptable blandness.

'You're not giving up already, are you?' Henry looked expectantly at her. She wished she had the guts to look expectantly back instead of wittering on obligingly. It was the same at dinner parties, she thought. Ten people fell into simultaneous silence and Amelia felt wholly responsible for filling it.

'Or maybe it will work,' she added lamely. 'Oh I don't know.'

Henry smiled at her. 'What don't you know?'

Amelia laughed. 'Where do I start? I don't have any faith in my ability to carry anything through. You know when you're little and say, "I want to play the guitar", or "learn to ride" or "build a matchstick model of the Eiffel Tower" and some grown-up comes along and says "That's all fine and well, dear, but will you finish it?" Well I'm doing it all myself now. I've cut out the middleman. Each time I decide to do something, each time I get swept away with a new plan, I say, "That's fine and dandy Amelia dear but will you ever carry it through?" Serves me right too; I'm a project nymphomaniac, always looking over the heaving shoulder of one idea at the newer and better one beckoning in the distance.' She stopped. There he was again, fixing her with that keen round-eyed gaze as if what she said actually mattered. Disconcerted, she fiddled with the pearls round her neck. They had come out of a Christmas cracker and Gerald had said she couldn't possibly wear them. Amelia thought they were very pretty.

'I still think it's quite an interesting idea,' Henry said now. 'Just make up your mind to do it. Lots of retired people round here, holiday-makers too. All you need is to stock the book section with Hardy, Dick Francis and Jackie Collins, and you're away.'

Amelia finished her whisky with a little grimace; she was training herself to drink the stuff because she thought the world was too full already of women ordering dry white wine.

'The newsagent across from here sells books of course,' she said, 'but they hide them under such a mountain of speciality interest magazines and Ninja Turtle stationery that you'd need a sniffer dog to find them. I might stock the odd voucher or Talking Classic, but otherwise it'll be strictly books. I'd be liberal in my selection though: Sex and Shopping, Sex and Suffering, Sex and your Intellect, No Sex but a lot of Intellect; it'll all be there. I can see myself on top of some rickety old library steps reaching for a dusty volume on the top shelf, captivating my customers with my intellectual air and spectacular legs.'

'What about the pastries?'

'Oh don't you worry, I'll fit them in. That's if

I decide to go ahead of course.' She sighed. 'I don't suppose I will.'

'You sound as if you have no control in the matter.' Henry looked annoyed.

'Some of us are blessed with self-control,' Amelia said primly, 'and some of us are not. So don't mock the unafflicted.'

'Rubbish,' Henry said. 'Shall we eat?'

Every time Amelia came into the hotel restaurant she was struck by the determined brownness of it: brown beams bore down from the ceiling, brown tables and chairs were placed at nudging distance around the brown wooden floor, even the curtains and the seat cushions had a brown pattern. She wondered who the little devil was who had slipped in red napkins.

They sat down and were given the large menu covered in improbable suggestions: 'Butter fried Dover Sole and Banana, Breast of Wild Duckling with Kiwi sauce, Fillet Mignon with a garnish of lobster claws.'

'It will have to be Dover sole and banana,' Amelia smiled across the table at Henry. He was fiddling with his napkin, smoothing it down and folding it, smoothing it down again.

She put her hand over his. 'Having you as a friend through everything, potty grannies, errant lovers, it's been marvellous. I'm just so sorry about your father. I don't feel I was a great comfort there.'

For once Henry didn't seem to be listening.

Taking a deep breath as if he was about to launch himself off a ten foot rock in to the sea, he said, 'We sail Monday week. We'll be away for about six months. Longer maybe if there's a war.' He looked guilty, as if he felt he had let her down.

When Amelia didn't answer he asked, 'Are you all right?'

'Fine.' She smiled. 'I think I'm getting immune to men leaving, or at least I've come to expect it.' And she realized that what she had begun to say for effect was actually true. Daniel, her father, Willoughby and Gerald; they had all left. Pulling a face, she said, 'It's as if it's in the Trade Descriptions Act, Man: non-childbearing member of the species, lots of body hair, one willie, leaves a lot.'

There was a bit of indulgence, she thought, in Henry's laugh as he reached across the table for her hand. Pulling it to his lips, he began kissing her fingertips each in turn.

While she enjoyed the sensation of his warm dry lips against her skin, she tried hard to think of something to say, ready for the awkward silence she guessed would follow when he'd run out of fingers.

'Every radio and television priest worth his collar is telling us to pray for peace. I'm all for it of course, but...'

Henry stopped kissing and gave her her hand back. 'But what?'

'I don't understand it. I never have. We're

251

told God is almighty. So we all ask the same questions: why does He allow children to be tortured and murdered? Why does He allow mass starvation, wars, the holocaust? And we're all given the same answer give or take a hallelujah: God gave us free will. We're not puppets. If we are not free to choose evil, we will never be able to understand the meaning of goodness. He suffers with us but He does not interfere. That's fine we say nodding wisely. That is, until someone comes along and tells us to pray. Why, I ask myself, why pray in the face of this determined policy of non-interference?'

'Oh that. Easy peasy Japanesey.' Henry lifted his hands to make room for the plate of stilton and apple soup.

Amelia put her spoon into the rubbery flesh of her avocado Mary Rose. 'I'm waiting. And "God knows" won't do as an answer either.'

All of a sudden Henry looked serious. 'I can't give you an all-enveloping, iron-cast, bullet-proof answer, but then you knew that. But first of all, you have to look at prayer not as a shopping list: long life, happiness, a plague on Aunt Caroline, etc but a way of keeping in touch, of keeping the lines of communication open. Both ways too.' He tasted the soup and quickly drank some wine.

'The Bible describes prayer as something like a torchbeam through the darkness.' He sat quiet for a moment. 'This might seem like a cop out,' he said at last, 'but I was given a book once by a master when I was at prep school. It said that we shouldn't always want a reason for everything. Why should we expect to understand everything about God? In the last resort to be a Christian you must be a bit like a trapeze artist, prepared to take a leap across the gulf between what you know and what you believe, reject the safety net of certain knowledge and just go for it. Once you've done that you hang on to those beliefs and, as time goes by, little by little God's purpose will be revealed to you.' He looked up at her and smiled, touching her forehead with his fingertip and drawing it down the bridge of her nose to her lips. 'I've taken that leap,' he said.

Later, when they had finished their dinner and were walking along the quayside with a tepid breeze coming off the water, Amelia asked, 'If there is a war, will you be frightened?'

He thought for a moment. 'Probably.' He slipped his arm round her shoulders and said, with all his usual energy, 'Fear can be a very useful emotion.'

Amelia stopped abruptly. 'You wouldn't say that if you knew my mother. Fear has ruined her life. It hasn't exactly added reams of jollity to mine either.'

Henry pulled her along. A seagull squawked over head, circled and glided off over the water. 'Fear has to be husbanded, harnessed, then it becomes useful. Your mother, from what you've told me, fights ghosts, spending her fear wildly in every direction, achieving nothing.'

Amelia shrugged off his arm. 'You make it sound as if she had a choice in the matter. As if she blighted her life through sheer carelessness.'

'I'm sorry,' Henry said quietly. He stopped her and pulled her close. Framing her face with his hands he bent down and kissed her.

In the circle of light thrown by the street lamp, Amelia was smiling.

'What are you grinning about?' Henry dropped his hands.

'You don't want to know,' Amelia said matter of factly.

'Yes I do.'

She sighed and put her hands on his shoulders. 'I smiled because I enjoyed your kiss. You're the nicest man I think I've ever known. And ...' She looked down at the tip of her blue shoes.

'And ...?'

'And I enjoy feeling a strong man weaken in my arms, and that feeling is enhanced when the man is a priest,' she said quickly. 'There, I told you you wouldn't like it.' She turned pink. It had been a mistake being honest. It nearly always was.

Henry looked at her unsmiling. 'Us chaplains do a good line in bondage too if you think it would give you a kick.'

'See, now you're offended.'

254

'No I'm not.' They had walked round the block and were back at the hotel entrance. 'How long will you be down here?'

'I go back to my mother's tomorrow. I'll stay for a couple of weeks and then ...' She shrugged her shoulders as if life really was too much of an effort.

Henry took the telephone number of the flat and, after a moment's hesitation, kissed her again before walking her inside.

*   *   *

I'm like the Princess of Wales, he thought as he drove back to Devonport, making himself smile at the unlikely comparison. I would marry knowing that whatever the rest of the world gets up to, I could never get a divorce.

CHAPTER TWENTY

The next morning Amelia got the keys to the dairy from the estate agent and wandered round the empty shop playing Bach on her Walkman. She liked Bach, the orderliness that would erupt into passion. She hadn't got Selma's and Dagmar's ability to play music but she had got their love of it: Mozart, Chopin, Beethoven, Bach, their music played like drums of war whenever she wanted to attack a new idea, because if mere humans had created beauty like that surely everything was possible. Or so she thought as long as the music lasted.

She pulled her right index finger lazily across the dusty wooden shelves and thought of Henry returning from sea, surprising her as she served a customer or arranged books along the shelves. And what then, she thought sourly to herself? What do I do then? Rape him? Do I confess to needing love like a stomach needs lining, a base before anything else can be successfully added.

She climbed the creaking oak staircase and, as her favourite passage of the concerto played, she thought of Selma whose decline had been gentle until Willoughby died, then it became a free-fall.

She remembered coming with Selma to the dairy to restock their empty egg boxes. Selma would let her pick out the large, white eggs one by one, making sure she checked them for cracks. Amelia could almost feel the shell between her fingers now, cool and grainy as if covered in goose-pimples. Then they'd buy the cream, thick yellow cream, like soft butter. She sighed. Maybe it should stay a dairy. Remain as a stubborn unprofitable memorial to the days when people still found minutes in the day to queue up at more than one counter. God knows how they did she thought when, thanks to all the cholesterol-ridden dairy products, their days must have been fewer anyway.

As she walked upstairs to the flat, she thought that, to her, maybe to all the customers, Mrs Philips, owner of the dairy for more than thirty years, round and apron-clad, began and ended with the handing out of cream and butter and eggs, only to vanish like Brigadoon to the place where all the people in the service industry go when their customers have done their business. So standing there in Mrs Philips's flat, peeking through into the tiny kitchen, inspecting the narrow bedroom where the multi-coloured roses on the wallpaper waged war against the peonies on the curtains, was a little like glimpsing suddenly an actor's legs sticking out from underneath the television set.

Before she left, she stood for a moment by the sitting-room window looking out at the grey, foam-tipped waves. It was a good view for a poet.

Later that afternoon she told Selma, 'I'm thinking of buying the old dairy. Mrs Philips is selling up and moving to Portugal. I'd like to turn it into a bookshop with a café part. Or maybe it's a café with a bookshop part?'

'That's very nice, darling.' Selma paused and thought for a moment. 'But why don't you keep it as a dairy. People need good cream and eggs. Mrs Philips always had the best, fresh from the farm.'

Amelia laughed. It made her happy when Selma said something like that, something perfectly normal and quite logical. Rosalind smiled in much the same way when Ronnie waved his fat little hand in a goodbye or held his own bottle.

'I thought about that. But it was making a terrific loss. No-one uses the little shops any more, the speciality ones. It's simpler to go to the supermarket and get everything from one place.'

'Young women today are very lazy,' Selma said. 'They can't even be bothered to push a pram. They dress their poor little babies in boiler suits and strap them into these striped deck-chair things you trip over.' She lifted her coffee cup and saucer to her lips, her hand trembling so it seemed impossible that her lips and the rattling cup would ever meet.

After a small wait, Amelia took the cup and saucer gently from her and held the cup steady for Selma to drink. It was a simple enough movement but, as Selma sucked at the coffee, Amelia felt that at Cherryfield it was showing off the most precious commodity of all, youth and an obedient body.

'I've still got your old pram. It's in the garage I think,' Selma said. 'It should clean up beautifully.'

Miss White had been craning her neck in their direction for some time, her lips moving in sympathy with every sentence they spoke. Seeing an opening, she moved in. 'Expecting a little one, are we?' she twinkled at Amelia.

Selma gave her an evil look which Miss White studiously ignored.

Miss Hudd sat in the high-backed chair in the Admiral's old place by the replenished fish-tank. 'I like babies,' she said in her deep voice. 'Babies and rabbits, no bad in 'em.'

Amelia suddenly wished, as much for the two childless old ladies as for herself, that she could conjure up an infant to match the excitement in their eyes and their softening gaze. 'No baby just at the moment,' she said, not wanting to close the door on the idea completely.

'Don't worry about it, that's what I say.' Miss Hudd nodded knowingly. 'These things take time.'

'Particularly,' Selma said, 'when there's no father involved.'

'I absolutely must get some greens for the rabbit.' Miss Hudd made a show of ignoring Selma's scorn. 'You did get the oats, didn't you?' She leant towards Amelia, staring expectantly at her.

Amelia blushed. 'I'm terribly sorry, I forgot.'

Miss Hudd moved agitatedly in her chair. 'But that won't do. It won't do at all.'

'Oh shut up, you silly old woman,' Selma cried.

Miss Hudd opened her eyes wide, then burst into tears. Like boys, large girls don't cry, or so they are told. Miss Hudd, like someone having

259

their first taste of a forbidden luxury, wept diffidently, carefully at first. Then, as seconds passed and no thunderbolt struck, she abandoned herself to the experience, crying in great snuffling sobs until Sister Morris appeared in the doorway. Taking one look at the scene in front of her, she hailed a nurse, much in the way of a head waiter directing the attention of his staff towards a soiled ashtray, and Miss Hudd was removed.

Amelia was shocked at the pleasure that lit up Selma's eyes at Miss Hudd's humiliation. Miss White sat very quiet, her back pressed hard against the chair.

The evening sun was autumnal, its light paler than only a week before. Selma dozed: the enlivening effect of spite, like that of most pick-me-ups, was short-lived. Nurses clip-clopped in and out of the room, checking on the residents, sometimes removing one, as if they were dead-heading a plant, Amelia thought, and now and then they would check on Selma to see if she too was ready for plucking. The room was hot, they must have turned the heating on already, and the television droned away, not quiet enough to be ignored, yet not loud enough to make sense. Amelia wondered what had become of the Rosenthal coffee cups that Selma liked to drink her morning coffee from at home. Selma stirred uneasily in her chair as her stomach thundered. Amelia sighed, the price of life was high, that was for sure.

* * *

Back in Dagmar's flat she asked, 'Have you got the Rosenthal cups?'

Dagmar shook her head. 'They must be in store with the rest of the things. Why? Do you want them?'

'No, no it's OK, only asking.' Amelia turned over the page of her book, *How to Set up your own Business—Beat Recession at its own Game.*

'Play something please,' she said after a while, nodding towards the piano. Obediently, Dagmar got up from the sofa where she had sat leafing through *Vogue*.

Amelia listened to 'Traumerie' and thought that nothing, nothing at all, had changed in the neat little flat. Since her collapse, Dagmar had slowly returned to her old shape like a tired piece of elastic. She had lost what was probably her last chance of love and companionship and she had scattered her nerves all over her life, yet nothing at all had changed. What a waste of suffering.

When Dagmar had finished playing Amelia asked her, as she had asked Selma, 'Why did you not make a career of your music?'

Dagmar did not get up from the piano, but swivelled round slowly on the stool. She shrugged her shoulders with a little smile, poised for an excuse as always, Amelia

261

thought.

'I like music too much,' Dagmar said. 'I have too much respect for the great composers. They deserve to be performed only by the best. I was never going to be more than adequate.'

Amelia felt the old irritation spread like a rash inside her. 'How can you possibly know? You never tried hard enough. I read Dylan Thomas but I still dream of becoming a poet.'

Dagmar got up from the stool, scanning the seat cover, smoothing down her skirt. 'Well, then you're very brave, darling,' she said.

Amelia was crushed. After a short pause she said 'Have you got the address of the storage people? I promised Granny to check that everything was in good order.' Telling Dagmar a blatant lie made her feel better.

*   *   *

Three days later she was rummaging through the teachests full of china and silver and books, measuring the length and breadth of furniture that had once combined to create a home and were now just listed items in the store room of Grant & Son, Removals and Storage. The gilded lion's paw of Selma's empire chaise-longue peeked out from under a dust sheet, making Amelia think of those mortuary scenes from American films where all you could see of poor Mr X was his pallid, labelled toe sticking out from under a shroud on the trolley.

262

She found the ring-binders where Selma had pasted in magazine cuttings with pictures and information of all manner of beautiful and useful things: handpainted chairs, Victorian tiles, shoe-tidies, cut-price linen sheets, Edwardian storage jars, china tooth-brush mugs. There were ticks against the things she needed straight away, crosses against the things she hoped one day to acquire, and at the back of each binder was a section marked 'Babylon' after the Hanging Gardens. On those pages were pictures of the unattainable: a painting by Monet, a Chippendale chair or Flora Danica china. Yet Selma had never seemed materialistic, more an artist perfecting an ever-changing picture. 'Come in, come in,' she would say like a benevolent spider inviting a visitor into her enchanted web.

Wrapped in plastic and stacked behind a large sideboard were Selma's hatboxes. She had collected them for years; extravagant, inessential, striped and spotted, they had paraded along the shelves in the hall. 'Just a bit of fun, my dears,' Selma would say showing them off.

Amelia lifted the boxes from their plastic wrappings and stacked them on the chaise-longue. She pulled the whole lazy-looking, sumptuously gilded piece over to the only open space in the store-room and, looking around her, picked up her black notebook from her pocket and checked the list. She moved Selma's

263

favourite armchair across to the chaise-longue, together with two small coffee tables, a display cabinet, two smaller chairs and a foot stool. She pushed it all close together then measured the space it all took up. Ticking items off the list, she unpacked several tea-chests, picking some things out and adding them to the court around the chaise-longue, putting others back in the chests. Finally, before leaving, she brought out two large blankets to cover the collection of bits.

That night she telephoned Henry onboard his ship. She launched her question with little prelude. 'I know you're not a Jesuit, but in your view does the end ever justify the means?'

Henry did not seem surprised by her question nor did he ask why she wanted to know. Amelia liked him more than ever for that. 'It depends, I think, on the end you're trying to achieve and the means by which you intend to achieve it. Boring answer I know.'

Amelia paused before saying, 'That's all I'm going to get?'

'I'm afraid so.' Henry sounded amused. 'If you'd like to tell me more I'd be very happy to listen.'

'Oh Henry, I don't know. My first instinct in any situation is to confess, shift my great dripping burden on to someone else, but this time I think I'll wait.'

'If you're sure,' he said. 'We sail on Monday, first thing. I was going to ask if you'd like to spend the weekend with me. I've got a friend's cottage in Cornwall for a couple of days while he and his family are away. It would be great just spending some time with you.'

Amelia said she thought it was a lovely idea, and they arranged to meet at the flat on Saturday morning.

*   *   *

Maybe it's a mistake to think too hard about these things, Henry thought as he stepped into his car and started off towards Exeter. Maybe with Amelia too, it's just a question of faith, of taking the leap. He had been in love before, of course, with glowing cheerful girls who studied, or cooked or cared for little children, but most of all cared for him: Alice, Arabella, Olivia and Jane, nice girls with even teeth and even tempers who didn't complicate life unduly. And now there was Amelia. He had begun to see that one of the reasons he was falling in love with her was the way she made him feel about himself; like an engine on permanent boost. She made him feel, well ... He searched his mind for a word ... Essential, that was it. And she was so pretty. He sighed and pushed his hair back from his forehead with a hand that was becoming embarrassingly damp.

*   *   *

265

Amelia was finishing her packing. She looked at the small suitcase lying open on the floor. A moment ago it had been on the bed, but Dagmar had come in and shuddered and asked if she realized the amount of dirt a suitcase accumulated on its travels in the boots of cars and holds of aircraft, let alone on those filthy conveyor belts. And did she not see that all those germs and disgusting bits were transferring on to Dagmar's bedspread that had to be drycleaned. Amelia had pulled the case off on to the floor without protest and now she looked at it, shaking her head. It really wasn't very small at all. She always aimed to go away with just a holdall or, best of all, a rucksack with some clever mix and match in uncrumpable cotton that would take her everywhere. But she never did. There was the midnight-blue silk jacket; it just didn't roll up well. And the linen shorts and the chiffon skirt in a pattern of faded flowers, and shoes and make-up. She knew she looked good in the soft straw hat with the upturned brim. She glanced at her watch; it was eleven o'clock and she was expecting Henry to arrive at any moment.

He really was so nice. She knew that, to many of her friends, nice was not an adjective that made them adjust their clothes and put on fresh lipstick but, to her, it was about the best compliment she could give anyone. Henry was the nicest man she had ever met. His smile lit up his face and he laughed a lot. He listened to her.

He was so ... so positive. She had needed a friend and he had been there.

As she got her sponge-bag, she glanced at her folder with poems lying next to it on top of the chest of drawers. Some of the work in there was good, some of it, and not necessarily the best either, had been published in magazines, but there just wasn't enough there to send off to a publisher. On the cover of the folder she had quoted Elizabeth Smart: 'I must satisfy Nature before I invite God.'

That, Amelia had thought, is a slightly pompous way of saying what I've always felt: I have to get my love life sorted out before I can write; pompous but clever. But now, now she felt she knew the quotation across the folder for what it was; an excuse to put life on hold. It might in all fairness, she thought, have worked for Elizabeth Smart, but it's done nothing for me. What good anyway could come from inviting anyone, Nature or God, into a shaky building? She sighed as she packed her nightdress, smoothing out the folds of peach-coloured silk with the back of her hand; a shaky building, not a nice image to have of oneself, not an image she would ever want to see mirrored in Henry's eyes.

Then she thought of the trip ahead and, slamming the case shut, she said out loud, 'Bugger it! What harm can a weekend do?'

*   *   *

Henry took her for lunch at a small pub in Modbury, and not once did they mention Selma or the nursing home. It was, Amelia thought, as if they were testing each other out, making sure that they had somewhere to go beyond Cherryfield. She remembered Rosalind sitting in Amelia's kitchen with Ronnie on her lap saying sadly, 'All Chris and I can talk about is the baby. These days we seem to be rushing through life on different tracks, converging only on Ronnie, and when we run out of chat about him, we just sit there in polite silence, waiting for his next step, or tooth, or word, to rescue us.'

She thought suddenly of Gerald dressed in prickly silence as if it was a cactus skin. Henry would never be like that. He threw himself into every conversation like a puppy attacking a new friend. And all that energy: in a midday heat that made even the buzzing of the bees sound like a tired gesture, he made sitting down seem like freeze-framed action rather than a rest.

During lunch he had wanted to hear all about her plans for the dairy: was she serious about opening the café, was she continuing with her journalism?

Amelia began to feel like one of those middle-aged mothers with a miraculous first baby, exhausted, a little frustrated but charmed.

'I'd love to see some of your poems,' Henry

said.

Amelia gave him a lazy smile. 'Little Bo-Peep has lost her sense and doesn't know where to find it.'

'Ha, ha,' Henry said.

'You shouldn't ha ha,' Amelia said reproachfully. 'I've had to take on writing jingles for Happy Thoughts Greetings Cards, to support my granny habit.'

'Really?' Henry looked interested.

'Really,' Amelia said. 'They rejected my last lot though.'

'You must try again,' Henry said.

He kept humming as, later on, they drove towards Cornwall, happy little hummings from no particular song that Amelia knew. He didn't have a bad voice, deeper than his speaking voice. He would sound good in church, she thought. She pulled her fingers along the naked skin in the crook of his arm. It was a hot day and his skin was damp.

'You've got nice arms,' she said.

Henry turned pink. 'Apparently,' he smiled suddenly, 'my mother used to say that to my father. He couldn't work out why she had married him, he was almost fifty, twice her age, quite staid and boring he said. I remember him laughing about it. "It must have been my arms; she thought my arms were sexy."'

'All right, all right.' Now Amelia was laughing. 'Your arms are sexy too.'

She looked at her watch. It would be tea-time when they arrived. She wondered what the cottage was like. Henry had said that the Cowans would be leaving them some food, but she had still brought some cheese and grapes, a few scones and a pot of home-made jam. The jam was made in someone else's home admittedly, and it had probably done the rounds backwards and forwards between different bring-and-buy sales in Abbotslea, but it looked like nice jam: strawberry, and the pot had such a pretty cloth-cover over its lid. Amelia kept trying to ward off thoughts of Henry leaving, leaving so soon and maybe even going to war in the Gulf. The idea seemed quite absurd in the midst of all that sunshine and normality, the way, she thought suddenly with a little shudder, it must have seemed eight years earlier to the people waving off the men sailing for the Falklands.

She shook herself. 'Twenty-four hours,' she said. 'just think, twenty-four hours all to ourselves.' She smiled as he put his hand on hers.

CHAPTER TWENTY-ONE

As they got out of the car by the grey stone cottage with its garden all jumbled up with roses and fox-gloves and cabbages, the front door opened and a small boy ran down the path and out of the gate, flinging his arms round Henry's neck.

'Uncle Henry, Uncle Henry! Mummy said you wouldn't be pleased to see us but you are, aren't you?' The boy was five years old and quite convinced that his mother was being very silly.

'Elvira was sick all night.' He jumped up and down with excitement, stirring up little puffs of grey dusty soil from the road side. 'First she was sick in her bed. And then she got into mine because hers was all icky and then she was sick in mine.' His voice rose to a high pitched squeal, 'And then...'

Henry gave a pleading look over the child's blond head. 'This is Freddie, my godson.'

Amelia smiled back helplessly.

'Are you Amelia? Mummy said that you wanted to be on your own with Uncle Henry. You can come into my playroom, it's quite big. Come.' Freddie put his hand in hers.

Freddie's mother appeared at the door and, giving an embarrassed little wave, she called, 'I'm terribly sorry, really I am, but you can imagine ... camping with Elvira at the moment.'

Henry hurried towards Jenny Cowan and kissed her on both cheeks. 'Mark's inside watching the athletics,' Jenny said, before turning to Amelia, shaking hands. 'Come through, I'll show you your room.'

The trick is, Amelia thought, not to burst

271

into tears on the Cowans' doorstep.

'I'll get the bags,' Henry said and disappeared off towards the car.

'We know how things are with Henry's "calling" and all that, so we've got you in the spare room,' Jenny explained as she took Amelia through the house. 'But I'm afraid Henry will have to share with Freddie. Actually,' she smiled conspiratorially, 'the little chap can't believe his luck. He was so upset when he heard you were coming and he wasn't going to be allowed to be here.'

She opened the door into a small, sunny room dominated by a double bed that stood like an insult at the centre of the wall. 'I hope you'll be comfortable. I'll just go and check on Elvira. I'll have a cup of tea ready in a sec.'

Think positive, Amelia told herself as she hung up her clothes. It could be worse. How? She thought for a moment: at least the children make a change from Cherryfield, she tried. And Jenny does seem very nice. She brushed her teeth and tried out a smile before joining the others in the sitting room.

Mark asked her if she wanted a large gin and tonic rather than tea. 'To get over the shock.' He grinned at her, as if they were all sharing in a really good joke.

'Tea will be fine.'

She went over to Henry who sat smiling with a look in his eyes as if he'd been struck by someone he trusted. She took his hand and

272

said, trying to sound cheerful, 'It's lovely to have a chance to meet you both.' She smiled at her hosts. 'And the children of course.' She was rewarded with a grateful glance from Henry.

After tea Henry suggested Amelia came with him for a walk. 'Can I come, can I come?' Freddie, who had been busy building a Lego zoo, jumped up and began looking for his boots.

'You don't need boots, Freddie,' Jenny called after him, 'it's dry as a bone outside.'

Henry took her hand again as soon as they got out of the house. 'I'm so very sorry,' he whispered. 'Do you want to leave? We could go to a hotel.'

Freddie circled them like a cheerful vulture. 'There are planes on Uncle Henry's ship.'

'Helicopters,' Henry corrected automatically.

Freddie circled closer. 'Amelia, there are helicopters on Uncle Henry's ship. Hundreds and hundreds of helicopters.'

Amelia smiled at him. 'Isn't that wonderful?' And she whispered to Henry, 'We couldn't do that, could we? They'd be terribly hurt. It would be very rude.' She half hoped that Henry would contradict her but of course he didn't.

'And this business with the rooms too,' Henry put his arm round her shoulders. 'You see, Jenny knows how I feel, how I normally feel about...'

'Uncle Henry, does God love everybody?'

273

Freddie interrupted him. He had stopped circling and settled into their steps. His cheeks were bright pink and his hair was damp from the running.

'Yes Freddie. God loves everyone.' Henry looked unhappily at Amelia. 'It's all getting to be such a mess. If at least we'd had this one night...'

'Did God love the dinosaurs?' Freddie squeezed in between them and took both their hands.

'Yes!' Henry almost shouted. 'Yes, the dinosaurs too.'

Freddie frowned. 'But if he loved them, why did he let them get extinct?'

*   *   *

Freddie and Elvira were asleep and Amelia had helped tidy their toys away from the kitchen. She wandered into the garden to pick some flowers for the table and coming back with a bunch of foxgloves in her arms, she bumped into Henry on his way to get some wood.

'Digitalis,' she smiled at him. 'For the children.'

Henry let go of the woodbasket and put his arms round her, squashing the flowers. 'I adore you, do you know that?' he mumbled the words so quickly that they came out almost on top of each other. Then he let her go and hurried outside.

Amelia stood looking after him, the crushed flowers in her arms. She had been told she was loved quite a few times by quite a few men, but never before had she been adored. She smiled as she arranged the flowers in Jenny's vase.

Henry opened the bottle of wine and Jenny served lasagne with a corner missing that had gone to the children's supper. There were caramelized oranges to follow, and Amelia's cheese. As Mark spoke of the possibilities of war, probing every angle, pulling out morsels of information from press and television, chewing over the options, Amelia kept hacking off little wedges of the cheese and popping them into her mouth absent-mindedly. Throughout their lives, she thought, at any particular time a war was being fought somewhere. Yet they could as well be sitting there talking of witches or dragons or a haunted house, as of war, because somehow, deep down amongst the fear and the excitement, none of them really believed in it.

'Now Mark's on to the Gulf he'll go on for hours,' Jenny grimaced at Amelia. 'He used to be in the Navy too, that's how we all met.' She pushed her plate away and, putting her hand on Henry's shoulder, she said, 'You boys can do the washing-up. Come on Amelia, I'm dying for a chat.'

Amelia stood up obediently, thinking it was like a sticky spider's web, this kind hospitality, choking the life out of their weekend.

275

Henry got up too. 'Let's get on with the clearing up,' he said to Mark.

'Oh, there's no hurry,' Jenny smiled at him. 'You two hardly ever get a chance to have a really good talk. We'll be all right, won't we?' She turned to Amelia. As there was no reply she tried again, 'Won't we, Amelia?'

Amelia felt there was no more fight in her. She allowed herself to be seated on the sofa next to Jenny, allowed herself to be plied with coffee and mint flavoured matchsticks, the extra long variety. 'Don't you just love these?' Jenny giggled as she put a third chocolate in her mouth.

No, Amelia wanted to say. I hate them. I only like the orange ones. But she muttered and smiled agreement.

'You must be worried sick with all this talk of war.' Jenny reached for the box again. Then, before Amelia had time to answer, she went on, 'He's totally wrapped up in you, you know. We've seen him with quite a few girls, but nothing ever seemed this serious.' She added kindly, 'He's obviously been waiting for someone special and now it looks as if he's found her.'

'We don't know each other all that well,' Amelia said gracelessly, annoyed at having their tentative affections all tied up and despatched by Jenny. 'I mean most of our meetings have been in a nursing home. I'm older than him too,' she added for good

276

measure.

'And now you've got us around to spoil your last weekend,' Jenny said. 'Poor you.'

Amelia blushed and apologized, but Jenny just laughed.

Feeling hot, Amelia excused herself and hurried into the bathroom to put on fresh lipstick and some scent. When she returned, Jenny looked up at her and said, 'Gosh, I remember making all that effort before we were married. I give you two months, and you'll be as slack as the rest of us.'

She hadn't been listening at all, Amelia thought, but when Henry joined them at last, a tea towel slung over one shoulder, she felt as if the door to home had opened.

* * *

Eventually, Henry had thought, Jenny would suggest that he would be much more comfortable sharing the spare room with Amelia, but she hadn't. During dinner he had almost heard the clock ticking away their last night together as Amelia grew quieter and quieter. She had a way, he thought, of hunching her already narrow shoulders when she was unhappy or worried, which made her seem smaller than she really was. Next to her, Jenny had seemed indecently robust, dark-haired, pink-cheeked and so sturdily married that she seemed to have all but forgotten about people needing to be alone together. And Mark, Mark was his best friend, but he had been no better, going on and on about the Gulf. Henry thought of the young sailors and Wrens in his care sailing off with him that Monday, none of them knowing whether war was at the end of their journey. He felt suddenly furious with Mark and all the men like him who sat pontificating in the safety of their homes, wishing they were 'out there'.

On the bottom bunk below him, Freddie snuffled and snored, twisted and turned, legs and arms flailing; he was fast asleep though. Carefully, so as not to make a sound, Henry swung his legs over the side of the bunk, dropping down on to the soft carpet below.

'Uncle Henry.' Freddie sat bolt upright in the lower bunk. 'Where are you going? Mummy says big boys should last the night.'

'Go back to sleep, Freddie, please.'

'I can't.'

'Go back to sleep, Freddie, I mean it,' Henry hissed.

'You're being horrid.' Freddie began to cry. 'Mummy says that because you're a Chaplain you're extra nice, but you're not and I'm feeling sick. I want Mummy.'

Henry sighed and knelt down by the boy, stroking the damp cheek. 'I'm sorry, Freddie. I'll get Mummy. Come with me to the bathroom first though.'

Freddie gave a small smile and crawled out

of bed, putting his hand in Henry's.

*   *   *

'Did you sleep well?' Jenny enquired brightly
of Amelia the next morning. 'I'm afraid Henry
might have had enough of his godson for a
while. The poor little chap was awake most of
the night.' She smiled lovingly at Elvira who
sat, looking interested, in a bright red plastic
high-chair. 'Did my naughty girl give Freddie
her bugs?'

Amelia and Henry went to church on their
own, no-one followed them there. Seated in the
pew she looked sideways at Henry. Although
this was not his parish, here in church he ceased
being Henry and turned into a chaplain, public
property. The thought of their kisses and
mumbled endearments suddenly seemed nicely
improper, like sitting in court and being the
only one knowing that, under his gown, the
judge was naked. Amongst all the dubious
wisdom handed down to women, Amelia
thought, there must be one about not lusting
after officials.

Next to her, Henry was deep in prayer so she
stopped looking at him and mumbled Our
Father, lest her unworthy thoughts should
somehow   vibrate   across   into   his
contemplation.

*   *   *

After lunch with the Cowans they said their goodbyes and set off back to Exeter. 'I'll write with my new address,' Amelia called through the open window of the car. 'Promise you'll come and see me.'

Henry grinned at her. 'Such warm farewells could be caused only by a bad conscience. Actually,' he said, serious now, 'you were marvellous, and I'm very grateful.'

'I'll come and wave you off tomorrow.' Amelia stroked his hair, smoothing it behind his ear. 'Isn't your hair too long? Won't you be ticked off?'

'Probably,' he smiled. 'I'll be very busy, you won't mind?'

She shook her head.

They stayed for a while in the car outside Dagmar's flat. Henry sat with his arm round Amelia's shoulders, looking out across the park. Suddenly he took his arm away and, putting his hand in his pocket, pulled out a heart-shaped locket on a chain. Holding it out to her he said, 'This belonged to my mother. I would like to think of you wearing it.'

Amelia touched the matt gold of the heart gingerly with the tip of her finger. 'It's a beautiful locket.'

'Please take it.'

Relaxing a bit, she took the necklace, making a fist around it.

Henry touched her cheek lightly, tracing her jawline round to her lips. 'You've got what is known in the trade as an expressive face, so what's wrong? Am I going too fast?'

As Amelia looked away, he said softly, 'You're a very nice person, Amelia, and you don't want to do anything to upset me because I'm going away and there might be a war, is that not right? But you see that's why it's especially important that you're honest with me.' He took her hand. 'I suppose what I'm saying is, that I'd like to know how you feel about me.'

'It's funny,' Amelia said, 'you're five years younger than me, but compared to you I feel unformed. And ... What's the opposite of self-possessed?' she smiled. 'Unpossessed? That too.'

She lifted his hand to her face, pressing it against her cheek. 'I don't know how I would have coped the last few months without you. And as you have probably guessed,' she let go of his hand, 'I would have loved going to bed with you. But you see, it wasn't very long ago that I thought I was going to spend the rest of my life with Gerald.' She paused.

'I've only just finished driving him away. I ought to have a break before I start on someone else.'

'If that last bit was an attempt to lighten the atmosphere,' Henry said, 'it wasn't very successful.' But he was smiling again.

'Henry, that locket belonged to your mother.'

'I know, I told you.'

Then he looked at her with such understanding sympathy that she wished that there was nothing for him to try to understand. She unfolded her fingers and picked the necklace up, about to put it on.

Henry stopped her. 'Truth, remember?' he said.

Amelia looked unhappily at him. 'Why do you want truth at a time like this? I've been nicely brought up, I'm not used to it.'

Henry began to laugh. 'Take it and keep it safe for me anyway.' He slipped the locket into her handbag.

'I had always planned to meet the ship when you all return, if you wanted me to that is; we're friends,' Amelia said. 'And I listen to you. It was you who told me that I drifted around expecting others to bring me the things I wanted from life. Like one of those women who sits around in middle-age thinking bitterly: I should have been a managing director's wife, or I should have been the mother of a doctor.'

'Did I say that?'

She grinned at him. 'Maybe not exactly, but something like it anyway, and you were right. And it won't do any more. I'm thirty-one years old and most of those years I've been flapping round like a homing pigeon whose loft has been demolished, trying to edge on to someone else's perch. It hasn't proved a great success.

I'm not very proud of myself, in fact I come pretty low down the list of people I'd choose to spend an evening with.'

She leant forward and kissed him lightly on the cheek. 'And the thing is, soon you'd feel the same.'

As Henry was about to protest, she put her finger softly across his mouth.

'No, I mean it. I will have to like myself a little before I start all over again asking someone else to.' She pressed her finger harder against his lips. 'Please, Henry.'

'You make me sound like some medieval princess,' Henry said at last, 'waiting for her sodding knight errant.'

Amelia leant her head on his shoulder. 'Some princess,' she said.

Henry twisted free and looking her straight in the eyes, he cupped her face in his hands and kissed her. 'So I'll wait,' he said.

CHAPTER TWENTY-TWO

The lines of the large grey frigate seemed fluid in the mist of the September morning, making it seem to Amelia, standing at the brow, as if at any moment it would dematerialize, leaving the small crowd of women and children isolated in the drizzle. But the leaving was slow; the brow was removed, the riggers let go wires and ropes leaving a single wire attaching the ship's fo'c's'le to the jetty: a rush of water as the engines eased the stern out. Three short blasts of the siren, the final wire detached from the bollard and the Union Flag was lowered. Now the ship was off, disappearing through the Narrows, past Devil's Point and out into the Sound. Everyone was waving, the goodbye kind; no throwing up of the arm with the hand whisking the air in excitement but a slow salute held for a long while as if, while they waved, the ship had not yet really gone.

*　　　*　　　*

'Henry has left. Admiral Mallett's son, he's sailed for the Gulf,' Amelia said to Selma. 'I watched them leave this morning.' She was hoping for a miracle, for Selma to understand and say wise and comforting words.

Selma said nothing but watched Amelia intently, her hand trembling in her lap.

Amelia felt angry again, she couldn't help it. What right did Selma have to look so enticingly herself? On Amelia's own instruction the visiting hairdresser had carefully blue-toned Selma's hair, and set it in loose waves. Her nails had been cut and she was wearing the nicer of the two polyester dresses. She was a Huldra, the Swedish fairy-tale creature who, in the guise of a lovely young girl, would appear in the woods before a lost

284

traveller, beckoning him to follow, leading him further and further from the track, deep into the forest where the massed crowns of the pine trees obliterated the sky. Then, only then would she turn her back on him and in that moment the traveller knew he was doomed, knew that it was the Huldra, because where her back should be, there was just a hollow.

The Huldra at Cherryfield looked so much like Amelia's wise and loving grandmother that Amelia was beckoned further into her confidence. 'He gave me his mother's locket to keep for him, it's all very confusing. And so soon after Gerald too.' She looked up at Selma who was looking intently at her. 'You know, Grandma, I can't just keep dropping in and out of relationships. I'm beginning to feel like a baton in a relay race, always the baton but never the runner. Then again, I was beginning to get very fond of Henry, and now there might be a war and I might never see him again.' She sighed. 'He would insist on me being honest too and you know how wretched that can make one feel.'

Selma blinked as if she'd just woken up. 'Oh darling, let's not talk about the war, you know how I hate it. All these films and television programmes, making it out to be exciting and romantic when it was all so horrible.'

Be gone with you Huldra, Amelia thought resignedly.

Selma made an effort; 'And how are you

anyway darling? Been to any nice parties lately?' as if she was racking her brains for suitable topics of conversation with a dull guest.

Amelia sighed, then she covered up quickly with a smile. 'I'm fine, absolutely fine.' Physical contact, she thought, that's the thing, that's the way of getting through. She looked surreptitiously at Selma's hands, the one that trembled and the one that was still, like a visitor picking a child from the line of abandoned urchins in an orphanage. If she picked the pathetic one, the most helpless, she would show up all the clearer the weakness of the whole and embarrass Selma. She took the good hand.

Selma's eyelids kept drooping, she seemed content. It occurred to Amelia that at Cherryfield the only touching you got, the only time you felt someone's arms around you or their skin against yours, was in the course of maintenance; when hands lifted you on to the loo or from your bed, washed you, wiped you. But no-one touched you just because they wanted to.

A while later, Nurse Williams popped her head through the door, and when she saw Selma and Amelia she smiled and called, 'Ah, there you are Mrs Merryman, I was looking for you.' She sounded as if she thought Selma had been playing Hide and Seek and she stepped briskly towards them with an empty wheelchair. 'It's time for your bandages to be seen to.'

Selma shrank back in her chair. 'I can't come with you now, I'm afraid. I've got my granddaughter here.' She relaxed a little. 'I don't believe you've met.'

'Of course we've met, dear, haven't we Miss Lindsay.' Nurse Williams winked at Amelia. 'We won't take a moment, Mrs Merryman, I'm sure your granddaughter will wait.' She began to haul Selma up from the chair.

Suddenly Amelia felt Selma's nails digging into her arm. 'You must take me away from here. I want to go home,' and she began to cry.

With an expertly executed pull and twist, Nurse Williams plonked her in the wheelchair. 'There we are,' she sing-songed. 'Nothing to it, is there Mrs Merryman?'

Amelia thought the nurses must develop the same selective deafness as mothers of young children. 'Just wait a moment could you Nurse Williams?' she said. 'My grandmother seems distressed.'

The nurse leant closer to Amelia. 'I know dear, it's upsetting, but she'll soon forget all about it and be back bright as a button and as sweet smelling.' And as Amelia gaped at her she released the brake of the wheelchair with a little kick of her sturdy white lace-ups.

Amelia put her hand on Selma's shoulder.

'She's fine, you know,' Nurse Williams said, and her large brown eyes had a hurt look in

287

them. They were the same eyes, Amelia thought, as those of Mrs King, the kindly neighbour Dagmar sometimes left her with as a child. Amelia hated going to Mrs King, having taken an instant, virulent and completely unfounded dislike to her, and each time as Dagmar prepared to leave, she'd begin to howl. That same confused hurt look would fill poor Mrs King's eyes as she tried to defend herself against the accusations of ill-treatment that were never made. And Dagmar had been embarrassed in the same way as Amelia was now; right in the middle of feeling sorry for Selma she felt embarrassed at the tactlessness of her tears.

Amelia patted Selma's shoulder awkwardly and said to Nurse Williams, 'I know you all look after her, it's not that.' She patted Selma some more. 'It's all right,' she mumbled, 'it's all right.'

Selma lifted her head. 'It's not bloody well all right!' Then she began to cry again. 'I don't understand anything any more. Robert said it would only be for a short while, but no-one takes any notice of what I say, no-one seems to listen when they see it's me talking.' She pulled a soiled pink tissue from the sleeve of her cardigan and wiped her nose.

It was the small, slightly upturned nose of a pretty young girl, Amelia thought sadly: noses just didn't age. She knelt down and put her arms round her grandmother. 'I'm listening,'

288

she said, then she looked up at Nurse Williams. 'I'll bring her to you in a moment, if I may?'

Nurse Williams still looked hurt, but she did leave them.

'I'm frightened, Amelia.' Selma hung her head like a small child. When she looked up again she was pleading. 'I'm frightened I'm going to die in this place.'

It was the first time Selma had mentioned death. Some old people never stopped talking about it, their own and others', in a busy possessive way as if dying was an exclusive hobby. Selma, though, had avoided the subject as if it was a bad smell. 'Ignore it dear, and it'll soon go away.'

Her uneven nails dug deep into the fleshy part of Amelia's arm, her eyes were locked on Amelia's face, anxiously following every flicker of her eyes, every twitch; as if the conclusion of her life is written in my features, Amelia thought, looking helplessly back at her. And what was she to say? 'Nonsense, you're not going to die. You've got years left in you.' Was that what she was meant to say? She had planned and schemed for weeks, enjoyed what was nothing but a state of madness or an over active day-dream. And now Selma, who not so long ago had been the serene and loving centre of her life, was begging like no-one should have to beg, for her help.

Amelia closed her eyes for a moment then she leant across and took both Selma's hands in hers. 'You'll be home for Christmas, I promise you that.'

Selma sighed a deep shuddering sigh as she relaxed back in her chair. 'Thank you, darling.' She added almost nonchalantly, 'I don't know what I'd do without you.'

Amelia felt as if she had just risked life and limb rescuing someone from an approaching steamroller only to find out when it rolled past that it was a *Potemkin* cut-out. Her heart still thumping, she wheeled Selma out to Nurse Williams who was waiting in the corridor outside Honeysuckle. Selma greeted the nurse with a gracious little smile and went off as if she hadn't a care in the world.

She's put them all on me, Amelia thought as she wandered out into the garden. At Cherryfield you grabbed your fresh air when you could. There was a moment, as she stepped out on to the lawn, when she expected to see Henry standing under the cherry tree in one of his awful shirts. With his head a little to one side, he'd look at her with those keen brown eyes, so different from Selma's, where age, confusion, sadness, had each, drop by drop, diluted the colour. As for Nurse Williams, Amelia thought, kicking a stone across the lawn and indulging her desire to be ten again, she had the large mournful eyes of a cow who had just been shooed off her favourite patch of grass.

'There's just no right way with old people,'

Amelia wanted to complain, basking in Henry's warm interest. She sat down under the tree and thought how right she was. You put them in a Cherryfield and you break their hearts. You take them to live with you and they break your spirit and make you fellow prisoners in their decline. 'No thank you Rosalind I can't go to London with you, Granny doesn't fit in the train,' and, 'Dear Editor, I hope you like my article on Japanese businessmen in Milton Keynes. I had to guess what Milton Keynes is like because there's only me at home with granny.'

How long would Selma have lasted, Amelia wondered, if they had all left her at home at Ashcombe, if they had never interfered?

She sat under the tree trying to think of all the reasons why she should not fulfil her promise to Selma and she remembered Henry saying once that doing nothing could be a grave sin too. The worst maybe, she thought, because you're so seldom brought to justice. She looked at her watch and got up, feeling her skirt all damp at the back. I'm one of life's hand-wringers she thought. You can see people like me at every bad happening through history, be it big or small. 'Oh dear, oh dear,' is our motto, as we stand at the foot of the cradle, squashed between the bad and the good fairy, peering down anxiously, 'Oh dear, oh dear.'

'Your gran is having a little snooze,' Nurse Williams told Amelia who came looking for her in the hall. 'It always takes a lot out of her I'm afraid, seeing those legs when the bandages are changed.' Then with surprising speed she dived after Miss Hudd who was arranging herself in the chairlift, and wrenched a small paper parcel from her fingers.

'Boiled carrots from the kitchen,' she mouthed at Amelia.

'You'll rot, you murderer,' Miss Hudd said calmly and clearly before propelling herself around and starting to walk back to the lounge. She looked straight past Amelia as she met her in the doorway and settled herself in a chair a little removed from the others.

Amelia waited a moment, then she walked up to her and asked, 'The carrots, were they for the rabbit?'

Miss Hudd turned slowly to face Amelia with an expression of such raw pain that Amelia flinched as if slapped by Miss Hudd's large, blue veined hand.

'I'm so very sorry about forgetting the food the other day. Would you please let me run down and get some now?' I'm taking the easy way out, she thought, joining in her disillusions: buy a smile now, pay later.

'It's too late.' Miss Hudd wasn't looking at her any more and she spoke more to herself than to Amelia. 'The carrots wouldn't have been any use either, but I felt I owed it to him to try.'

Amelia was wondering what to say when

Miss Hudd looked directly at her. 'Come and see for yourself, it doesn't matter now.' She heaved herself up from the chair.

Upstairs in her room Miss Hudd walked over to the chest of drawers on the bare wall opposite the narrow bed. Letting go of one stick, supporting herself on the other, she pulled out the top drawer. She looked up at Amelia. 'Here,' was all she said.

Thinking hard of fluffy toys, Amelia took a step closer and looked down. On a piece of thick green velvet lay what seemed at first to be an untidy mesh of pale grey wool. Then she saw the silky ear and the small front paws. 'Oh my God!' Amelia slapped her hand across her mouth and took a step back.

Miss Hudd dropped the second stick and, leaning her side against the wall, put her large hands into the drawer. Gently she lifted the little creature out and, shifting so that her back was supported by the wall, she stood, holding the rabbit tight against her flat chest. Amelia turned away for a moment, the expression in Miss Hudd's eyes was hard to bear. Then, coming up closer, she whispered, 'Is he dead?'

Miss Hudd bent her neck and kissed the rabbit's head. For a moment his sparse lashes fluttered as he struggled to open his eyes. Then he lay still.

'I didn't really mind coming here,' Miss Hudd said, in an even voice. 'I know I was becoming a nuisance; always scalding myself,

293

falling over. I had agreed to go when my nephew told me pets weren't allowed.' She buried her nose in the tousled fur, and when she looked up again there were tears in her eyes. 'I couldn't go without him, you understand that, don't you?' She looked as if she was going to sink to the floor.

Amelia reached out and steadied her, guiding her across to the chair. Still clutching the rabbit to her chest, Miss Hudd collapsed on to it. She sat, silently stroking the rabbit, her big hand covering the animal like a heavy blanket. Then suddenly she cried out.

'Look how big I am! Look at me. "Let Hudd do it," the teacher at school said, "she's a big strong girl." And my mother, "Trust Elizabeth, Elizabeth will cope, she's so sensible, so capable," she said. Look at me!' Miss Hudd cried again, stretching her long arms out, showing the emaciated rabbit laying motionless on her large palms. 'I'm no use,' she whispered, 'no use at all.' She began to cry, tears falling down her cheeks, dropping one by one on to the rabbit's face.

Amelia knelt by the chair and put her hand gently on Miss Hudd's shoulder. 'I'm so sorry I didn't believe you. I'm so very sorry. Let me take him to the vet, please.'

Miss Hudd shook her large head violently like a distraught child and her plaits uncoiled and dropped down her back. 'It's too late. He's gone.' She rubbed her wet cheeks against him, kissing him over and over, then with a shudder she held him out to Amelia. 'You take him. Bury him for me, would you? Please. Under the cherry tree.'

*   *   *

'I'd like you to use my car while I'm away,' Henry had said as he sailed that morning. 'It will actually be a help for me. I would have to sell it otherwise or pay for garaging.' So Amelia placed the dead rabbit on the floor of Henry's car and, as Selma was still sleeping, drove off to pass the time until dark fell. She took tea down by the harbour and had another look round the dairy. Then she drove back to Cherryfield and sat at Selma's side until the cherry tree at the centre of the lawn grew fainter and disappeared in the darkening evening.

She had taken the gardener's shovel from the shed before it was locked up and now she brought it from its hiding place under the rhododendrons. She carried the rabbit from the car wrapped in a white Cherryfield towel, and she could feel its bones under the cloth, as fragile as a feather pen. Glancing up at the dull, starless sky she pushed the shovel into the hard soil and, as the crust broke, the sickly-sweet smell of mud and rotting leaves rose from the ground.

She placed the rabbit in the shallow hole

295

she'd dug, still in his towelling shroud. The small theft gave her some pleasure. The wind rustled the branches of the tree and fresh leaves floated to the ground, some settling on the small white bundle in its shallow grave. Amelia had a sudden image of Sister Morris, blackcloaked and wild, toiling away over a much bigger grave. She shook herself. Sister Morris was nothing if not orderly. Every body that passed through Cherryfield was sure to be properly accounted for.

'Everyone but you,' she whispered to the rabbit. She covered him with black soil, shovelful after shovelful, until it was impossible to see that someone was buried under the cherry tree.

CHAPTER TWENTY-THREE

'Doreen? Amelia Lindsay here. Yes, we're all well thank you.' Amelia held the receiver a little away from her ear as Doreen Hamilton seemed not to trust the telephone to carry her voice all the way to Exeter. 'I'm calling on behalf of my uncle,' she lied. 'He's living out in Brazil at the moment but he's asked me to make sure that everything is satisfactory.'

She fiddled with her key-ring, gazing out through the open window at the street. The dry autumn leaves rattled along the pavement like a plague of brightly coloured cockroaches, while Doreen, her voice stiff with complaints, told her about cracks, damp patches, loose tiles and funny smells in the cellar.

'Well that's excellent then,' Amelia said breezily, 'I can tell him everything is fine.' Ignoring any complaints with cheerful resolution was a trick she'd learnt from the builders that had worked on the Old Rectory.

'Oh, by the way,' she said quickly, as Doreen, sounding confused, was preparing to hang up, 'I hear you're spending Christmas in the sun this year. Over the actual holiday is it?' She tucked the question in with her goodbyes. 'Until the sixth, lovely.' She put the phone down and went to find her diary.

The red ribbon marker running along the inside spine of the blue leather diary (she always bought the best in diaries ever since reading Mrs Miniver when she was fourteen) was placed to make it fall open on the twenty-third of December. The red-ringed date made her jump as if it had announced itself in a ringing baritone; only two months away. Time, these days, was money in more than the obvious sense, she thought, as she sat down on her bed with the open diary in her lap. Ever larger amounts of it disappeared faster and faster. Two hot summer weeks when you were seventeen were time to be reckoned with; you got a lot for fourteen days when you were very young. Now, it was nothing but small change,

297

and she squandered it, as if she still had riches of years ahead of her, when instead she should be making the minutes go a long way, like a pensioner counting coins at a check-out counter.

She sighed and got up, putting the diary on her desk with the letters from Henry. For him, time seemed suspended as he sailed in the ship, closer and closer maybe to war. There was already a small pile of his letters to her. Funny, clever, sometimes beautiful letters, each written with that last weekend like an unanswered question between them.

Later that day, Amelia stood by the window in Selma's room looking out at the gentle dying of the leaves that were at their loveliest just before dropping to the ground. Then she looked at Selma.

There was no more talk now of her moving back to her old room. The darkening evenings and the cold winds were kept at bay by electric light and central heating but, like wolves howling at the door, they still seemed to threaten the residents of Cherryfield.

'We always lose a few more in winter,' Nurse Williams said.

A week later Mrs Ambrose died. They had brought her husband in to sit with her and Selma spent the day in the Residents' Lounge before being allowed back to the room with its empty second bed. She didn't ask about Mrs Ambrose, so no-one told her.

The new vicar went his rounds though, and he even mentioned a rabbi friend to Amelia. 'When the devil gets old he becomes religious,' Selma used to say. But she was in no more mood for religion now in her dying days than she had been before. Amelia thought it was because she didn't know she was old.

'Your grandmother seems much more settled these days, don't you think?' Sister Morris moved her lips in the direction of a smile as she passed Amelia in the passage.

'I was thinking of taking her over to my mother's flat for the day,' Amelia said.

Sister Morris had only paused briefly on her clip-clop along the glossy floor, but now she stopped again. 'I don't know Miss Lindsay. We normally encourage outings, but with those burns only just beginning to heal ... The skin is as fragile as tissue paper.'

Back at the flat, Dagmar washed her hands three times at the news. 'I feel guilty. You don't know how many snide little remarks I get from people. Some of mother's old cronies have even called up to tell me they think I'm a bad daughter for not having her to live with me.' She rubbed some handcream into the cracking skin on her hands. 'Not one of them, other than old Evelyn, of course, has bothered to visit her but they all know that I should have mother here with me.'

Amelia had written an article for the local paper on the importance of helping old people

299

to keep their pets. She had since been asked to do another on the topic of old age. The editor had suggested 'The Care of Our Elderly: Shame or Shambles?'

'Shame and Shambles,' Amelia had corrected him mildly. But she had admitted she could think of no clever alternatives to that particular mess.

'How to care for Selma?' she asked now, more to herself than to Dagmar, as she followed her into the sitting room. She knew it was one of life's unanswerables.

'I love William Hurt, don't you?' Dagmar put a tape in the video and settled into the sofa, her long legs tucked under her. As the credits were running she asked Amelia, 'Are you sure you want to settle in a little hole like Kingsmouth? Isn't London really the place?'

About to answer, Amelia felt all wrong, like a pink button on an orange cardigan. She knew she should love London for its galleries and theatres, its shops and restaurants. And she did love it, as a visitor. But she had tried living there and the loneliness froze her, slowing her down until just getting out of bed was an effort.

'I only like the rich extravagant bits I can't afford,' she said, portioning out the truth to her mother in bite-sized chunks because who wanted, at thirty-one, to admit to their mother that living in a big city frightened them? 'I've tried to like the squalid bits. Tried calling them cosmopolitan and full of flavour, real and

300

alive.' She threw herself down on the small sofa. 'Anyway, why is it that what's scruffy is described as real as if anything else is not? Why are quiet leafy terraces and tea at the Ritz not deserving of the label? It is the reality for some. Lucky sods.'

'Hush.' Dagmar turned the sound up on the video.

*   *   *

In her bed, Selma rolled about uneasily and when her arm hit the hard edge of the bedside table she woke. For a few moments her thoughts floated round pleasurably as if in a warm lagoon, then unease seeped through. This was not just another day, pleasantly filled with family routines, about to begin.

Bang! It hit her like a tidal wave of misery and she struggled to sit up. Daniel, Daniel was dead, that letter had said so. She opened her mouth and screamed, 'Daniel!'

Footsteps hurried towards her and a bright striplight was switched on. 'Mrs Merryman, Mrs Merryman! What's the matter? Are you all right?'

There was much shaking of heads that afternoon when Dagmar and Amelia visited. Nurse Williams sucked in air through the gaps in her teeth and said, 'She was totally confused. Going on and on in some foreign language...'

'Swedish,' Amelia said.

301

'. . . then she switched to English but we were hardly any the wiser because she kept on talking about her husband having just died and calling him Daniel but we all know her husband was called Willoughby.'

After that, Selma's decline seemed to Amelia like one of those speeded-up sequences in a nature film; almost before her eyes she folded and wizened. She always recognized Dagmar and Amelia but the smile now seemed joyless, accusing almost, and each time Amelia stood up to leave she felt the barrier come down between the visitor free to go and the prisoner who was not. Sometimes she wondered if Selma hated her.

She bought the dairy. She had to call in a removal firm to bring her things down from Abbotslea. The day she was there packing it all up, Gerald took a couple of hours off work to be there too. He made her sad by the charm and kindness he exuded so carelessly in her direction, smiling at her with a warmth he had not shown since he stopped loving her. By showing his pleasure with her for disappearing from his life with comparatively little fuss (as he so rightly pointed out, you could hardly see the scratches on the car from when she had parked it in the sitting room and the carpet cleaned up beautifully) he came close to rekindling her love for him.

When, a day later, she shopped in the supermarket next to her new home, she looked enviously at the tired looking young woman in front of her stacking the conveyor high with food, her two small children squabbling somewhere at hip level. Amelia looked at her own basket, she didn't even merit a trolley, and thought, I'm turning into that awful cliché: the one-chop woman.

Soon, though, she got into a soothing routine and she found, as always, that inactivity had one busy trait; it begot more of the same. She got up no earlier than eight and padded down the bare-board stairs to the front door where the papers waited on the mat. She took three papers, two national and one local, and she read them all while she ate slices of toasted wholemeal bread with butter and Devon honey. At around ten she was dressed and ready to work on her articles before going for a long walk along the cliffs. She had forgotten how much she enjoyed the sight and smell of the sea. The walk was the time for some fairly vigorous day-dreaming of poetry readings in the café, and of bus loads of London critics squeezed in around the little tables downstairs. She hadn't yet found furniture that she both liked and could afford, so the tables and chairs these phantom poets and journalists were offered varied: sometimes the chairs were bentwood, placed round cloth-covered tables and sometimes the tables were oak and the chairs became pews.

After lunch she would work some more on

303

her articles and she studied her correspondence course in accountancy, and around tea-time most days she wandered up the hill to Cherryfield.

No, for me, all is for the best, in this the most static of all possible worlds, she sighed, as she sat by Selma in the Residents' Lounge; and what would Henry think of me now, after all my bold words when we parted?

All through the autumn, Amelia had gathered the brightest autumn leaves off the ground and pressed them between the pages of Strindberg's *Collected Plays*, and by the time the Christmas lights had replaced the last leaves on the oaks in the little park by the harbour, she had put them in a huge padded envelope and sent them to Henry. He loved autumn in England, he'd said, just before the ship sailed, and now he wrote to her of the heat that lay like cling-film across the ship, suppressing all spare energy, and of how instead of dolphins playing on the pressure waves at the bow, there were the bloated bodies of dead sheep tossed overboard from some livestock transporter bound for Daman.

When Amelia walked in the garden at Cherryfield she found little pieces of boiled carrot in the grass under the Cherry tree where Miss Hudd's rabbit lay buried.

'I'm taking my grandmother home for Christmas,' she said to Sister Morris.

Sister Morris puckered her lips. 'We do

encourage Christmas visits with friends and family but Mrs Merryman really isn't in a fit state to be moved. She's such a weight for a start, I doubt you'll even get her out of the car and as you know she's quite unable to help herself in the smallest way now.'

'She sort of dresses herself. A bit.'

Sister Morris didn't answer.

'The burns are healed now. I really can't see why nothing is being done about the foot. It's been getting steadily worse since she came here.' Amelia felt that for once she had Sister Morris on the run.

'Come into my office would you, Miss Lindsay?' Sister Morris said.

She offered one of the two hard chairs in the closet-sized room to Amelia and sat down herself. No fees had been siphoned off in the direction of the office, Amelia thought, handing a sour little portion of approval to Sister Morris as she waited for her to speak.

'The gangrene is spreading.' Sister Morris looked straight at Amelia, a business-like tone in her voice. 'We could amputate but that would almost certainly kill her. Her blood pressure is very high, she's got early signs of Parkinson's. I'm sorry but there really is very little we can do. We are managing the pain very successfully and, quite honestly, all we can do now is continue to make her comfortable and hope the infection doesn't spread above the knee.'

305

'How long has she got?' Amelia asked and she blushed as she realized that a part of her felt it would be easier if it, death, happened before Christmas. Then she remembered Selma's face when she had begged her not to let her die at Cherryfield.

Sister Morris sighed and shrugged her shoulders. 'It could be a few weeks, it could be months. Who's to say?'

'There seems to be a general assumption that it's God,' Amelia snapped. 'And by what right, I sometimes ask myself.' She enjoyed Sister Morris's look of horror before getting up to leave.

She walked past the Residents' Lounge with its smell of stale urine, its grunts and murmurings, through the corridor to Selma's room. Hell, she thought, was most probably not fire and brimstone, but acres of passages with super-polished floors where each poor sinner's footsteps showed against the high gloss, and the air was heavy with disinfectant.

CHAPTER TWENTY-FOUR

On the twenty-third of December Amelia stood in the hall at Ashcombe for the first time since the house had been sold back in the spring. She had put her old key in the lock, turned it easily, and here she was inside, running her hand along the familiar ochre walls that were lit by milky winter sunlight. She wandered round the house, amazed at how little seemed to have changed. There was less dust around than in Selma's latter days and the smell of cats had gone, allowing the pot-pourris that Doreen, like Selma, kept in bowls around the rooms, to exude their scent unchallenged. It was a blessing that Doreen had always admired what she called, the Country-House style. The rooms themselves: the study with its bookshelves and carved pine fire-place, the sitting room with its deep bay looking out over the garden, the sunny passages, they all had character of their own so that any change of furnishings altered them only slightly, like discreet make-up on a strong featured face. Only the dining room was really different, not golden yellow any more as if it had its own sun in residence, but dark green and hunting-print adorned.

Having toured the house, Amelia went outside again and, as she unloaded the hired van she had parked in front of the garage, she felt thankful for the tall yew hedges that shielded the house and drive from the lane, and the neighbouring gardens.

She worked hard, singing as she went, 'The bells of hell go ding-a-ling-a-ling,' returned for a second armchair, 'for you but not for me.' She dragged the chaise-longue along the gravel path and into the study. 'Ding-a-ling-a-ling,' put the tea-chests in the hall and dumped the pile of sheets and blankets on the old card table. When she stopped for a moment to wipe the damp hair from her forehead she decided that if she did go to hell as a result of what she was doing, she'd at least go there a better person.

By the time the light was going, she stood in the sitting room, a bunch of holly twigs in her arms, surveying her work. Unfamiliar tables had become Selma's again because Amelia had draped them with the Christmas cloths Willoughby's mother had embroidered. The two Swedish oils of Gothenburg and the west coast archipelago flanked the fire-place and Selma's armchair was in its place by the bay window.

Once, long ago, Amelia had asked Selma if she wasn't offending her Jewish faith by celebrating Christmas with such enthusiasm. Selma had been decorating the tall tree, standing on top of the library steps, a box of baubles in her hand. Amelia could see her now, looking down at her, smiling. 'Jesus was a great Jewish man, why should I not join in the celebrations?' and she had fixed the final decoration, a gold star Amelia had helped her make, at the top of the tree.

The last thing Amelia had brought from the van outside was a six-foot Christmas tree. She had decorated it with the contents of four cardboard boxes that she'd found amongst

Selma's stored belongings. The star, a simple shape cut in cardboard and covered with gold paper, caught the light from the electric candles and Amelia saw now that it was remarkably like a Star of David.

'Tasteful Christmas trees are an aberration,' Selma had always said. She would like Amelia's tree. It stood in the bay so laden with tinsel, lights and baubles that it had become one solid glittering pyramid. Amelia took one final look around before slipping out of the front door and locking it behind her.

*   *   *

In the Residents' Lounge at Cherryfield, a plastic tree twinkled in the gloom. The traffic-light colours of the fairy lights flashed, throwing their colour across the magnolia walls and the grey faces of the residents, and jazzed-up carols played from a cassette recorder on the coffee table.

'You shouldn't worry about your gran,' Nurse Williams said. 'We do a lovely Christmas here: turkey with all the trimmings, it has to be carved the day before of course on account of the kitchen staff but they always do us proud, Christmas pud, no charms because of our teeth, but everyone gets a pressie.' She dazzled off a smile at Amelia.

'You think of everything.'

'Oh yes. I almost forgot, there's the crackers:

green and gold this year.'

'With paper hats?' Amelia asked in a voice as if a lead weight had been attached to her vocal chords.

'Of course with hats.' A wailing noise came from a small woman hunched in a chair by the French windows and, hurrying away, Nurse Williams said, 'Your gran is having a little rest in bed today, so you'll find her in her room.'

Amelia turned in the doorway. 'What if they don't like paper hats?'

Nurse Williams looked puzzled for a moment then her face cleared. 'Everyone likes a hat for Christmas, don't they?'

Amelia had not slept well. She had kept on waking with her mouth dry and her heart going so fast it seemed it was trying to run right out of her chest and she was sure she had acquired at least one extra arm expressly to get squashed under her body as she tried to ease herself into a comfortable position.

As she went to find Selma, she tried to calm herself. Nothing had been done yet that couldn't easily be undone. When it came to it, maybe Selma didn't really want to leave. After all, she was used to Cherryfield now. It was warm and quite comfortable and ... there was always someone about.

I shall tell her that I'll spend the whole of Christmas Day here with her, she decided. I can bring chocolates, dried fruit, cake, champagne even. She opened the door to

Selma's room.

'There you are at last, Amelia. I've been waiting.' Selma sat in bed, a shabby Gucci headscarf tied under her chin, an accusing look on her face. She seemed to be wearing the entire contents of her jewellery case; two gold chains hung round her neck and three sizeable brooches were pinned any how across the chest of her purple cardigan, the gem-stones twinkling amongst the spills and stains.

'I'm all packed,' she said, pointing.

Amelia looked at the small suitcase lying on the chair, bits of material sticking out from under the soft bulging lid, a stocking foot peeking out at one side, then she looked back at Selma. She took a deep breath and, moulding her voice into something cheerful, sensible sounding, she asked, 'Are you sure you wouldn't rather stay here where you are all snug and comfortable?'

Selma's laugh was scathing. 'Of course not. I want to go home.'

'Ah.' Amelia nodded emphatically as if the rhythmic movement could calm her. 'Right.' She picked up the suitcase and a bead necklace dropped out, falling rattling to the floor.

Amelia pushed the wheelchair out from Honeysuckle. She stopped outside the Residents' Lounge. 'Do you want to say goodbye to anyone. I can see Miss White and Mr Ambrose there.'

Sister Morris too was in the Lounge. She

311

looked at the suitcase in Amelia's hand and said, 'Mrs Merryman is going off for the festivities then.' She opened her eyes wide making them round and incensed looking and the loose flesh under her chin trembled.

Christmas time, Amelia thought, and even Sister Morris makes me think of turkey.

'You'll miss all the fun,' chirruped Miss White. 'We've been promised a party.'

Sister Morris's expression softened as if she was hearing the words of a favourite child. 'Indeed you have Miss White, and a very jolly party it will be too.'

Selma had been looking from one speaker to another, her fingers gripping tighter round the arm of her wheelchair. She opened her mouth and a shriek came out. 'I'm not staying here, do you understand? I'm not staying!' Her arms flayed about her as she tried to twist round to see Amelia behind her. 'I'm going home.'

Apart from Miss White who looked up at Sister Morris as if to say, Now there's a naughty girl for you, no-one took any notice but continued to stare at the walls or the turned off television. The carols played on from the tinny sounding tape recorder.

It's like the New York subway here, Amelia thought as she moved in front of the wheelchair; nobody dares to care. She took Selma's hands. 'It's you who decide,' she said in a clear slow voice and, as she spoke, she felt those words were about as important as anything she'd ever said.

'Would you be so good as to stop by my office on your way out.' Sister Morris spoke in the dangerously perky voice of a teacher who has finally given up on a pupil.

'Wait here,' Amelia said unnecessarily to Selma before hurrying off.

Sister Morris handed Amelia a form. 'Sign here please.' She indicated a gap in the print towards the bottom of the page. 'It's to say you accept that Cherryfield carries no responsibility whatsoever for your grandmother whilst she is in your care. Have a nice Christmas, Miss Lindsay.'

CHAPTER TWENTY-FIVE

Many years before, Willoughby's old boxer had come home after a journey to the vet's from which no-one had expected he would return. Lifted out from the back seat of the car, he had limped inside with all the speed he could muster, making straight for his favourite spot on the hearth rug. He had circled it once before lying down and then, with a little wag of his stumpy tail and a sigh of contentment so deep it sent a shudder through his whole body, he closed his eyes and fell asleep.

Some things were the same for people as they were for dogs; coming home after you've had a bad time when you thought you might never make it, was one of them, Amelia thought as she put another log on the fire. Selma, dozing in her old armchair, stirred and mumbled and, even as she slept, the smile was there at the corners of her mouth together with the froth from the milk she'd been drinking. By her side on the three-tier cake-stand stood her mug with Willoughby's mend running like a black thread through the marmalade fur of the painted cat. Amelia thought Willoughby would be amused to think that his repair had lasted longer than him.

On the drive back to Ashcombe, Amelia had explained to Selma by way of cunning little lies that seemed to spawn ever more intricate deceptions, why she would find her home changed. 'Someone has been living at the house whilst you've been away. Sort of house-sitting. They moved quite a lot of their own things in with them. Their own house got flooded so that seemed the sensible thing to do. Of course the woman is allergic to cats ... and we haven't quite got it all back to normal yet ...' Hearing the thinness of her explanation stretched to breaking point, Amelia shot Selma a worried glance as she parked the car by the front door. But Selma just smiled and nodded and said she understood perfectly and Amelia wondered at the need for self-delusion, every bit as strong as the will to live.

'I've made up the chaise-longue for you in

314

the study,' she said now as Selma woke in her chair and smiled hazily at her. 'Just until your leg gets better.'

It was a large room, the study, but it had never been heavily furnished; books, the chaise-longue with an old Chinese screen to partition it off from the rest of the room, Willoughby's old desk by the window, and the room belonged to the Merrymans once more.

Selma was undressed and resting between her own patched and thinning linen sheets. Amelia was about to leave the room when she noticed Selma's lower lip wobbling and the pale brown eyes brimming with tears. Amelia stood, looking at her horrified, like a mother who's carefully picked, beautifully wrapped gift has just been kicked across the room by her darling's sandalled foot.

'What's wrong? Oh dear, whatever is wrong now?' she pleaded, scratching at the small chapped patch on her hand until a tiny, almost transparent, drop of blood appeared.

Selma sniffed and smiled, holding her good left hand out to Amelia. 'Nothing is wrong, darling. I'm just so happy to be back.' She gave Amelia's hand a trembling squeeze and said with a little laugh, 'I know it was silly of me, darling, but I was beginning to think I was never going to come back home.' The tears ran down her cheeks, making snail-trails in the thick powder and her hand shook so hard it was as if she was trying to shake it right off the arm. 'Darling, I was so frightened.'

And I was about to tell her that she'd have to go back to Cherryfield after Christmas; Amelia looked helplessly at Selma who was smiling again. 'Well you're home now, that's all that matters.' Amelia stood up, tucking the sheet in tighter round Selma, raising the pillow a touch. 'Comfortable?'

'Mmm,' Selma's smile glowed. 'Thank you, darling.'

*　　　*　　　*

Dagmar thought the call from Amelia strange. 'What do you mean, come and spend Christmas at Ashcombe instead of your place? All right I won't ask questions. I'll be there tomorrow. Twelve o'clock.' Dagmar put the phone down and went to fill the kettle. She was intensely curious as to what Amelia was up to. Who wouldn't be under the circumstances, she thought. The whole thing sounded like an adventure. Dagmar had always felt that she was meant to be quite a different person from how she'd turned out: bright, exciting, like a Renaissance painting before the grime of centuries distorted the intentions of its creator. Someone who would love adventure, that is, if she'd allow herself five consecutive care-free minutes to do so.

So what could Amelia be doing? Dagmar poured herself a cup of tea and curled up in the large armchair by the window, ready for pleasurable contemplation, but her thoughts wouldn't play ball. Since her Little Turn, as she referred to her breakdown, her fear of germs and worms had faded a little, turned soft at the edges. But there had been no respite, because a new enemy had formed out of the anxiety that lurked in the layer just beneath reason: I'm sure there was something I was meant to remember, she would fret, what was it now? She felt she had to catch and hold every thought: amongst the flotsam and jetsam of the mind something of importance might be hiding. Something that, if not dealt with, could cause harm, but the thoughts would drift off, just out of reach, like thoughts will, leaving her scrabbling in the dark.

Now she packed her bag with clothes and parcels, called her neighbour to say she'd be at a different address if anything should happen, wrote the note to cancel the milk, all while she scratched round inside her mind: the bank, maybe that was it? Or was it to do with work? Anyway, how had Amelia got the Hamiltons to let them spend Christmas at Ashcombe? Long red skirt for Christmas Day, red blouse, pine-needle green velvet jacket. She loved Christmas and every year she hoped she might enjoy it.

*   *   *

Christmas Eve morning was mild and misty. Dagmar rang the doorbell at Ashcombe and Amelia opened, snatching her inside. 'Did anyone see you?'

Dagmar looked offended. 'Happy Christmas, Amelia. What do you mean, "Did anyone see me?"?'

Amelia took her into the kitchen and Dagmar wrinkled her nose at the newly installed, leaded, dark oak cupboards that had replaced Selma's white and blue painted ones. 'Ye Olde Yuk,' she said, sitting down.

When Amelia had finished explaining, Dagmar burst out laughing. Then she said, 'How will you get her to go back?'

Amelia was pouring water into Selma's silver coffee pot. 'I don't know.' She put the kettle at the side of the old beige Aga, left from Selma's days, and sat down. She smiled at Dagmar but she kept rubbing her forehead hard with her fingers. 'I don't know,' she said finally. 'I just don't know.'

'But that's no good,' Dagmar said getting up and pouring herself a cup of coffee.

'All right!' Amelia shouted. 'I'll tell more lies, that's how I'll do it. I'll tell lies until I can't tell any more and then I'll have to drag her back and that'll destroy her and Sister Morris will tell me she always knew it would end like that, and you'll say something helpful like "Amelia, that's no good", and bloody Uncle Robert will make a miraculous return to

318

England just in time to tell me I should never have interfered. Of course the only person who won't come back is Henry because he really would be of some use and we can't have anything nice happen now, can we?'

'Now you're being silly,' Dagmar said.

Amelia buried her head in her arms for a short comforting while, inhaling the faint traces of her favourite jasmine scent.

'Sorry,' she said, lifting her head again and smiling across at her mother. 'But at least something Selma wanted to happen is happening. She wanted to spend Christmas at home and now that's what she'll do. That must count for something. It will show her she's not entirely without say in her own life. When you have no control you have no hope. When you have no hope you're better off dead.' She stood up looking at her watch. 'Come and say hello. It's time for her pills anyway.'

*   *   *

It was Christmas Day, and the mist from the day before lay frozen across the lawn, and the sun shone pale and wintry as it should.

'Thank you, God,' Amelia said as she stood by the open window in her old bedroom. 'Can we please go on this way?'

Selma drank her cup of tea in bed, with Amelia and Dagmar sitting at the foot of the chaise-longue. 'I'm afraid I haven't made you up a stocking this year, darling,' Selma said, lifting the cup to her lips and snatching a drink before it came clattering back down on the saucer. 'I don't seem to have had as much time as usual.' She caught an irritated glance from Dagmar and put her hand over her mouth. 'I didn't say something I shouldn't?' Then she laughed. 'Of course I didn't. You've known for ages it was granny.'

Amelia wondered why Lewis Carroll felt he had to use a white rabbit to take Alice into Wonderland; a white-haired grandmother would have been quite sufficient.

At twelve o'clock the doorbell rang. Amelia, kneeling by the oven, basting the turkey, kept down. The bell kept ringing, drilling through the voice of the boy soprano carolling on the radio. Amelia stayed kneeling, knees aching, praying her mother would stay out of sight. There was a pause, then another ring. Amelia reached up with one hand, searching the worktop above her head for her glass of champagne. Feeling her fingers touch the cold crystal she pulled the glass along the surface, lifting it down. She sat back against the cupboard and sipped the wine. Selma never cooked a Christmas lunch without several glasses of champagne to spur her on. 'It's a good way of getting through the less exciting bits of the day,' she used to say. By the time Amelia had finished the glass, the door bell had stopped ringing.

Moments later Dagmar hurried into the kitchen glancing over her shoulder several times. Checking for wolves, Amelia thought.

'Fill up?' Still on the floor she reached up for the bottle.

Dagmar shook her head. 'I've still got some. So has Mummy. I'm sure she shouldn't really have any.' She opened the oven door and glanced absent-mindedly at the sizzling turkey. 'Maybe we should have answered the door. If whoever it was asked, we could have said we'd just popped in on our way from church to make sure everything was all right. Or something.' Her voice rose a little. 'Maybe whoever it was had already seen us and is ringing the police this very moment.'

Amelia looked at her mother and took a long gulp from her glass. Actually, she thought, at this precise moment, Gerald and Clarissa are celebrating Christmas together in my home. My Gerald, my home; all gone.

'You'll get tipsy.' Dagmar raised a pencilled eyebrow.

'I hope so.' Amelia got up from the floor and put the water on for the sprouts.

In the sitting room the white Christmas lights sent a shimmering haze through the baubled branches of the tree, holly twigs rested on the gilded picture frames and a fire burnt in the grate. Amelia had covered the Hamiltons' table with a red cloth embroidered with cross-stitch holly leaves and snowflakes, and set it for

321

three with Selma's blue and gold china.

'I hope you don't mind eating in here,' Amelia had said to Selma. 'But the heating doesn't seem to be working in the dining room.' It was another lie of course.

Selma didn't mind at all. Amelia and Dagmar had helped her dress in a loose-fitting peacock-blue cashmere dress that they had given her that morning, and now she sat, a smile on her face like someone three lines behind in the telling of an amusing anecdote.

'No pad?' Dagmar had hissed after Amelia had placed Selma in the chair.

'No pad,' Amelia had whispered back. 'I want the seat of her dress to touch the seat of her chair with no go-between.'

'Why?' Dagmar had signalled back. Amelia wasn't sure. 'Just a feeling.' She shrugged her shoulders.

When Amelia put a plate of smoked salmon in front of her, Selma looked up with that puzzled look in her eyes again, although she was smiling. 'I've been away you know.' The smile turned shaky. 'I didn't enjoy myself very much at all.' After that she ate with quiet concentration, crumbs of turkey, rivulets of gravy and flakes of sprouts settling in the soft folds of her dress. Dagmar had cut the food in neat little squares on her plate and Selma had made no objections. She had come to accept her reliance on others, that much Cherryfield had done for her.

322

Amelia had lit candles all across the room: on the coffee table and the card table, in the window-seats of the bay and on top of the chimney-piece. They sat circled by candles while outside the light slowly died.

'Though I say it myself,' Selma said, her cheeks a little pink from the wine and the warmth of the fire, 'it really is a lovely turkey.'

She's happy, Amelia thought. She sits there, an old woman with a rotting leg, dying of at least three separate complaints, and she's happy. And it's all thanks to me. She got up to fetch the Christmas pudding and returned, holding it high over her head to show off the blue-burning flame.

'Bravo the cook!' Selma laughed and clapped as Amelia put the pudding in front of her and they watched as the blue flames sank and drowned in the sugary liquid.

'Don't throw the left-overs away now, will you?' Selma said, nodding at the sticky heap left on the serving plate. 'It will be delicious fried tomorrow.'

Laughing and thinking about tomorrow, Amelia continued saying to herself as she cleared the plates: And it's all my doing.

When they had finished eating, Selma asked Amelia to get her jewellery box. 'It's still in my case I think.' She looked up, explaining, 'I've been away you see.'

Amelia remembered unpacking the small leather case and she fetched it in from the study.

Selma bent low over the box, riffling through its contents. 'I've got some little things for you.'

'But you've already given us some lovely presents.' Amelia gesticulated towards the little heap of things; a couple of books, a scarf, a bottle of scent, lying on the seat by the fire. Gifts from Selma to her and Dagmar that Amelia herself had carefully chosen and wrapped.

'Oh those, that's nothing.' Selma waved her hand dismissively. 'I don't seem to have had much time to do my shopping this Christmas,' she turned to Dagmar, 'but I'd like you to have this, it's from your father's family, from Germany.'

The brooch was shaped like a basket of flowers and set with diamonds and rubies and Dagmar fastened it on to her red blouse. 'It's beautiful. I've always loved it,' and she got up to kiss her mother.

Selma gave Amelia a jade bracelet and lastly she brought out a large signet ring. 'It was Willoughby's. You remember it don't you, darling? Robert has got his grandfather's, so I'd like your young man to have this. It should be worn. It's no use lying here in this box.'

Amelia glanced across the table at Dagmar. They both wondered which young man it was that Selma was thinking of.

'Come on darling, take it,' Selma prompted. So Amelia took it and thanked her. 'That's wonderful, he'll be thrilled.'

Selma looked pleased. 'You didn't think I had forgotten your presents now, did you?' she said and then she added, 'I don't think I've had a proper look at my cards.'

Amelia tried to avoid her eyes. 'No,' she said weakly, 'nor you have.'

Selma turned her head to the chimney-piece, then back to Amelia. 'In fact I can't even remember opening them. Aren't I silly?'

Not really, Amelia thought, seeing that I put them there straight from the packets just before you came.

'So darling, could you take them down for me?' A touch of impatience had crept into Selma's voice. 'I don't seem to be able to get up as easily as I normally do. Too much good food I expect.'

'Shall I crack a nut for you?' Dagmar asked, reaching for the bowl that she had made in woodwork when she was nine.

Selma ignored her and kept on looking keenly at the row of cards. With a deep sigh she couldn't help, Amelia got up from the table and picked out a winter scene in a Dickensian Trafalgar Square. She had thought carefully before buying it as it had cost over a pound just for the one.

'I'll read it, shall I?' she said. 'It's rather dim in here and I don't know where you put your glasses.' Selma didn't object, so she began, reeling off polite, Christmassy phrases of good

325

cheer and well wishes, recalling the names of Selma and Willoughby's friends, as she went along. '. . . all the best, Gordon and Sheila.'

Selma had smiled and nodded at each familiar name but now she looked up with a frown. 'Gordon's dead.'

Amelia felt like a captain of a ship illicitly slipping anchor under the protection of fog only to find beams of sunlight breaking through, scattering the mist and making his deception clear to the world.

'Sheila, she must have signed automatically for both of them, it happens, I hear,' she added weakly.

'Not from the grave it doesn't,' Selma said. 'Poor Gordon was a widower for years.'

Amelia was tired. And why, she thought viciously, is it that your memory gets busy only when it's not wanted?

'Are you sure you don't want me to prepare a pecan for you? They're lovely,' Dagmar insisted.

'And here's one from the Hammonds,' Amelia exclaimed, waving a glossy, gold-edged card at Selma. The Hammonds were definitely not dead, she'd seen them in the supermarket only the other morning. But Selma had lost interest by now. The colour had gone from her cheeks, turning them the shade of unbleached writing paper, and her eyelids kept closing. Dagmar got up and began clearing the discarded wrappings from the floor. She was about to drop a shiny green sheet into the fire when Selma put out her hand and said, 'Don't darling. It'll do for next year,' and she took the paper and placed it across her chubby knees, carefully smoothing the creases with trembling fingers.

By eight o'clock she lay in bed smiling at Amelia like a contented child. 'I've had a lovely day.' Then she frowned. 'But where did your young man get to? I'm sure you said he was coming.'

Amelia kissed her lightly on the cheek. 'He had to work over Christmas,' she said. 'He was terribly disappointed.' But Selma had gone to sleep.

Amelia looked down at her for a long time, then with a shudder she turned away. I was willing her to die, she thought. I was standing here thinking it would be just perfect if she never woke up.

She looked up to see her mother in the doorway. As they walked from the room Dagmar whispered, 'It would be kinder all round if she just died.'

Amelia looked at her with a small smile. Then she said, 'I can't help wondering why what is right and what is kind so often seem to be quite different things?'

CHAPTER TWENTY-SIX

Of course Selma did wake the next morning, and the morning after and each day she seemed to grow stronger. It was as if with every touch of a familiar surface, every feel of her lips round the rim of her own china cups, each sight of the trees and shrubs outside, life seeped back into her.

'We'll have to ask these people to move their things out now I'm back,' she said as Amelia brought her breakfast on the fourth day. 'I still don't quite see why they had it all moved here in the first place.'

When Amelia told Dagmar she rolled her eyes and sighed, 'I told you you hadn't thought this through. We're meant to take her back tomorrow and she still believes the place is hers and that she's back for keeps.'

'You go back to Exeter as planned,' Amelia said. 'We might stay on a day or two. The Hamiltons aren't back for another ten days.'

'It's not going to get any easier telling her,' Dagmar warned.

'I don't expect it will, but each good day when you have only a hundred or so left, is a gift.' Amelia improvised the answer and ended up quite pleased with it.

So Dagmar left and Amelia was alone at Ashcombe with Selma. That was the problem, she was alone. Selma's new lease of life had been as brief as a Swedish summer, and now, once more, the dark and muddled moments of her mind grew longer. She slept so much that Amelia became worried. Was it good for her to doze away large chunks of the day? Should she be stimulated like an overdoser, kept awake and aware? There was no-one to ask. She telephoned Dagmar every day but Dagmar's only advice was 'Take her back.'

She wrote to Henry. She imagined herself talking to him, she asked his opinion and got so carried away at times, sitting in the window-seat chatting to him, that she felt quite let down when she paused and there was no answer.

Sometimes, when she walked through the silent house, she imagined it floating in space, as whole and separate as a planet. She ventured out into the garden only after dark and she realized that if no-one knew about you, you had only your own word that you actually existed. Other times though, in the early morning or when evening fell so depressingly early at four o'clock, her thoughts would race like crazy horses through her mind; discovery, newspaper reporters, prison. She wished she hadn't left Willoughby's law books in storage, they would have told her if trespassing was a tort or a criminal offence. Surely she couldn't be charged with theft; even the brandy on the Christmas pudding had been her own. But what about electricity and gas? One early morning she lay in bed wriggling and sighing until she thought her chest would split open, releasing this great putrid stream of worries.

There was a poverty of light too over the days between Christmas and New Year. Each morning Amelia pulled the curtains back as far as they would go but still there was an air of evening about the house any hour of the day.

'Those hedges need clipping,' Selma said one morning when Amelia brought her breakfast. 'I'll have a word with Mr Edwards in the New Year.' Amelia thought her grandmother's voice sounded faint, as if the words were spoken from a much greater distance than halfway across a small room.

'I'm not doing as good a job of looking after you as they do at Cherryfield,' she said, 'and I'm late with your pills again.'

'I hate pills. My father died because of the wretched things. Too many and none of them agreeing with the others.' She smiled weakly and held her hand out to Amelia who had to grab it quickly before it fell back on to the sheets. 'There's nothing much wrong with me you know. Nothing a few days' rest here in my own home, with my little granddaughter to look after me, won't cure.' She shifted in the bed, trying to reach the tray at her side.

'Anyway,' she said dropping a piece of buttered toast on to her chest, 'wild horses wouldn't drag me back to that awful place. You know I hated boarding school as a girl.'

She closed her eyes and mumbled, 'Hated it.'

Amelia heaved herself up from the foot of the chaise-longue as if she was fighting her way up from under a mountain of rubble. I'll tell her tomorrow. She sighed. I'll get everything packed and ready and then just tell her and go, leave her no time to argue or worry.

The next morning was New Year's Eve and Amelia had to shake Selma gently by the shoulder to wake her. Even then, she opened her eyes only to smile and close them again, and her breathing was quick and shallow. Amelia stood looking at her and as she looked she grew more and more scared. She was like a whist player from the village hall caught up in a game of poker in Las Vegas: out of her league. Pale faced, she turned and ran to the phone, dialling the number of the health centre.

Putting her stethoscope away, Dr Donaldson turned a grave face to Amelia, beckoning her away from the chaise-longue where Selma lay drifting between sleep and waking.

'She's very poorly I'm afraid, not really responding to the medication. Her blood pressure is right up, as for her leg . . .' Again she shook her head. 'I'd like to consult with her own doctor but he's not on again until the second.' She looked up from her notes. 'We've got her registered as living at Cherryfield Nursing Home though.' She glanced at Selma. 'I really think she would be better off there

331

now. When were you planning to take her back?'

'A week ago, but she fears and dreads that place.' Amelia felt the lump in her throat swelling. 'How long has she got?'

Dr Donaldson, like Sister Morris, shrugged her shoulders. 'It's impossible to say, days, weeks, maybe more.'

Well, we've only got five days, Amelia thought, close to tears. Five days for Selma to die in peace. She gave her grandmother a long look, then she turned away and followed Dr Donaldson into the sitting room.

'Which are the vital pills, the ones she couldn't do without? I mean maybe she's taking too many.'

Dr Donaldson looked at her. 'They're all vital in keeping her alive, all but the painkillers of course.' Then she looked around her. 'I thought the Hamiltons lived here.'

'They do,' Amelia assured her. 'But they're completely neurotic about burglars, so I'm house-sitting. I had to bring my grandmother with me.'

Dr Donaldson seemed satisfied with the answer. 'How long before the Hamiltons come back?'

'A couple of days or so,' Amelia was deliberately evasive. 'You couldn't spare a commode, could you? It's my back.'

'If you're quite sure your grandmother prefers staying with you here, I'll send the

332

community nurse along twice a day and I'll try to come myself at the end of each morning surgery. We won't be able to keep it up for ever though. I'll see about the commode, they might be able to lend us one from the Cottage Hospital.'

The nurse came that evening. She helped wash Selma, checked her blood pressure and changed the dressing on her leg.

'I'd like to get up today,' Selma said on the second day of the nurse's visits. 'I'm feeling much better.'

They dressed her in a warm, emerald-green housecoat and lifted her into the wheelchair. She winced as her leg touched the side of the chaise-longue but she didn't complain, instead she said, 'I'm afraid I haven't been able to do as much of the cooking as I usually do this Christmas. My little granddaughter has managed beautifully though.' She tried to turn to give Amelia an encouraging smile.

When she left, the nurse said to Amelia, 'You soldier on if you can, dear. Allow them to die in their own place, that's what I always say.'

'When do you think it will be, this dying?' Amelia caught the nurse's surprised look and gave a little apologetic shrug. 'What I mean is, I'd like to be prepared.'

The nurse's brow cleared. 'Of course you do. But who's to say? But you'll find the strength when the time comes, don't you worry.'

Amelia didn't want her to go; all that

cheerful competence, all that approval, the whiff of the real world where young women of thirty-one did not break into people's houses to spend Christmas with their dying grandmother. She lingered in the doorway, watching the nurse stride off towards her car and, as the little red mini drove off, she felt as if her own sanity had gone with the nurse, riding away cheerfully in the passenger seat. 'Wear a seat-belt,' she murmured. 'I might need you again.'

She was in the kitchen the next morning, preparing Selma's milky coffee when she heard the front door slam shut. It was too early for the nurse and anyway she didn't have a key. Automatically Amelia had sunk her knuckle into the milk to test the temperature and now as she heard footsteps in the passage she stayed that way, staring at the door. The steps hesitated then stopped, the door was pushed open and a long pale face peered round. 'Oh my Gawd,' it said as it caught sight of Amelia. 'Who would you be?'

Amelia remembered that attack was the smartest way of defence and said, 'May I ask who you are?' Adding truthfully, 'We weren't expecting anyone.'

The woman had obviously decided that if Amelia was dangerous she would by now have put down the coffee cup and picked up a knife, so she stepped inside but remained close to the open door just in case. 'I'm Mrs Clover. I do for Mrs Hamilton every Tuesday and Thursday.' She crossed her thin arms over the smooth tongue of her flower-sprigged apron. 'This is Tuesday.'

'Well don't let me stop you,' Amelia said. 'With the Hamiltons returning Sunday, I'm sure you've got lots to do. I've hoovered the sitting room by the way.' And she made for the door, her heart thumping so hard she felt sure Mrs Clover could hear it.

Mrs Clover barred her way, braver now. 'Mrs Hamilton said nothing to me about someone staying in her house.'

'That was remiss of her.' Amelia shook her head. 'One likes to be told about these things I know. I'm Mr and Mrs Merryman's granddaughter, Amelia Lindsay. My grandparents used to live here and the Hamiltons asked me to house-sit. Are you sure they didn't tell you?' she asked sympathetically.

'They most certainly did not.' Mrs Clover looked aggrieved, then her thin face softened. 'I remember Mr and Mrs Merryman. I used to do for friends of theirs, the Franklins. I thought the old couple passed away.'

'Not quite,' Amelia said bitterly. 'Now I mustn't keep you from your work. By the way, the study is best left for now I think.' She slid past and out of the door.

Selma had gone to sleep again in her chair in the sitting room, so Amelia went upstairs to the

335

bedroom to fetch her writing case. 'I need you Henry Mallett,' she said to herself as she hurried back down to Selma. 'A chaplain would do wonders for my credibility just now.'

She sat down in the window-seat and began to write:

'My Dear Henry, Wish you were here.'

She paused, chewing the cap of her pen, listening to the sound of the vacuum cleaner coming closer.

'There's something going on here.' Mrs Clover appeared dragging the hoover behind her. 'Look at this place. It's different.'

'My grandmother is asleep.'

Mrs Clover glanced in Selma's direction, then lowered her voice to a hiss. 'I'm calling the Hamiltons. I've got their number in case of burglary or fire.'

'Well this is neither,' Amelia said in a tired voice, 'so why worry them?'

Selma snored and shuddered, her head lolling against the wing of the chair, her mouth hanging open. Her face looked so small and her skin was grey. The grey of a corpse on a mortuary slab before the undertaker had got to work with colour and brushes, Amelia thought with a shiver.

'Please don't call.' She looked intently at Mrs Clover, as if she hoped pity was catching. 'Please. We'll be gone by Saturday.'

Mrs Clover's eyes narrowed. 'You're squatters, that's what you are. I should call the police, really I should.' And as Amelia stood up and moved towards her she fled from the room.

Amelia sat down again and buried her head in her hands. Soon they'd come and take Selma from her beloved Ashcombe, drag her from her chair, away from the view over the garden and the sea. Drag her back to Cherryfield to die with all her hopes gone and her illusions shattered.

'They know who you are.' Mrs Clover was back, speaking to Amelia from the doorway ready to retreat again. 'They said to tell you to leave immediately and they'll deal with you when they return. Lucky for you they don't want the police. Not at the moment they don't.'

Amelia lifted her head and looked at her. 'We're staying.' There, she thought, I've done it. As she got up from the seat, Mrs Clover took a step backwards and when she saw Amelia come towards her she turned and ran. Amelia heard a clanging noise, then a yell and as she hurried out into the hall she almost tripped over Mrs Clover lying prostrate on the floor her right foot tangled in the flex of the hoover.

'Here.' Amelia put her hand out.

Looking as if she knew she was going to regret it any moment, Mrs Clover allowed herself to be helped up.

'I'm quite harmless really.' Amelia smiled at her. 'But we're not leaving.' It all seemed quite simple now, simpler by far than taking Selma back to Cherryfield.

Mrs Clover shrugged her shoulders. 'Suit yourself, but I'm not stopping here a minute longer, not with a criminal in the house.'

'That's fine,' Amelia said tiredly. 'I'll finish the vacuuming.'

CHAPTER TWENTY-SEVEN

Outside, the sky was an unbroken dome of grey, allowing night to creep up with such stealth, Amelia thought. Selma had drunk some broth and now she sat in bed propped up against the pillows. She held on to Amelia's hand and didn't want to let go, so Amelia stayed and talked, their conversation weaving in and out of Selma's memories like a needle and thread.

'Of course you never knew your grandfather,' Selma said suddenly and in a clear strong voice. 'He died in Germany you know, before the war.'

'I'd love to know more about him,' Amelia said, realizing that for the first time she meant it. But Selma had gone back to sleep.

The nurse, her name was Mary she told Amelia, stood looking at Selma. She was smiling. 'I wish all my old people could go like her, in their own place with a relative to care for

338

them.'

Amelia was smiling too. It doesn't matter a bit that it's all an illusion, she thought. Selma believed she was in her own home, the lady of the house with tomorrow to plan for, and not a helpless inmate of a nursing home where tomorrow seemed more like a surcharge than a bonus. Mary certainly didn't know any different, so perhaps illusion had turned into reality. Amelia waited as the nurse took Selma's blood pressure and checked the dressing on her leg. Wasn't a well-maintained, oiled and running illusion a must for a happy life? If we all saw ourselves and others and life itself for what it truly was, would any of us have the heart to carry on?

She realized that Mary was speaking to her.

'Her heart is remarkably strong, she could go on for weeks you know. Will you be able to cope? Isn't there someone else who could come and stay with you for a bit?'

Amelia shook her head. 'Weeks did you say?'

'It could be, then again she could go at any time. But she's not suffering. She's quite contented, isn't she?' Mary looked up at Amelia, her round face all smiles and approval, but Amelia returned to the study near to tears.

'If you're going to die, do it now please,' she whispered between clenched teeth. 'I'm like a juggler adding the last plate to an impossible number already spinning over my head, I've

339

peaked. Any more and it'll all come tumbling down, crash, crash, crash,' she mumbled, banging her fist against her forehead. Selma snorted and turned over in her sleep, a small smile passing her lips.

Amelia telephoned her mother.

'You're still there,' Dagmar said. 'I was just about to call Cherryfield to see how Mummy's settled back in. You really must take her back immediately. I can't take any more of this worrying.' She sounded affronted, as if Selma's continued stay at Ashcombe was a deliberate attack on her nervous system. 'You know I'm sure there was something absolutely vital I had to tell you but I just can't remember … Anyway, I've said what I think, now I wash my hands of you, Amelia, I really do.'

'Ho, ho, ho,' Amelia said and Dagmar hung up.

A neighbour came to the door; Mr Squire who knew Amelia from the Merrymans' days at the house. 'Mrs Clover's told us you're squatting or something.' Mr Squire, tall and stooping, scratched his bald patch. 'It's not really the sort of thing we go in for around here you know.' He looked unhappily at a point to the left of Amelia's ear.

Amelia stood in the doorway saying nothing. I'll smile him away, she thought.

Mr Squire looked disturbed. 'Ah well, I suppose it's between you and the Hamiltons,' and he left. Amelia went back to the study and

340

continued reading *Emma* to Selma who knew the book so well she could drift off comfortably at any point in the story and come back as if she'd never been away.

*   *   *

The night before the Hamiltons' return, Amelia stayed all night in a chair in the study watching over Selma, listening to her breaths that came as quick and light as a runner's steps. She had opened the window, letting in an icy wind from the sea, but Selma was warm, covered up with several blankets. Amelia felt she knew somehow that when you were dying you didn't want silence and sterility but air and movement, smells of flowers and of cooking, voices and music; all the sounds and sights of life as long as you were still a part of it.

Earlier in the day, when Dr Donaldson had told Amelia it was unlikely that Selma would get up again, she had tidied away the Christmas decorations and loaded the van with Selma's furniture. She had taken the sheets off the bed in her old room and put them on the chair in the study. All the china except a cup and saucer and plate was boxed up and back in the van. Only the study she left as it was.

Now she stretched and yawned in her chair and, leaning across the chaise-longue, pulled the covers up higher across Selma's shoulders. She was about to open the writing case to continue her letter to Henry, when she paused and got her handbag instead. In the small zipped compartment was Henry's locket; she picked it up and, looking at it for a moment, hung it round her neck. With a little sigh she sat back and started to write:

'Selma is dying and, loving her as I do, I wish you'd tell me what the purpose is of making it such a drawn-out affair. Soon I'll find out if the Hamiltons are prepared to drag a dying woman from her bed. Life that once seemed quite a decent length now appears pitifully short. She lies there, her breathing is so quick and shallow, her time here almost up. I bet it didn't seem much more than a moment to her. I don't suppose it ever does.

'If I escape the consequences of my actions, which I very much hope I will, I don't think I shall stay in Kingsmouth, not once Selma is gone. I don't expect I'd be very welcome either. I'll probably go back to London and find a job. I suppose down here I have actually done something at last. I've taken action. I've lied and cheated and broken into a house, and do you know, for the first time in my life I feel proud of myself. I remember saying to you once that there was no such thing as a happy ending in life, no such thing as a happy death. Well maybe I was wrong. Maybe Selma is having a happy death, or as near to it as one can get, and I've had something to do with it.

'... I enclose my grandfather's signet ring; I would like to think of you wearing it, and so would Selma. It's really a present from her.

'... As I write, I can feel your locket against my skin. Keep safe Henry, I pray each night that there will not be a war...'

Selma stirred and mumbled. Amelia put her pen down and went up to the window, parting the curtains to let in the morning light. Then she went in to the kitchen and made a pot of tea and buttered some white bread. There was no more of their food left in the freezer now and only one pint of long-life milk. She carried the tray back into the study and put it down on the table by the chaise-longue. A little later Selma opened her eyes and tried to sit up. As her head fell back against the pillow she whispered, 'Could you do meals on wheels for me today, darling? I don't think I'm feeling terribly well.'

It was eight o'clock and Amelia wandered out into the garden. Two camelias, one red, one pink, grew against the south-facing wall at the back. The pink one was already flowering; un-English, un-blushing pink against lush green leaves. She picked a few blooms and brought them inside for Selma, placing them close to her.

At ten, Selma woke and drank a little warm

milk from the flask Amelia had made up. 'I must tell Willoughby the camelias are out already,' she said.

Soon after that the front door opened and slammed shut.

'And what, Miss Lindsay, is your grandmother still doing on my settee?' Doreen Hamilton, wrapped in a white mohair coat, stood in the study doorway framed by light from the sitting-room bay, her bleached hair streaked further by a tropical sun, her turquoise eyes, fringed by mascara'd lashes stiff and furry as flies' legs.

Amelia got up from Selma's bedside and pulled the screen closer. Then she walked across the room to Doreen. 'She's still dying,' she said in a quiet voice, 'and the chaise-longue is hers. If you make her leave you'll most probably speed up the process: I believe lost hope and a broken heart are tried and tested killers.' She forced herself to stay calm in the face of the image of Selma being taken back, confused and terrified, to Cherryfield, of her whispering, 'My mother died in a place like this.'

'She's dying, did you say?' Doreen hissed. Nudged by Amelia she backed out of the room and turned to her husband who had appeared behind her, only his round sleek head visible above the huge collar of his sheepskin coat.

'Desmond, Mrs Merryman is dying in our study and it's not even acute.'

344

'I'll phone the nursing home.' Desmond Hamilton glared at Amelia. 'And the police.'

'No!' Amelia ran past him and yanked the phone from its socket.

'What the hell do you think you are doing?' He strode out to the hall where the second telephone stood.

'It wouldn't look good in the paper,' Amelia called out after him. '"Local property developer hurls dying woman on to street".'

Desmond Hamilton's head appeared around the door.

'I'm not hurling your grandmother anywhere. I'm getting her back to the nursing home where she belongs.'

For a moment Amelia did nothing, feeling her will to fight dissolve; what Desmond had just said was so reasonable. Then she thought of Selma, dying so contentedly in the study of her beloved Ashcombe. Would she cry and beg? She'd be so frightened. With a little sob, Amelia rushed past Doreen and into the study, locking the door behind her. Panting she ran up to the window and shut it, sliding the double-glazing pane across. She stood there for a moment looking out at the garden where the mist was breaking up revealing the familiar shapes of shrubs and trees. Her heartbeat slowed down and she began to breath normally.

'Hello darling.' Selma had opened her eyes and was smiling at her. 'Is it morning already?'

She put her hand out, tipping over one of the medicine bottles on the small table by her side.

Amelia automatically checked the time on her watch; it was about time for the first lot of pills of the day. She stayed sitting down, resting her head against the back of the chair, closing her eyes. The pills could wait a minute or two. When she opened her eyes a short while later, Selma was sleeping again, and she could hear murmuring voices from the other room. There was a knock on the door making her jump. With a glance at Selma she hurried across the room up to the door.

'Yes?'

'Miss Lindsay, Amelia,' the voice was coaxing. 'It's Doreen here. We've called the nursing home and spoken to the Matron and they're sending transport, so you might as well open the door.'

Amelia began to cry, fat salty tears rolled down her cheeks. What could she do now? What could she do to stop Selma's poor old body, barely able to contain her soul, from being stretchered off to Cherryfield where a suitable dying, a well-ordered, well-mannered and, above all else, legal dying was being arranged?

'Just give us a moment, will you Doreen?' Her voice broke. 'Please.'

There was silence, then Doreen's voice again, measured and reasonable. 'Very well then, Amelia, five more minutes but then you'll have to open the door.'

Five minutes passed and then five more. Amelia stopped crying and put some music on. She sat down by Selma, watching her, listening to the two violins making love to each other. She put her hand in her pocket and traced the outline of the signet ring that lay with the letter, waiting to be sent to Henry. There was another knock on the door.

'Desmond says they'll be here any minute now.'

Amelia didn't answer and miraculously, so that Amelia began to believe miracles really happened, nothing was heard for a good half hour other than the music and the wind blowing through the chimney.

Then: 'Miss Lindsay, there's someone to see you.' Doreen, on the other side of the door, sounded inviting.

'Leave us alone, please.'

'Miss Lindsay, this is Sister Morris. I think you're not quite yourself. You'd better let us in, your grandmother needs professional care.'

Exhausted, Amelia went up close to the door. In a quiet, even voice she said, 'You're right, I'm not myself and I'm all the better for it and if you don't stop bothering us I will kill her. Now, will you please GO AWAY?'

As she waited, Amelia was pleased that she had made a store of sandwiches and drinks. She ate some at lunchtime, but she cried when she couldn't get Selma even to drink.

'Miss Lindsay,' again a voice beckoned her to the door. 'It's Dr Donaldson here. Sister Morris from Cherryfield has left now. I told her that there was no overwhelming medical reason for your grandmother to go back.'

'Desmond will call the police, I'm warning you.' That was Doreen.

'So I'm afraid you've got to sort out your differences with the Hamiltons, Miss Lindsay.' Dr Donaldson spoke again. 'I'll be back in a little while, if you're still here. In the meantime please check your grandmother's dressing and make sure she's not in pain.'

Again, Amelia heard nothing from the Hamiltons for a while and she managed to put clean dry sheets on Selma's chaise-longue. Changing the sheet with Selma on top wasn't easy, but Selma woke for a moment and helped by easing up her legs and shoulders. She smiled weakly at Amelia. 'I'll be better tomorrow, you'll see, darling.' Then she closed her eyes and fell back into a deep sleep.

Amelia needed a pee and, checking to see there was no-one in the garden, she opened the window, climbed out and hurried along the wall of the house to the shrubbery on the corner. Coming back again, locking the window behind her, she heard Doreen calling.

'Amelia, have you come to your senses yet? We don't want a scene.'

'Can't you think of us as guests?' Amelia pleaded, pressing her face to the small crack in
348

the door. 'You've got the whole rest of the house and it's not as it we're complete strangers.'

'You're not guests, you're squatters or housebreakers, or whatever. Anyway, my guests don't come here to die.'

Amelia started to laugh. She laughed so much that Doreen had to shout at her to stop. Selma mumbled something Amelia couldn't make out, but she didn't wake.

Then it wasn't long before she saw Desmond Hamilton's face at the window. He looked grey and unfocused in the dusk and he mouthed something, holding up a piece of paper for her to read: 'You have until 7.00 a.m. to think things over. Then we call the police.' His sleek head nodded emphatically and disappeared into the darkness. Amelia settled down to wait.

'Has she eaten?' Dr Donaldson asked through the door some hours later. 'And what about you? Have you had anything?'

'She had a teaspoon of broth a little while ago.' Amelia's voice broke. 'I can't get any more down her. She sleeps the whole time, it's such a deep sleep.'

'It's all right.' Dr Donaldson's voice was calm, soothing like calamine lotion. 'Try her with some water and make sure you have some of that broth yourself. Has she had her pills?'

'I missed this morning's lot ... I tried a while ago but I could only get her to take the white one, you know the one for her blood pressure,

349

and the black and yellow capsule. She doesn't seem to be in any pain.'

'That's not so bad then. Try to sleep. And Miss Lindsay, they do intend to get you out tomorrow, one way or the other. I'm sorry.'

Amelia sat on the floor, her back against the side of the chaise-longue and her fingers clasping the locket round her neck. Now and then she would doze off only to wake with a start, her mouth dry and her heart pounding.

It was six o'clock when she got up, stiff-legged and aching, to open the window. She leant out, feeling the cold morning air on her face. As she turned around her gaze fell on the soft pillow supporting Selma's head; already Selma's breath was as fragile as a glass thread, it wouldn't take much, a quick movement, the slightest of pressure and the flow would be cut. Amelia walked across the room with little quick steps, up to the chaise-longue, putting her hands on the pillow. She stayed there looking at her grandmother, then she closed her eyes as if she was standing at the edge of a cliff, preparing to leap into the cold clear sea below. When she opened her eyes again she found Selma looking back at her.

'Is that you, darling?' Selma's voice sounded as if it came from a long way away. 'Darling, are you there?' Her voice was a little anxious now and Amelia knew she could be addressing any number of her darlings: Daniel, Dagmar, Willoughby, Robert, or Amelia herself, it
350

didn't matter whom really, as long as one of them, one of those people that belonged to her, was there.

With a little sigh she bent down and kissed Selma's cheek, it felt papery and hot against her lips.

'It's time for your pills,' she said, 'time for your pills.' She stretched across the pillow and reached for the first of the bottles, shaking out two small red capsules into her sticky palm.

Selma opened her eyes wide. Raising herself from the pillow she looked straight at Amelia and whispered, 'Bugger the pills.' She slumped back and, with a little frown, she died.

Slowly a tear appeared in Amelia's eyes then another. She kneeled by the bed and p[u]t her arms round Selma, holding her for a wh[ile] then, when she heard the sound of a car on [the] gravel, she got up and unlocked the door.
351

the door. 'You've got the whole rest of the house and it's not as it we're complete strangers.'

'You're not guests, you're squatters or housebreakers, or whatever. Anyway, my guests don't come here to die.'

Amelia started to laugh. She laughed so much that Doreen had to shout at her to stop. Selma mumbled something Amelia couldn't make out, but she didn't wake.

Then it wasn't long before she saw Desmond Hamilton's face at the window. He looked grey and unfocused in the dusk and he mouthed something, holding up a piece of paper for her to read: 'You have until 7.00 a.m. to think things over. Then we call the police.' His sleek head nodded emphatically and disappeared into the darkness. Amelia settled down to wait.

'Has she eaten?' Dr Donaldson asked through the door some hours later. 'And what about you? Have you had anything?'

'She had a teaspoon of broth a little while ago.' Amelia's voice broke. 'I can't get any more down her. She sleeps the whole time, it's such a deep sleep.'

'It's all right.' Dr Donaldson's voice was calm, soothing like calamine lotion. 'Try her with some water and make sure you have some of that broth yourself. Has she had her pills?'

'I missed this morning's lot . . . I tried a while ago but I could only get her to take the white one, you know the one for her blood pressure, and the black and yellow capsule. She doesn't seem to be in any pain.'

'That's not so bad then. Try to sleep. And Miss Lindsay, they do intend to get you out tomorrow, one way or the other. I'm sorry.'

Amelia sat on the floor, her back against the side of the chaise-longue and her fingers clasping the locket round her neck. Now and then she would doze off only to wake with a start, her mouth dry and her heart pounding.

It was six o'clock when she got up, stiff-legged and aching, to open the window. She leant out, feeling the cold morning air on her face. As she turned around her gaze fell on the soft pillow supporting Selma's head; already Selma's breath was as fragile as a glass thread, it wouldn't take much, a quick movement, the slightest of pressure and the flow would be cut. Amelia walked across the room with little quick steps, up to the chaise-longue, putting her hands on the pillow. She stayed there looking at her grandmother, then she closed her eyes as if she was standing at the edge of a cliff, preparing to leap into the cold clear sea below. When she opened her eyes again she found Selma looking back at her.

'Is that you, darling?' Selma's voice sounded as if it came from a long way away. 'Darling, are you there?' Her voice was a little anxious now and Amelia knew she could be addressing any number of her darlings: Daniel, Dagmar, Willoughby, Robert, or Amelia herself, it didn't matter whom really, as long as one of them, one of those people that belonged to her, was there.

With a little sigh she bent down and kissed Selma's cheek, it felt papery and hot against her lips.

'It's time for your pills,' she said, 'time for your pills.' She stretched across the pillow and reached for the first of the bottles, shaking out two small red capsules into her sticky palm.

Selma opened her eyes wide. Raising herself from the pillow she looked straight at Amelia and whispered, 'Bugger the pills.' She slumped back and, with a little frown, she died.

Slowly a tear appeared in Amelia's eyes, then another. She kneeled by the bed and put her arms round Selma, holding her for a while then, when she heard the sound of a car on the gravel, she got up and unlocked the door.